OLDE REIGN

DAMIEN FEGAN

CREDITS

Originally conceived and created by the wonderful brain box of Scott Myers, without you my brother none of this would exist.
Lovingly rewritten, expanded, and updated by yours truly - Damien Fegan

Cover by Dean Spencer
Interior Art by Dean Spencer, Daniel Comerci, Jeremy Mohler & Blake Davis
Some artwork © 2013 Earl Geier, used with permission. All rights reserved.
Some artwork copyright William McAusland, used with permission

Edited by Sinead Fegan & Luke Griffiths

Published by Damien Fegan under the Open Game License version 1.0a
Copyright 2000 Wizards of the Coast, Inc.

The name Olde Swords Reign is used under license and with permission from Scott Myers © 2020

Special thanks to those on the Kanaz server that have played and helped shape this game - Caelin Araven, Luke Griffiths, Cainly, Keljorn, Kev, Le Gromp, Thom, Fred, Jason.

CONTENTS

INTRODUCTION

A few years ago my friend, Scott Myers from Workhorse RPG Studio, wrote a game. It was close to not being released but he knew if he did release it at least I would play it. That was Olde Swords Reign 1.0. It was 5th edition reimagined to play like the original 1974 edition of the world's greatest roleplaying game.

And play it I did! The game you've got in your hands is the result of 100's of hours at the table. The original game was more faithful to the 1974 version but has inevitably grown and morphed into something slightly more. I've tried to write it so you can strip it back to that original feel, but if you choose not to, there are options galore here for you to play the game that you want.

I've made every effort to capture and explain the importance of procedures that were essential to emergent gameplay, such as dungeon and wilderness exploration, and adapted them to the universal mechanics and difficulty systems that run through the entire game.

This is now your game! Take what you want and adapt what you need to fit your table. There is no right or wrong way to play. If you and your table enjoy what you're doing, then that is all that counts

Damien

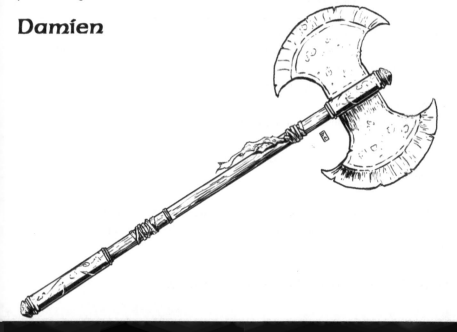

What is Olde Swords Reign?

Olde Swords Reign is a tabletop roleplaying game based on 5th Edition but designed with emergent gameplay in mind. It's faster, a tad deadlier, and relies more on player creativity to problem-solve than the options on a character sheet. Universal mechanics run through the game that speed up gameplay, make improvisation easier for both players and GMs as well as helping to make rulings a little more intuitive and consistent.

You can pick up and play any old-school module or OSR adventure but still have that 5e framework.

Being based on the 5e ruleset, it can be played with any of the bigger Virtual Table Tops (VTTs) that have 5e rulesets and most of the rules can also be easily dropped into your regular 5e game.

So steal what you want, that's what it's here for.

What Are Some of the Differences Between 5E and OSR?

Simplified Classes and Races

Only 4 classes and 4 races but *all* have a huge amount of flexibility

No Subclasses

Subclasses are gone, speeding up character creation and allowing you to change direction as your character develops

Classes stop at level 12

This is a game of adventurers, *not* superheroes. You get what you earn, and if you're lucky, retire as a legend.

Skills Replaced by Backgrounds

Who you are and what you know **matters**. Add your proficiency bonus to any non-combat related checks that relate to your background, this, combined with straight ability checks replaces skills.

Feats & Hindrances

The feat system allows you to create any character concept you can come up with using the 4 base classes. Hindrances add a little more flavor to make your character more creating more opportunities for shenanigans.

Simplified Difficulty Classes (DC)

An intuitive fixed DC system makes ruling much easier.

Simplified Range and Movement

Movement and Speed are split into simple ranges

Spell List

Over 120 spells that go to level 6.

Monster Hit Dice

Monsters all have d8 Hit Die, like the original rules supplements.

Simplified Monster Creation and Conversion

Monsters XP, to hit bonus, saving throw, and more are all based on their Hit Die, making running, converting, and creating them a breeze.

CHARACTER CREATION

CHARACTER CREATION BASICS

1. Roll Ability Scores
2. Choose a Race
3. Choose a Class
4. Choose a Background
5. If you qualify pick feats
6. Choose Additional Languages
7. Choose Spells for Clerics & Magic-Users
8. Buy Additional Equipment
9. Gain an Inspiration for completing your character

The Basics

Before creating characters we need to put the whole thing in context.

Olde Swords Reign is a tabletop role playing game where a group of friends get together and create a communal story.

There are 2 main roles within the group - a Game Master (GM) or Referee, and players. The GM creates the world and all of the creatures that live in it. The Players create characters that they then use to traverse the world, overcoming obstacles and gaining experience as they do. Simple!

The gameplay tends to unfold according to this basic pattern.

1.   The Referee describes the environment. Giving the players a detailed description of their surroundings.

2.   The players describe what they want to do. This can either be as a group or individually. It could be to search a treasure chest while a second keeps watch for monsters. Sometimes, resolving a task is easy but if there is a risk of failure the referee might ask the player to roll a die to determine the results of an action.

3.   The Referee narrates the results of the adventurers' actions.

Game Dice

The game uses polyhedral dice with different numbers of sides.

They are referred to by the letter d followed by the number of sides: d4, d6, d8, d10, d12, and d20. So, a d6 is a six- sided die (the typical cube many games use).

Percentile dice, or d100, work a little differently. A number between 1 and 100 is generated by rolling two different ten-sided dice numbered from 0 to 9. One die (designated before you roll) gives the tens digit, and the other gives the ones digit.

When you need to roll dice, the rules tell you how many dice to roll of a certain type, as well as what modifiers to add. For example, "3d8 + 5" means you roll three eight-sided dice, add them together, and add 5 to the total.

When to roll

When the outcome of a task is not certain then, generally, you have to roll dice to confirm the outcome of that task.

The GM may assign a Difficulty Class (DC) to the task or it may be set by another factor, e.g. the difficulty in hitting an enemy is determined by their Armor Class (AC). The player then rolls a dice, normally a d20, adds any relevant modifiers and, if they meet or exceed the target, then the task succeeds.

Ability Scores

The majority of tasks that a player, or monster, attempts are covered by one of their 6 ability scores, covering the 6 areas where their characters are naturally gifted. The better you are in a particular area, the higher the chance of you succeeding in a task that relates to that area.

USING ABILITY SCORES

When attempting a task that is not an attack, and the result is not certain, the referee may call for an ability check. They will give the task a difficulty level e.g. Normal (12) and the player will roll a d20 adding or subtracting their proficiency bonus (if applicable) and ability score modifier (see page 9) trying to meet or beat that target.

The six ability scores are:

Strength (STR) - physical power, athletics, brute force

Examples of strength checks would be climbing, jumping, swimming, forcing something open, pushing something over, breaking out of bonds...

Combat: Strength is added to both your attack rolls and damage rolls when you are involved in Melee (close) combat.

Encumbrance: How much you can carry is based on your strength. A character can carry their Strength ability score in weapons and items, and an additional 10 items with a backpack. (see Encumbrance p.102)

Dexterity (DEX) - agility, reflexes, balance, nimbleness

Examples of dexterity checks would be attempting to stay on your feet, balance, acrobatics, picking a pocket, hiding, concealing an object, moving silently, sneaking, tying knots, steering a cart, wiggling out of bonds....

Combat: Dexterity is generally added to your attack rolls and damage rolls when you are in Ranged combat, there are some exceptions with thrown weapons (see Combat p.121). You can also choose to use dexterity for Melee attacks when using a weapon with the finesse property, such as a dagger or short-sword.

Armor Class: Your dexterity represents your ability to avoid blows, so is it added to your armor class.

Constitution (CON) - health, stamina, vital force

Examples of constitution checks would be pushing yourself beyond normal limits, holding your breath, forced march or labor, going without sleep, surviving without food or water, surviving poison, fighting disease, resisting the effects of drugs or alcohol.

Hit Points: Your constitution modifier is added to your hit points for every level you gain, making it either harder or easier to kill you, depending on whether it is positive or negative. If your Constitution modifier changes, you apply this change to every level.

Eg. If you were a 4th level character and your Constitution modifier increased by 1 you would add 4 points to your max hp, one for every level.

Intelligence (INT) - measuring, reasoning, memory, mental acuity

Examples of intelligence checks would be recalling lore/historical events or something read in a book, deducing the location of a hidden object, discerning from the appearance of a wound what kind of weapon dealt it, or determining the weakest point in a tunnel that could cause it to collapse, appraise an item, forge a document.

Spellcasting Ability: Magic-users use Intelligence as their spellcasting ability, which helps determine the saving throw DCs of spells they cast.

Wisdom (WIS) - perception, intuition, insight

Examples of wisdom checks would be reading body language, understanding someone's feelings, noticing things about the environment, calming down a domesticated animal, intuiting an animal's intentions, stabilizing a dying companion, diagnosing an illness, spot or hear things, follow tracks, hunt wild game, predict the weather, avoid natural hazards.

Spellcasting Ability: Clerics use Wisdom as their spellcasting ability, which helps determine the saving throw DCs of spells they cast.

Charisma (CHA) - force of personality, confidence, eloquence, charm, command

Examples of charisma checks would be influencing or entertaining others, finding hirelings, making an impression, telling a convincing lie, performing music, dance, acting, storytelling, finding the best person to talk to for news, rumors, and gossip.

Hirelings: Your charisma score influences hiring retainers to work for you and watch your back.

Ability Score Modifiers

Ability scores have two facets, the score itself and a modifier that is derived from the score. It is this modifier that is added or subtracted to rolls made for that ability (see table). The maximum ability score for a player is 20 but some monsters are far more powerful.

E.g. If a character was trying to lift a heavy boulder the GM might give the task a difficulty class (DC) of 12. If that player had a 16 STR they would roll a d20 and add +3 to the roll attempting to roll a total of 12 or more.

To put ability scores into perspective, the average person would have an ability score of 10.

ROLLING ABILITY SCORES

Roll 3d6 six times and place the results for your 6 ability scores. Your race will grant you further ability score bonuses.

Down the Line: Optional

In our games I often give the players an option to declare "down the line" before they roll their scores.
This removes the ability to move their scores around. The first roll goes in STR, then next in DEX, and so on.
This tends to generate less optimized but more interesting characters, which seem to be far more fun to play. As a reward for putting their fates in the hands of the dice gods, I let them pick an extra feat to start the campaign with (see Feats p.30).

Proficiency Bonus

Characters have a proficiency bonus that they can apply to certain rolls.
A player's background, class, or feats determine what they are proficient in and this bonus gets added to these rolls. As they go up in levels this bonus increases (see Advancement Table p.22)

Your proficiency bonus can only be added once to any die roll.

Use of these modifiers will be covered in more detail in later sections.

Ability Score Modifier Table

Score	Mod	Score	Mod
1	-5	16-17	+3
2-3	-4	18-19	+4
4-5	-3	20-21	+5
6-7	-2	22-23	+6
8-9	-1	24-25	+7
10-11	0	26-27	+8
12-13	+1	28-29	+9
14-15	+2	30	+10

Races

Dwarf

Ability Score Bonus. Your Constitution score increases by 1.

Speed. You have a walking speed of Normal (30ft).

Age. Dwarves mature at the same rate as humans, but they're considered young until they reach the age of 50. On average, they live about 350 years.

Size. Dwarves stand between 4 and 5 feet tall and average about 150 pounds. Your size is Medium.

Languages. You can speak, read and write Common and Dwarvish.

SPECIAL

Darkvision. Dwarves have darkvision (30ft).

Dwarven Resistance. You have advantage on saving throws against spells and spell-like effects.

Giant Fighter. All dwarves add +1 to hit and +1 to their Armor Class when fighting giants.

Stone Sense. Dwarves easily take note of certain features of stonework: sloping corridors, moving walls, and traps made of stone — in particular: falling blocks, rigged ceilings, and tiny arrow slits designed to release poison gas or darts. They can also identify whether stonework is recent or not. A dwarf merely passing within 5 feet of any of the above is entitled to an Intelligence check to spot the feature (can be EASY, NORMAL, or HARD DC), as if the dwarf were actively looking for it (these checks are normally best rolled in secret by the GM not to alert the player). When a dwarf actively searches for such features, this check is done with advantage.

ELF

Ability Score Bonus. Your Charisma score increases by 1.
Speed. Your base walking speed is Normal (30ft).
Age. Although elves reach physical maturity at about the same age as humans, the elven understanding of adulthood goes beyond physical growth to encompass worldly experience. An elf typically claims adulthood and an adult name around the age of 100 and can live to be 750 years old.
Size. Elves range from under 5 to over 6 feet tall and have slender builds. Your size is Medium.
Languages. You can speak, read and write Common and Elvish.

SPECIAL

Elven Senses. Elves can see and hear further than humans in just about every circumstance and visual and audible checks for them are always EASY.
Find Secret Doors. Elvish vision and keen senses allow them to spot secret, hidden, and concealed doorways. An elf merely passing within 5 feet of a secret, hidden or concealed doorway is entitled to a Wisdom check to spot the door (can be EASY, NORMAL, or HARD DC), as if the elf were actively looking for it (these checks are normally best rolled in secret by the GM not to alert the player). When an elf actively searches for such doorways, this check is done with advantage.
Defenses. Elves cannot be paralyzed by ghouls.
Elven Weapon Training. All elves are proficient with swords and bows. They gain +1 to their attacks and damage rolls with these weapons

Halfling

Ability Score Bonus. Your Dexterity score increases by 1.

Speed. Years of keeping up with the tall ones have made Halfling's fleet of foot. Your base walking speed is Normal (30ft).

Age. A halfling reaches adulthood at the age of 20 and generally lives into the middle of his or her second century.

Size. Halflings average about 3 feet tall and weigh about 40 pounds. Your size is Small.

Languages. You can speak, read and write Common and Halfling.

SPECIAL

Attack Bonus. You gain +1 to hit with ranged weapons.

Halfling Resistance. You have advantage on saving throws against spells and spell-like effects.

Sling Training. All halflings add +3 to hit when using a sling (not damage).

Human

Abilities. Choose 2 ability scores from Strength, Dexterity, Constitution, Intelligence, Wisdom, and Charisma to increase by 1.

Speed. Your base walking speed is Normal (30ft).

Age. Reach adulthood in their late teens and live less than a century.

Size. Vary widely in height and build, from barely 5 feet to well over 6 feet tall. Regardless of your position in that range, your size is Medium.

Languages. You can speak, read, and write Common and one extra language of your choice.

SPECIAL

Saving Throw Proficiency. All characters gain two saving throws from their class, but because of humanity's adaptable nature they can choose a third saving throw proficiency at character creation (see Proficiencies p.9).

Classes

The description of each class includes class features common to members of that class. The following entries appear among the features of each class.

Hit Points.

Hit Dice: The dice size used to generate your hitpoints.

Hit Points: Are an indication of how hard you are to kill. Every time you gain a level your hit points increase. You can either roll your Hit Die or take the average rounded down (in brackets) then add or subtract your constitution modifier. At first level you can take the maximum of your hit die.

Proficiencies.

When you are proficient in something, you get to add your proficiency bonus to associated rolls (see Advancement Table p.22).

Armor: The armors this class can use

Weapons: The weapons this class can use and are proficient with.

Saving Throws: Each class is proficient in 2 saving throws

Each class gains a +1 increase to one ability score and also has a table that shows their level and any features they gain at that level.

Cleric

As a cleric, you gain the following class features:

Hit Points.

Hit Dice: 1d6 per Cleric level

Hit Points: 1st Level: 6 + CON, higher levels 1d6 (or 3) + CON

Proficiencies.

Armor: Light armor, medium armor, shields.

Weapons: Club, mace, flail, sling.

Saving Throws: Wisdom, Charisma

Equipment.

You start with the following equipment:

(a)Mace or (b) Flail

Chainmail and Shield

Backpack, Rations, 1 person/ 1 week, 6 Torches and Water/ Wine Skin

(a)Sling and Sling Stones or (b) Holy Water/Vial

(a)Wooden Holy Symbol or (b) Silver Holy Symbol

Healing Kit

15 gp

Alternatively, you may want to start with 4d4x10 gp to buy your own equipment.

Ability Score Bonus. Your Wisdom score increases by 1.

Saving Throw Bonus. Clerics gain advantage on saving throws against being paralyzed or poisoned.

Turn Undead. By presenting your holy symbol and speaking a prayer you send undead fleeing.

Turn undead targets monsters starting with the lowest HD first. You may turn undead beings as long as their HD is less than your level +2. Make a Wisdom Check (see table for DC), if you succeed 3d6 Hit Dice of creatures flee. You can repeat this each round until your god fails you.

A turned creature will flee for 3d6 rounds spending its actions moving as far away from you as it can. If there's nowhere to move, the creature will cower.

Check	HD
Easy	Level
Normal	Level +1
Hard	Level +2

Spellcasting. As a conduit for divine power, you can cast cleric spells.

Cleric Spellcasting

Wisdom is the ability you use for casting cleric spells. You add your Wisdom modifier and proficiency bonus to any spell attacks, and any saving throws an enemy might need to make to avoid the full effects of your spells.

Spell save DC = 8 + your proficiency bonus + your Wisdom modifier
Spell attack modifier = your proficiency bonus + your Wisdom modifier

Preparing Cleric Spells

A cleric's powers come from their god, and every morning they can prepare the spells they want to cast that day through prayer and meditation. Preparing their spells readies the spell to be cast at will later in the day.

Every morning a cleric has access to all the spells that are available to their level but can only prepare a limited amount each day. The total number is equal to the Wisdom modifier + their cleric level. *So, a 3rd level cleric with a wisdom modifier of +2 can prepare 3 + 2 = 5 different spells for casting each day.*

Every time a spell is cast they consume a spell slot (see Magic p.57). Every time you finish a short or long rest you regain any spent spell slots and can prepare different spells, it takes at least 1 minute per spell to level to prepare so a 4th level spell would take 4 minutes.

Spellcasting Focus

You must use a holy symbol (see Equipment p.43) as a spellcasting focus for your cleric spells.

Lvl	Feature	Lvl	Feature
1	1st level spells, turn undead	7	4th level spells
2		8	+1 to any one ability score
3	2nd level spells	9	5th level spells
4	+1 to any one ability score	10	
5	3rd level spells	11	6th level spells
6		12	+1 to any one ability score

Fighter

As a fighter, you gain the following class features.

Hit Points.

Hit Dice: 1d8 per Fighter level
Hit Points: 1st Level 8 + CON, higher levels 1d8 (or 4) + CON

Proficiencies.

Armor: Light armor, medium armor, heavy armor, shields.
Weapons: Simple weapons, martial weapons.
Saving Throws: Strength, Constitution

Equipment.

You start with the following equipment:
Chainmail or (b) Leather Armor, Long Bow and Quiver of 20 Arrows
(a) any martial weapon and shield or (b) two martial weapons
(a) Light Crossbow and Case with 30 Quarrels or (b) two Hand Axes
6 Torches, Backpack, Rations - 1 person/ 1 week and Water/ Wineskin
5 gp
Alternatively, you may start with 4d4x10 gp to buy your own equipment.

Ability Score Increase. Your Strength score increases by 1.
Feats. See Fighter Feats p.33 for list of feats.

Lvl	Feature	Lvl	Feature
1	Fighter Feat	7	Fighter Feat
2		8	+1 to any one ability score
3	Fighter Feat	9	Fighter Feat
4	+1 to any one ability score	10	
5	Fighter Feat	11	Fighter Feat
6		12	+1 to any one ability score

If you wish to play with a fighter class closer to the original supplements then add the feat weapon focus at first level and do not add any fighter feats on subsequent levels.

Expert

As an Expert, you gain the following class features:

Hit Points.
Hit Dice: 1d4 per Expert level
Hit Points: 1st Level: 4 + CON, higher levels 1d4 (or 2) + CON

Proficiencies.
Armor: Light armor.
Weapons: Simple weapons, martial weapons.
Saving Throws: Dexterity, Intelligence

Equipment.

You start with the following equipment, in addition to the equipment granted by your background:

(a) Sword or (b) Shortsword
Quiver of 20 Arrows and Short Bow
Leather Armor, two Daggers and Thieves' Tools
6 Torches, Backpack, Rations - 1 person/ 1 week and Water/ Wineskin
25 gp
Alternatively, you may start with 4d4 x 10 gp to buy your own equipment.

Ability Score Increase. Your Dexterity score increases by 1.
Feats. See Expert Feats p.31 for list of feats.

Lvl	Feature	Lvl	Feature
1	6 x Expert Feats	7	Expert Feat
2		8	+1 to any one ability score
3	Expert Feat	9	Expert Feat
4	+1 to any one ability score	10	
5	Expert Feat	11	Expert Feat
6		12	+1 to any one ability score

If you wish to play with a thief class closer to the original supplements then add the feats Backstab, Hear Noise, Open Locks, Move Silently, Hide in Shadows, Pick Pocket & Traps at first level and do not add any expert feats on subsequent levels.

Magic-User

As a magic-user, you gain the following class features:
Hit Points.
Hit Dice: 1d4 per magic-user level
Hit Points: 1st Level: 4 + CON, higher levels 1d4 (or 2) + CON
Proficiencies.
Armor: None
Weapons: Dagger, Staff.
Saving Throws: Intelligence, Wisdom

Equipment.
You start with the following equipment:
Dagger and Arcane Staff
Spellbook
Rations, 1 person/ 1 week, Backpack and Water/ Wineskin
10 gp
Alternatively, you may start with 4d4 x 10 gp to buy your own equipment.

Ability Score Increase. Your Intelligence score increases by 1.
Spellcasting. As a student of arcane magic, you have a spellbook containing spells. See Spells Rules for the general rules of spellcasting and the Spells Listing for the magic-user spell list.
Saving Throw Bonus. Magic-Users gain advantage on all saving throw rolls against spells, including spells from magic wands and staffs.

Lvl	Feature	Lvl	Feature
1	1st level spells	7	4th level spells
2		8	+1 to any one ability score
3	2nd level spells	9	5th level spells
4	+1 to any one ability score	10	
5	3rd level spells	11	6th level spells
6		12	+1 to any one ability score

Magic-User Spell-casting

Intelligence is the ability you use for casting magic-user spells. You add your Intelligence modifier and proficiency bonus to any spell attacks and any saving throws an enemy might need to make to avoid the full effects of your spells.

Spell save DC = 8 + your proficiency bonus + your Intelligence modifier
Spell attack modifier = your proficiency bonus + your Intelligence modifier

Cantrips
At 1st level, you know and can cast Wizard Bolt and Prestidigitation.

Spellbook
At first level you have a spellbook containing read magic and 1 + your Intelligence modifier spells. These can be rolled randomly, chosen by the referee, or picked by the player depending on the type of campaign that is being run.
For more on spell books and acquiring spells see the Magic pg.62.

Preparing and Casting Spells

A magic-user must read their spell book every morning to fix their spells in their mind. Preparing their spells readies the spell to be cast at will later in the day.

Magic-users can pick any spell in their spell book to prepare.
Spells Prepared. is equal to their Intelligence modifier + magic-user level.
So a 3rd level magic-user with an intelligence modifier of +2 can prepare 3 + 2 = 5 spells for casting each day.

Every time you finish a short or long rest you can prepare different spells, it takes at least 1 minute per spell to level to prepare so a 4th level spell would take 4 minutes.

Spellcasting Focus
You use an arcane focus (see Equipment p.43) as a spellcasting focus for your magic-user spells

Beyond 1st Level

As your character advances through the game going on adventures and overcoming challenges they gain experience points, and when they reach a certain level of experience points (XP) they can advance to the next level. XP is awarded for both overcoming foes and returning to safety with riches. Your GM may award XP for other actions or outcomes as they see fit.

A character must take a long rest to gain a new level unless the referee is using the training option below.

When your character gains a level, they gain one additional hit die. To find their new maximum hit point, roll that die and add the total along with their constitution modifier to their current hit points.

Alternatively, you can use the fixed value shown on your class HD section in brackets which is the average roll rounded down.

Your constitution modifier is added to your hit points for every level you gain, making it either harder or easier to kill you depending on whether it is positive or negative. If your Constitution modifier changes, you apply this change to every level.

The character advancement table shows the relevant XP needed to acquire new levels.

Training: Optional

This option adds a little more verisimilitude whilst pushing characters to go out in the world, explore and acquire wealth.

When a character meets XP requirement for their next level they must undergo training in order to gain that level. Training takes 2 weeks and costs their *current level X 100gp per week*. So training costs to advance from level 2 to 3 would cost *2 x 100gp = 200gp per week*. At the end of that period, the character would need to make an EASY check using their main ability score to show they have gained the required skills. Failure requires another week's training followed by another check.

Advancement Table

Lvl	XP Needed	Prof. Bonus	Lvl	XP Needed	Prof. Bonus
1	0	+2	7	23,000	+3
2	300	+2	8	34,000	+3
3	900	+2	9	48,000	+4
4	2,700	+2	10	64,000	+4
5	6,500	+3	11	85,000	+4
6	14,000	+3	12	100,000	+4

Multiclassing (optional)

Multiclassing allows you to gain levels in multiple classes. Doing so lets you mix the abilities of those classes to realize a character concept that might not be reflected in one of the standard class options.

With this rule, you have the option of gaining a level in a new class whenever you advance instead of your current class. Your levels in all your classes are added together to determine your character level. For example, if you have three levels in magic-user and two in fighter, you're a 5th-level character.

Experience Points

The experience point cost to gain a level is always based on your total character level (as shown in the Character Advancement table) not your level in a particular class. So, if you are a cleric 6/fighter 1, you must gain 34,000 XP to reach 8th level before you can take your second level as a fighter, or your seventh level as a cleric.

Hit Points and Hit Dice

You only gain maximum hit points for your first character level. After that, you roll or take the average regardless of if it's your first level in that class.

You add together the Hit Dice granted by all your classes to form your pool of Hit Dice. If the Hit Dice are the same die type, you can simply pool them together.

For example, both the expert and the magic-user have a d4, so if you are an expert 5/magic- user 5, you have ten d4 Hit Dice.
If you are a fighter 5/cleric 5 you have five d8 Hit Dice and five d6 Hit Dice.

Proficiency Bonus

Your proficiency bonus is always based on your total character level, as shown in the Character Advancement Table, not your level in a particular class. For example, if you are a fighter 3/expert 2, you have the proficiency bonus of a 5th-level character, which is +3.

Proficiencies

When you gain your first character level you gain all of the benefits of that class, if you later multiclass, you gain only some of the starting proficiencies of the new class, as shown in the Multiclassing Proficiencies table below.

Class	Proficiencies Gained
Cleric	Light armor, medium armor, shields
Fighter	Light armor, medium armor, shields, simple, martial weapons
Magic-User	
Expert	Light armor

Expert Feats

When a first level character starts as an expert they receive all 6 expert feats, due to the training they have received prior to starting the game. If you multiclass into the Expert class then you only receive 3 expert feats on your initial expert level.

Backgrounds

At character creation, players choose one background for their character, or randomly roll a d20 and check the list below. These are only a few options for guidance, so feel free to create your own.

Using Backgrounds

Backgrounds let a player add their proficiency bonus to any, non-combat related, checks that would fall under the backgrounds skillset. For Example, a tracking check by a hunter, a smith repairing armor, a barbarian searching the wilds for food, etc. These entirely replace the skill proficiencies in 5e making your background a vital part of who your characters are.

Players should tell the referee that they would like to use their background, but the final call on whether it's applicable to the current check is always the referees.

Background Table

Roll	Background	Roll	Background
1	Acrobat	11	Noble Blood
2	Alchemist	12	Sailor
3	Assassin	13	Scoundrel
4	Barbarian	14	Scribe
5	Bard	15	Seducer
6	Beast Trainer	16	Sellsword
7	Beggar	17	Smith
8	Farmer	18	Soldier
9	Healer	19	Trader
10	Hunter	20	Worker

Background Descriptions

Acrobat

Juggling, tumbling, and entertainment are important in the world. Ceremonies and feasts will have tumblers, jugglers, acrobats, and the like. Acrobats are athletic, showing feats of skill, agility, and coordination. Some tumblers extend their skills to a few sleight-of-hand and juggling tricks, and others to feats of contortion.

Alchemist

They are master brewers and herbalists; mixing and blending various ingredients together to create potions and tinctures. Their work with herbs, fungi, venoms, and oils enables them to produce perfumes, potions, powders, poisons, poultices, and other amazing creations.

Assassin

Blades-for-hire, perhaps agents in the service of a noble house or guild, spies and assassins make killing and stealing discreetly a way of life. They are adept at information gathering, disguises, city lore, persuasion and poisons.

Barbarian

Barbarians are wild and untamed, much like the lands they live in. They have natural skills in wilderness lore, survival, beast riding, intimidation, natural instincts, and so on.

Bard

Wandering or employed by a lord, the Bard is an accomplished artist and scholar who knows legends of past heroes, and who may even be ready to join an adventure themself, just to get a good story out of it. Some extend their art to a bit of juggling and, possibly, sleight-of-hand trickery.

Because they travel and are great at gossip, they learn ancient legends, are good orators, and have some knowledge of city and world lore.

Beast Trainer

Beast Trainers are in demand the world over for their special empathy and skill with animals. They train animals for riding, pulling wagons, combat, and even gladiatorial and pit-fighting. They can calm maddened creatures, are expert riders and wagoneers, can recognize whether creatures are dangerous and about to attack or not, and often have some skill in healing them if injured or sick.

Beggar

Beggars are vagrants or tramps, aimlessly wandering from place to place. They may do casual work here and there, they may sell a few small trinkets that they carry about in their backpacks, or they may have to beg for a few coins when times are really hard. Some even turn their hands to less honest pursuits. They are experts at going unnoticed in cities, living for free and making use of anything they find.

Farmer

Farmers live outside of large settlements but often within a half day's travel so that they are able to get their produce to market. They are hardy, hardworking and skilled in basic plant and animal lore, animal handling, cooking, baking, brewing, trading for basic goods, and the like.

Healer

Healers maintain the medical traditions of their ancestors; knowledge passed down through the generations. This is not magic, but rather a good working knowledge of the body and its functions: a healer knows how to set a broken bone, stitch a wound, and defeat an infection. They knows how the organs work, and of remedies that relieve pain.

Hunter

The Hunter is a master of tracking prey through the wilderness and wastelands. Once hunters locate their target, they'll use stealth, traps and/or expert bowmanship to bring it down. They are at home in the wild and can survive there for long periods, returning to more civilized areas only when they have furs and hides to sell, or when they require the company of their fellow men (or women).

Noble Blood

Often holding homes in cities and towns, and estates or hunting lodges in the countryside, these characters are usually titled (though not necessarily deserving) and have some authority over the common people, peasants, and thralls. Those of noble blood are often able to obtain credit, have high-ranking contacts, and are skilled in such things as bribery, browbeating, dress sense, and etiquette.

Sailor

Sailors are sea warriors and adventurers who are skilled in sea lore, navigation by stars, and boat handling, and have a good knowledge of local ports and nearby coastlines and islands. Skilled mariners are always in demand and will rarely be refused working passage on board a ship. Some sailors lust for gold and become pirates.

Scoundrel

Perhaps you fell into a life of crime or began as a young street urchin. In either case, you have a certain unique set of skills that most find unsavory. Scoundrels and other ne'er-do-wells will have skill in such things as city lore, climbing, burglary, gambling, and other skullduggery, and may be part of some "guild" or order. You will almost certainly be robbed at some time or another, if you stay in the city for any length of time, because of some Scoundrel.

Scribe

Scribes are chroniclers and teachers, well-educated and knowledgeable on a wide variety of subjects — they are cartographers, astronomers, linguists, historians, and philosophers. Scribes are also skilled at debate as they discuss at length a variety of topics with other enlightened individuals.

Seducer

There are some who have honed seduction and manipulation down to an art form. The Seducer may be a lover, an ambitious courtier, or a power-hungry advisor who tries to gain power over others through flattery and various forms of enticement. A Seducer is skilled in etiquette, intuition, conversation, manipulation, and seduction.

Sellsword

These warriors work for anyone who will pay for their services. Some form themselves into companies under a strong leader and others travel individually or in small bands to seek employment. Often these mercenary groups turn to banditry when not gainfully employed.

Just about all noble houses have used these mercenaries and Sellswords in past conflicts and will continue to do so. They tend to have skill in living rough, riding, intimidation, carousing, and in basic upkeep and repair of weapons and armor.

Smith

These craftspeople work hard at their forges — melting, melding, bending, shaping, and fixing metal objects. They are skilled at weapon and armor smithing and repair. They craft tools and implements and manufacture many other metallic items and objects, from shackles and cages to the metal parts of ships and wagons. Their skills lie in metallurgy and the knowledge of weapons, armor, and metal goods.

Soldier

Soldiers are the guards in a town or in the standing armies of rich nobles. They are often stoic but of limited imagination. They will have knowledge of some city lore, perhaps skills in intimidation and riding, as well as a limited amount of authority — especially the officers.

Trader

Traders are not shopkeepers — they are wide-traveled adventurers, who seek new and exotic goods to sell from faraway places. As such, trader characters pick up a range of useful skills like trading, appraisal, obtaining rare or unusual goods, persuasion, knowledge of city lore, distant places, and guild membership. If you want a strange or unusual item, speak to a trader first.

Worker

Workers are unskilled laborers — men who erect palisades, dig ditches, build homes, city walls, and temples, or who load and unload wagons and riverboats. Workers often move around doing a range of odd jobs here and there, many of which are seasonal or temporary. Workers will be skilled in heavy lifting, intimidation, carousing, and hard labor.

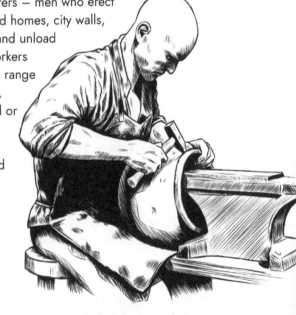

Feats (optional)

This is where the game really moves away from the original whitebox. I have to stress that feats are completely optional, the game works perfectly well without them. Both the expert and the fighter classes have options for using them without feats in keeping with the whitebox. But if you want your players to have nearly limitless options here is where you look.

Both fighters and experts have specific feats they can add as their characters gain levels. They have been designed to coincide with the casting classes getting new spell levels so everyone gets to feel they're progressing at the same time.

There are also additional feats that you can include in your game but how you use them is up to you. Below are a few options. Feel free to use any combination that fits the type of game you want to play, or make up your own;

- » Let all players take an extra feat at levels 2, 6 & 10
- » Play the original classes and add feats at every odd level
- » Let the players roll a hindrance at character creation and take a feat as a reward
- » If a player rolls their stats "down the line" at character creation let them take a feat
- » Make learning a non-class related feat costs 2,500gp, requires a teacher and takes 10 days.
- » Limit feats to 5 additional feats on top of those granted by their class.

As you can see there are a nearly limitless number of ways to build these into your game and it's easy to fit them into your campaign world.

By combining backgrounds, feats and multiclassing you cease to be restricted by the idea of traditional character classes, if you want a character who is a story-telling bard, then flies into a rage then feels guilty and heals their victims, it's all there.

Feats with an asterisk * can be taken more than once.

Expert Feats

Backstab - When attacking with surprise, from behind, the Expert gains advantage on the attack roll and a successful attack inflicts double damage. At levels 5-8, damage is tripled, and above level 8 such an attack inflicts quadruple damage.

Charmer - Charisma rolls to make a first impression, get on someone's good side and open social doors are done with advantage

Chemist - Hurling oil, alchemist fire, or any kind of exploding potions or bombs, will explode in a radius 5 ft wider than normal.

Contacts (High) - You have friends among the Nobles or Merchant Class in the better parts of towns and cities. They may help you by sharing information, giving aid, etc. but with the rich there is always a price of some kind.

Contacts (Low) - You have friends in the seedier parts of towns and cities, who may help you find what you are looking for, sometimes for a price.

Disguise - Whenever you are attempting to conceal your true identity, rolls are Easy (DC 8). In addition, if you would like to suddenly appear in an encounter you are not in, spend an Inspiration (see page 97) and, if feasible, you appear in the scene, having been there in disguise the entire time.

Escape Artist - You can escape from any prison or manacles, no roll necessary.

Hear Noise (WIS) - Listening intently an Expert can hear the slightest sound in a range of NEAR. This requires a successful WIS Check and maybe EASY, NORMAL, or HARD. They can discern numbers, details of conversations, and far more than someone unskilled.

Hide in Shadows (DEX) - Hide in Shadows requires a DEX Check and is compared to the NPC or Monsters passive Perception. You must break line of sight to hide.

Mimic - you have an ear for sounds and the ability to recreate them. Whether it's an accent, a specific person's voice, or even an animal call.

Move Silently (DEX) - Moving Silently requires a DEX Check and is compared to the NPC or Monsters passive Perception.

Open Locks (DEX) - Picking a lock requires Thieve's Tools and a DEX Check. Locks are EASY (DC 8), NORMAL (DC 12), or HARD (DC 16).

Parkour - Tests of climbing/balance are always EASY and if you fall complete an easy DEX save to half damage and land on your feet.

Pick Pocket (DEX) - Picking a pocket requires a DEX Check and maybe EASY, NORMAL or HARD.

Poised to strike - Advantage on initiative rolls

Poison Use - You are well versed in poison making and identification, and use double your proficiency bonus on most any checks involving poison.

Read Normal Languages - You can figure out the gist of most written languages, and have an 80% chance to comprehend treasure maps or written documents. This does not mean they can automatically decipher codes or solve riddles, although it would allow them to understand what a riddle says, for example.

Traps (INT or DEX) - Finding a trap requires an INT Check. Disarming a trap requires a DEX Check and Thieve's Tools and setting a trap requires 1d4 rounds and a successful INT Check Finding, disarming, and setting a trap may be EASY, NORMAL, or HARD.

Weaponless Damage - You are an expert in fighting with your bare hands. Unarmed strikes do d6 damage modified by either your strength or dex bonus.

Wise Mouth - You have the ability to get under people's skin. By saying a wise comment you force opposition to make a Charisma save to keep their cool. This may result in them flying into a rage, showing their hand, or forgetting their tactics for a short period.

Fighter Feats

Battlecry - Terrify all Near opponents with a successful Charisma roll vs. their DC (Easy, Normal, Hard). You and your allies' actions against them have advantage for one full round.

Blind Fighting - You can close combat (melee) fight in utter darkness, even magical, with no penalty.

Bodyguard - Once per combat round you may choose to take damage that would have hit an adjacent ally.

Brawler - Add proficiency to engaging, holding, and escaping grapple checks.

Cutting Edge - You may reroll an attack's damage once per combat.

Death Strike - When you strike an enemy dead, immediately make an attack against another Near enemy.

Deflect Missiles - You are an expert at using your position to minimize the chances of being hit by missile fire. You gain +3 to your AC for any missile weapon attack against you that you are aware of.

Feint - You are an expert at dodging and lulling your opponent in. You have advantage on any melee attack the round after you perform the dodge action

Hurl Weapon - Can throw any proficient weapon out to Near with no penalty.

Marksman - Use your action to aim and get advantage on your next ranged attack. You may not move while aiming.

Mounted Combat - You gain +1 to-hit and damage while fighting mounted on an animal.

Poised to strike - Advantage on initiative rolls

Quick Fire - Once per round on a natural 19 or 20 you can fire a second shot. This works for any ranged attack.

Rage - You can choose to enter a rage at the start of your turn, or in response to taking damage. While in a rage, you have +1 attack rolls, and your melee attacks inflict +1 damage and are immune to pain and fear. While raging, you cannot do anything defensive, curative, or tactical with your allies. All you can do is attempt to kill things. Rage lasts for 1 minute (10 rounds). You can will yourself to stop raging with a Hard (DC 16) Wisdom check. If one of your allies has injured you in this fight they count as an enemy. If all enemies are slain before your rage ends you attack your allies if willing yourself to stop fails.

Second Attack - May be taken at 7th fighter level or above

Shield Specialist - (Requirement: shield proficiency) You gain an additional +1 bonus to Armor Class with shields.

Vital Strikes - You inflict critical hits on a d20 roll of 19 or 20.

Weapon Focus* - You gain +1 attack bonus with one weapon; repeatable with different weapons.

Weapon Mastery * - (Requirement: Must have the Weapon Focus Feat for the weapon) You gain a +2 bonus to damage with one weapon; repeatable with different weapons.

Weaponless Damage - You are an expert in fighting with your bare hands. Unarmed strikes do d6 damage modified by either your strength or dex bonus.

General Feats

Most of these feats are available to every class, any restrictions are in parenthesis after the feat name eg **Armored Caster (Magic-User)**

Alertness - Add 5 to your passive Perception when it comes to being surprised.

Ancient Lore - When studying ancient texts, recalling history, reading arcane scripts, etc. all rolls are Easy (DC 8).

Animal Companion* - Your character has a small (1 HD or less) animal companion. This animal can understand simple commands. If you lose the animal you can find a new one but it takes d8 weeks to fully train them. If you take the Animal Companion Feat a second time you can have a larger animal companion, up to 2 HD.

Armor Proficiency* - You may now wear Armor one step above what your Class allows, plus a shield (i.e. None to Light, Light to Medium, etc.). This can be taken multiple times, 1 time per armor type.

Armored Caster (Magic-User) - You may cast spells while wearing armor, and you gain proficiency with, Light armor.

Attractive - Rolls are Easy (DC 8) in situations where your physical beauty may be important.

Blessed by the Gods - You can store up to 3 Inspirations.

Blessing (Cleric) - Choose an ally, on a successful Normal Wisdom Check (DC 12) their next check, attack, or saving throw is done with advantage.

Channel (Cleric) - Use one of your spell slots to heal everyone within a Near radius for 1d3 hit points per spell level.

Detect Evil (Cleric) - As an action and with a successful Normal (DC 12) Wisdom Check you can detect any evil creatures or items out to Near.

Disease Immunity - You are immune to all diseases, even magical ones.

Divine Favor* (Cleric) - Saving throws against one of your spells are at Disadvantage: repeatable with different spells.

Dodge - You gain a +1 bonus to Armor Class.

Exhort Greatness - Speak (or sing) to an ally, make a Normal (DC 12) Charisma check, on a success they gain 5 temporary Hit Points that last up to 10 rounds. This can only be used once per ally per combat and the ally must be conscious.

Faith Healing (Cleric) - When attempting to Stabilize a downed character if your roll is successful they stabilize and gain 1d4 Hit Points.

Fast - When performing the dash action, you may move up to 3 times your normal speed (Instead of 2).

Favored Enemy* - Choose a specific enemy (Hobgoblin, Orc, etc) attack rolls against them are now done with Advantage.

Fearless - When making any checks against Fear, magical or otherwise, saves or checks are done with Advantage.

Fearsome - When attempting to intimidate opponents or others, rolls are done with Advantage.

Great Eyesight - When making sight-based checks, rolls are done with Advantage.

Great Hearing - When making hearing-based checks, rolls are done with Advantage.

Great Sense of Smell - When making smell-based checks, rolls are done with Advantage.

Hardy Caster (Magic-User, Cleric) - You get Easy (DC 8) checks on any attempt to break your concentration while maintaining a spell.

Healer - Reviving a downed character is Easy (DC 8) instead of Normal.

Hearty Eater (Halfling) - Heal 1d4 hit point every time you eat a full meal.

Holy Aura (Cleric) - Make a Normal (DC 12) Wisdom Check, on a success all attacks against Close allies have Disadvantage until your next turn. This can only be performed once per encounter.

Inspire - Use your Action to inspire a teammate. Make a Normal Charisma Check (DC 12), on a success the inspired teammate gets Advantage on their next roll. Once per teammate per scene.

Known Spell* - Choose one 1st level spell from either the Cleric or Magic-User lists. You can cast this spell once per Short Rest. You can take this multiple times to gain new spells.

Lay on Hands* - Once per day you can cure others of 3 hit points of damage. This can be taken several times

Learned* - When recalling facts from a chosen specialty your roll is Easy (DC 8).

Linguist * - You may learn an additional language of your choice.

Luck - Once per Short Rest you may re-roll any Natural 1 (Does not include death saves)

Lucky Halfling (Halfling) - All party members within Near gain +1 to saving throws.

Magic Resistance - When making saving throws versus spells and magic, rolls have Advantage.

Night Sight - You can see in near darkness out to Near as if it was Dim Light.

Persuasive - When trying to persuade someone, checks are done with Advantage.

Precise Shot - When you fire into melee combat, you never hit an ally.

Presence - You roll with advantage on all initial Charisma reaction rolls.

Protection from Poison - Rolls are Easy (DC 8) when trying to resist the effects of any magical or non-magical poison, toxin, or venom.

Quickness - Your speed is Fast.

Resilient - You gain a +1 bonus to all saving throws.

Resist Elements - All checks and saving throws against elemental damage are done with Advantage. You are unaffected by the weather.

Sharp Senses - All checks to spot an illusion or the invisible are done with Advantage.

Smite (Cleric) - Fighting Attacks against Undead, Demons & Devils are done with Advantage.

Tracking - You are able to track down other creatures in the wild, in cities, and even through underground passages. When making tracking checks you add double your proficiency bonus to the roll. On a success, you also learn their exact number, their sizes, and how long ago they passed through the area.

Tunnel Vision (Dwarf) - Your darkvision has a range of Far.

Undead Scourge (Cleric) - Your rolls to turn undead are done with advantage.

Vigor - You gain 1 extra hit point per level.

Weapon Proficiency* - Choose a weapon that is not allowed by your class, you are now proficient with it and can use it without a penalty.

Remember, these are just a small selection of possible feats. Use them as building blocks to create your own or steal ideas from other games.

If there's something cool someone really wants to do and it fits your game then create a feat and add it to the collection.

Hindrances (optional)

Hindrances, although completely optional, add a little depth and interest to characters creating great opportunities for roll play. PC's in Olde Swords Reign are not perfectly optimized heroes they tend to be more flawed adventurers who do the best they can.

If players roll a random hindrance using the hindrance table let them pick a general feat to start the game with. Try to stay true to the results and be creative with how you implement them.

We've had an assassin who was a coward and a magic-user librarian addicted to the glue from book bindings!

Addiction - You are addicted to some substance, and rolls are HARD for most actions after 24 hours of not having access to your addiction.

All Thumbs - When attempting delicate tasks like lock picking, firing a crossbow, etc rolls have Disadvantage.

Arrogant - You are better than everyone. Roll with Disadvantage in most any social interaction.

Arsonist - You love fire, taking any opportunity you can to set things ablaze even if it is a very bad idea.

Cannot Lie - You can never lie. No matter the consequence.

City Dweller - When outside of the safety of a city, roll with Disadvantage when attempting anything to do with wilderness survival.

Clumsy - When attempting any action that involves balance, roll with Disadvantage.

Combat Paralysis - When combat starts make a Hard (DC16) Charisma check or you freeze for 1d3 rounds. While frozen you can defend yourself but you cannot make an attack.

Coward - Roll with Disadvantage when making checks against fear or intimidation. You are easily spooked.

Cursed - You never gain Inspiration.

Distrusts Magic - Roll with Disadvantage when socially interacting with magic-users.

Drunk - At the start of each session roll a d6 on a 1 you are drunk and all rolls associated with balance and coordination are rolled with disadvantage.

Dumb - You are weak of mind. Lose one point of Intelligence and cannot raise Intelligence above 18.

Elderly - You are old. If pushed physically and without rest, roll with Disadvantage on most checks and attempts.

Fanatic - You are a zealous believer. Roll with Disadvantage when dealing with non-believers in most situations.

Fear of... - Choose something you have an irrational fear of. When in its presence all your rolls are at Disadvantage.

Forgetful - You have a terrible memory and have difficulty remembering names, dates, appointments etc., usually at the most inopportune time.

Fragile - You are delicate of build. Subtract 2 Hit Points from your total.

Greedy - You cannot resist the chance to make money. Roll with Disadvantage when trying to resist being tempted by gold.

Gullible - You tend to believe anything. Roll with Disadvantage when someone tries to persuade you into doing something that's a terrible idea.

Illiterate - You cannot read or write.

Insane - You are afflicted with some kind of madness. Work with the Referee to determine its effects.

Landlover - Whenever you are on water you get ill. Roll with Disadvantage for any activity while at sea.

Lazy - You do everything you can to avoid anything that feels like work, regardless of the impact this has on other people.

Lecherous - You find it difficult to resist a pretty face. Roll with Disadvantage when tempted by others with sex or when trying to resist the advances or persuasiveness of those you'd find attractive.

Missing Arm - You can only use 1 handed weapons and are unable to use a shield while fighting.

Missing Leg - Roll with Disadvantage in situations where the Referee determines its appropriate.

Natural Fool - You have a great gift of creating the most hysterical insults, unfortunately, you don't share this gift voluntarily.

Obsessed - You are completely obsessed with something. Whenever you are in its presence your roll with Disadvantage when trying any task that would cause you to ignore your obsession.

Pacifist - You will not fight. You can defend yourself but under no circumstance will you raise a blade.

Petty Liar - You constantly lie about the smallest things, sticking to these lies even when they are pointed out.

Poor Eyesight - Roll with Disadvantage when attempting any sight-based checks.

Poor Hearing - Roll with Disadvantage when attempting any hearing-based checks.

Poor Sense of Smell - Roll with Disadvantage when attempting any scent-based checks.

Poor Stamina - You have a terrible constitution. Lose one point of Constitution and you can never raise your Constitution above 18.

Quiet - You very, very rarely speak. Roll with Disadvantage in most social situations.

Repugnant - Your personality and presence is horrible. Lose one point of Charisma and you can never raise your Charisma above 18.

Slow - Your agility is low. Lose one point of Dexterity and you can never raise your Dexterity above an 18.

Socially Mute - You struggle to speak to strangers. You roll with Disadvantage in social situations where you are trying to be understood.

Talkative - You overshare in almost any situation. Including giving away intentions, plans, and secrets

Temper - Your anger often gets the better of you, roll with Disadvantage when attempting to not fly off the handle when insulted, etc.

Ugly - Roll with Disadvantage anytime your looks are important.

Unaware - Your passive Perception is 5 points lower when used to see if you are Surprised.

Unsettling - Something about you isn't quite right. Roll with Disadvantage in social situations or when dealing with animals.

Uncoordinated - You fumble with shooting weapons. You have Disadvantage on any attack rolls with ranged weapons.

Wanted - You are wanted by authorities or by some criminal organization. When entering a new town or city roll the Referee rolls a d6, on a 1, agents of those authorities or organizations will make your life unpleasant.

Weak - You are weak of body. Lose 1 point of Strength and you can never raise your Strength above an 18.

Yokel - When outside of the safety of your rural environment, your rolls have Disadvantage when attempting anything to do with urban survival.

Young - You are young, unsettlingly so to be adventuring. Your rolls have Disadvantage when you are in social situations where you are dealing with 'grown-ups'.

Zealot - You have absolute faith in your religion. All the others are wrong and you don't mind telling them. You believe that the more followers you convert the higher your rewards in the afterlife.

Hindrance Table

Result	Hindrance	Result	Hindrance
1-2	Addiction	51-52	Missing Arm
3-4	All Thumbs	53-54	Missing Leg
5-6	Arrogant	55-56	Natural Fool
7-8	Arsonist	57-58	Obsessed
9-10	Cannot Lie	59-60	Pacifist
11-12	City Dweller	61-62	Petty Liar
13-14	Clumsy	63-64	Poor Eyesight
15-16	Combat Paralysis	65-66	Poor Hearing
17-18	Coward	67-68	Poor Sense of Smell
19-20	Cursed	69-70	Poor Stamina
21-22	Distrusts Magic	71-72	Quiet
23-24	Drunk	73-74	Repugnant
25-26	Dumb	75-76	Slow
27-28	Elderly	77-78	Socially Mute
29-30	Fanatic	79-80	Talkative
31-32	Fear of...	81-82	Temper
33-34	Forgetful	83-84	Ugly
35-36	Fragile	85-86	Unaware
37-38	Greedy	87-88	Uncoordinated
39-40	Gullible	89-90	Unsettling
41-42	Illiterate	91-92	Wanted
43-44	Insane	93-94	Weak
45-46	Landlover	95-96	Yokel
47-48	Lazy	97-98	Young
49-50	Lecherous	99-100	Zealot

Languages

Your race indicates the languages your character can speak by default. Characters can also choose one additional language for each +1 Intelligence modifier they have above +1. *i.e. a character with a +3 INT modifier gains two additional languages.*

Choose your languages from the Standard Languages table, or choose one that is common in your campaign.

Language	Typical Speakers
Common	Humans
Dwarvish	Dwarves
Elvish	Elves
Giant	Ogres, Giants
Goblin	Goblinoids
Halfling	Halflings
Orc	Orcs

With the referee's permission, you can instead choose a language from the Exotic Languages table.

Language	Typical Speakers
Abyssal	Demons
Celestial	Celestials
Draconic	Dragons, Kobolds
Deep Speech	Aboleth, Cloakers
Infernal	Devils
Primordial	Elementals
Sylvan	Fey Creatures, Gnomes
Undercommon	Drow, Underworld Traders

EQUIPMENT

Coins

The three most common coins are the gold piece (gp), the silver piece (sp), and the copper piece (cp).

One gold piece is worth 10 sp or 100 cp, and 1 sp is worth 10 cp.

Standard Exchange Rates

Coin	cp	sp	gp
Copper	1	1/10	1/100
Silver	10	1	1/10
Gold	100	10	1

Selling Treasure

Opportunities abound to find treasure, equipment, weapons, armor, and more in the dungeons you explore. Normally, you can sell your treasures and trinkets when you return to a town or other settlement, provided that you can find buyers and merchants interested in your loot.

Arms, Armor, and Other Equipment. Undamaged weapons, armor, and other equipment fetch half their cost when sold in a market.

Magic Items. Finding someone to buy a potion or a scroll isn't too hard, but other items are out of the realms of most but the wealthiest nobles. The value of magic is far beyond simple gold and should always be treated as such.

Gems, Jewelry, and Art Objects. These items retain their full value in the marketplace, and you can either trade them in for coin or use them as currency for other transactions.

Trade Goods. Many people conduct transactions through barter. Much like gems and art objects, trade goods — bars of iron, bags of salt, livestock, and so on—retain their full value in the market, and can be used as currency.

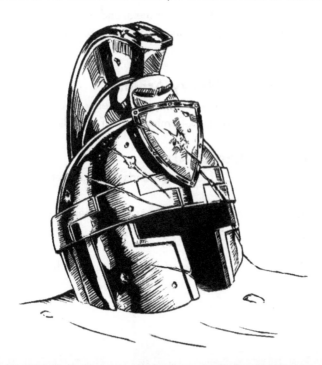

Armor

The Armor table shows the cost, inventory slots, and other properties of the common types of armor worn in fantasy gaming worlds.

Armor Proficiency. Anyone can put on a suit of armor or strap a shield to an arm, however, only those proficient in the armor's use know how to wear it effectively.

Your class gives you proficiency with certain types of armor. If you wear armor that you lack proficiency with, you have disadvantage on any ability check, saving throw, or attack roll that involves Strength or Dexterity.

Minimum Strength. Heavier armor interferes with the wearer's ability to move quickly, stealthily, and freely. Plate Mail armor reduces the wearer's speed by 10 feet unless the wearer has a Strength score equal to 12 or higher.

Stealth. If the Armor table shows "Disadvantage" in the Stealth column, the wearer has disadvantage on Dexterity checks to do with stealth.

Shields. A shield is made from wood or metal and is carried in one hand. Wielding a shield increases your Armor Class by 1. You can benefit from only one shield at a time.

Light, Medium, and Heavy Armors
No matter the armor you wear, you add your Dexterity modifier to the base number from your armor type to determine your Armor Class.

Getting Into and Out of Armor
The time it takes to don or doff armor depends on the armor's category.

Don. This is the time it takes to put on armor. You benefit from the armor's AC only if you take the full time to don the suit of armor.

Doff. This is the time it takes to take off armor. If you have help, reduce this time by half.

Sleeping in Armor (optional)

It is possible to sleep in most types of armor but, due to its size and unwieldy nature, if you sleep in heavy armor you must make a successful Normal (DC12) Constitution check in the morning to benefit from a short rest. If you roll a natural 1 you receive a level of exhaustion.

Armor	Cost	AC	Min	Don	Doff
None	-	10 + DEX mod	-	-	-
Leather (light)	15 gp	12 + DEX mod	-	1 minute	1 minute
Chain (medium)	30 gp	14 + DEX mod	9	5 minute	1 minute
Plate (heavy)*	50 gp	16 + DEX mod	12	10 minutes	5 minutes
Shield	10 gp	AC +1	-	1 action	1 action

* When wearing Heavy Plate Armor you have disadvantage on all stealth checks and it takes up 2 inventory slots

Weapons

The Weapons table shows the most common weapons, their price and size, the damage they deal when they hit, and any special properties they possess. Every weapon is classified as either melee or ranged. A melee weapon is used to attack a target within CLOSE (5ft) range of you, whereas a ranged weapon is used to attack a target at a distance.

Weapon Proficiency
Your race, class, and feats can grant you proficiency with certain weapons or categories of weapons.

Proficiency with a weapon allows you to add your proficiency bonus to the attack roll for any attack you make with that weapon. If you make an attack roll using a weapon with which you lack proficiency, you do not add your proficiency bonus to the attack roll.

Weapon Categories
The two categories are simple and martial.

Most people can use simple weapons with proficiency. These weapons include clubs, maces, and other weapons often found in the hands of commoners.

Martial weapons, including swords, axes, and polearms, require more specialized training to use effectively. Most fighters use martial weapons because these weapons put their fighting style and training to best use.

Weapon Properties
Many weapons have special properties related to their use, as shown in the Weapons table.

Ammunition. You must have ammunition to fire a weapon with this property, and each time you fire you expend one piece of ammunition. Drawing the ammunition from a quiver is part of the attack (you need a free hand to load a one-handed weapon). At the end of the battle, you can recover half your expended ammunition by taking a minute to search the battlefield.

Finesse. You can choose Strength or Dexterity modifier for the attack and damage rolls. You must use the same modifier for both rolls.

Heavy. Small creatures, like Halflings, have disadvantage on attack rolls with heavy weapons. A heavy weapon's size and bulk make it too large for a Small creature to use effectively. A heavy weapon takes up 2 inventory slots.

Light. A light weapon is small and easy to handle, making it ideal for use when fighting with two weapons.

Range. The maximum range of a weapon in parentheses is in the weapon properties column. Ranges in OSR are Close, Near, Far, and Very Far). When attacking a target beyond the weapons range, you have disadvantage on the attack roll, and going beyond range with certain weapons may be impossible (referee's discretion). You can't attack a target beyond double the weapons range.

Reach. This weapon adds 5 feet to your reach when you attack with it, as well as when determining your reach for opportunity attacks with it.

Thrown. You can throw the weapon to make a ranged attack. If the weapon is a melee weapon, you use the same ability modifier for that attack roll and damage roll that you would use for a melee attack with the weapon. The range for the weapon is in parentheses after the Thrown property. For example, if you throw a hand axe, you use your Strength, but if you throw a dagger, you can use either your Strength or your Dexterity, since the dagger has the finesse property.

Two-Handed. This weapon requires two hands when you attack with it.

Versatile. This weapon can be used with one or two hands. When used two-handed the damage value in parentheses is the two-handed damage.

Improvised Weapons

Sometimes characters don't have their weapons and have to attack with whatever is at hand. An improvised weapon includes any object you can wield in one or two hands, such as broken glass, a table leg, a frying pan, a wagon wheel, or a dead goblin.

Often, an improvised weapon is similar to an actual weapon and can be treated as such. For example, a table leg is akin to a club. At the Referee's adjudication, a character proficient with a weapon can use a similar object as if it were that weapon and use their proficiency bonus.

An object that bears no resemblance to a weapon deals 1d4 damage (the Referee assigns a damage type appropriate to the object). If a character uses a ranged weapon to make a melee attack or throws a melee weapon that does not have the thrown property, it also deals 1d4 damage. An improvised thrown weapon has a normal range of Near.

Silvered Weapons

Some monsters that have immunity or resistance to non-magical weapons are susceptible to silver weapons, so cautious adventurers invest extra coin to plate their weapons with silver. You can silver a single weapon or ten pieces of ammunition for 100 gp. This cost represents not only the price of the silver but the time and expertise needed to add silver to the weapon without making it less effective.

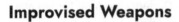

Simple Melee Weapons

Weapon	Cost	Damage	Properties
Dagger	3 gp	1d4 piercing	Thrown (Near), light, finesse
Hand Axe	3 gp	1d6 slashing	Thrown (Near), light
Wood Axe	3 gp	1d6 slashing	Two-handed, heavy
Mace	5 gp	1d6 (1d8) bludgeoning	Versatile
Spear	1 gp	1d6 (1d8) piercing	Thrown (Near), versatile
Staff	1 gp	1d6 bludgeoning	-

Simple Ranged Weapons

Weapon	Cost	Damage	Properties
Light Crossbow	15 gp	1d4+1 piercing	Ammunition, two-handed (Far)
Short Bow	25 gp	1d6 piercing	Ammunition, two-handed (Far)
Sling	1 sp	1d4 bludgeoning	Ammunition, two-handed (Near)

Ammunitions

Weapon	Cost	Range
Case with 30 Quarrels	10 gp	Far
Quiver of 20 Arrows	10 gp	Far
Silver Tipped Arrow	5 gp	Far
Sling Stones (50)	4 cp	Near

Martial Melee Weapons

Weapon	Cost	Damage	Properties
Battle Axe	3 gp	1d8 (1d10) slashing	Versatile, heavy
Flail	8 gp	1d8 bludgeoning	-
Halberd	7 gp	1d10 slashing	Two-handed, heavy, reach
Lance	4 gp	1d8 piercing	Heavy, reach
Morning Star	6 gp	1d8 piercing	-
Pike	5 gp	1d8 piercing	Two-handed, heavy, reach
Pole Arm	7 gp	1d8 piercing	Two- handed
Short Sword	8 gp	1d6 slashing	Light, finesse
Sword	10 gp	1d6 (1d8) slashing	Versatile
Two-handed Sword	15 gp	1d10 slashing	Two-handed, heavy

Martial Ranged Weapons

Weapon	Cost	Damage	Properties
Heavy Crossbow	25 gp	1d4+1 piercing	Ammunition, two-handed (Far)
Long Bow	40 gp	1d8 piercing	Ammunition, two-handed (Far)

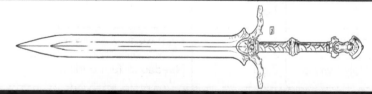

Adventuring Gear

Item	Cost	Properties
10' Pole	1 gp	Heavy
Iron Spikes (12)	1 gp	-
3 Stakes & Mallet	3 gp	-
50' of Rope	1 gp	-
Arcane Focus	15 gp	Arcane Focus
Backpack	5 gp	-
Flask of Oil	2 gp	Refill lanterns, fire
Holy Water	25 gp	1d8 damage to undead
Lantern	10 gp	Light to Near, Bullseye To Far
Large Sack	2 gp	Hold 20 additional items
Potion of Healing	75 gp	Heal 1d6+1 damage
Provisions (10)	10 gp	Food, water and first aid
Silver Holy Symbol	25 gp	Needed to Turn Undead
Silver Mirror, small	15 gp	-
Small Sack	1 gp	Hold 10 additional items
Spellbook	100 gp	Holds 20 spells
Steel Mirror	5 gp	-
Thieves' Tools	25 gp	Required to pick locks
Torches (6)	1 gp	Light to Near
Water/ Wine skin	1 gp	-
Wine (quart)	1 gp	-
Wolfsbane (bunch)	10 gp	Keep werewolves away
Wooden Holy Symbol	2 gp	Needed to Turn Undead

Adventuring Gear Descriptions

10' Pole. Used to prod around for traps.

12 Iron spikes. Used to climb, spike shut doors, etc.

3 Stakes & Mallet. For all your vampire hunting needs.

50' of Rope. Rope, made of hemp, has 2 hit points and can be burst with a Hard (DC 16) Strength check.

Arcane Focus. An arcane focus is a special item— an orb, a crystal, a rod, a specially constructed staff, a wand-like length of wood, or some similar item, designed to channel the power of arcane spells. A magic-user can use this item as a spellcasting focus.

Backpack. A backpack allows a character to carry 10 additional items (See Encumbrance pg.102).

Flask of Oil. Can be used as a Near ranged weapon for 1d6 fire damage per round until extinguished.

Holy Water. Causes 1d8 damage (thrown weapon attack, Near range) when thrown on most types of undead creatures and demons. This can be useful, since many of the more-powerful undead and demons can otherwise only be damaged with magical weapons.

Lantern. A lantern casts light in a Near radius. Once lit, it burns for 6 hours on a flask (1 pint) of oil. As an action, you can lower the hood, using it in a direct line out to Far.

Large Sack. Large sacks allow you to carry 20 additional items but they take up a hand, and DEX based moves are HARD.

Potion of Healing. This small vial or bottle heals 1d6+1 hit points of damage. Drinking or administering a potion takes an action.

Provisions. These are an amalgamation of food, water, and first aid supplies (see Provisions p112.).

Silver Holy Symbol. A holy symbol is a representation of a god or pantheon. It might be an amulet depicting a symbol representing a deity, the same symbol carefully engraved or inlaid as an emblem on a shield, or a tiny box holding a fragment of a sacred relic. A cleric can use a holy symbol as a spellcasting focus. To use the symbol in this way, the caster must hold it in hand, wear it visibly, or bear it on a shield.

Silver Mirror, small. A small (4-inch in diameter) mirror, can be used for signaling others from a distance and looking around corners.

Small Sack. Small sacks allow you to carry 10 additional items but they take up a hand, and DEX based moves are HARD.

Spellbook. Essential for magic-users, a spellbook is a leather-bound tome with 100 blank vellum pages suitable for recording spells. Holds up to 20 spells.

Steel Mirror. A sheet of mirrored steel, usually 2 ft. In diameter.

Thieves' Tools. A set of small lock picks, pliers, etc.

Torch. A torch burns for 1 hour, providing light out to Near. If you make a melee attack with a burning torch and hit, it deals 1d4 fire damage.

Transport, Tack & Harness

Item	Cost	Properties
Barding, (Horse Armor)	150 gp	Increases mounts AC to 17
Cart	100 gp	Transport up to 50 items
Large Galley	30,000 gp	-
Large Merchant Ship	20,000 gp	-
Mule	20 gp	Can carry 50 items
Riding Horse	40 gp	-
Saddle	25 gp	-
Saddle Bags	10 gp	Carry 20 items and rider
Small Boat	100 gp	Up to 6 passengers
Small Galley	10,000 gp	-
Small Merchant Ship	5,000 gp	-
Wagon	200 gp	Transport up to 100 items
Warhorse	200 gp	-

MAGIC

Magic permeates most fantasy worlds. In Olde Swords Reign, spells are split into two specific types - arcane and divine.

Arcane spells are cast by magic users and are the result of study and manipulation of the very fabric of creation.

Divine spells are granted to clerics from whatever deity they worship. As a result, they behave slightly differently. A cleric has access to all of the spells available for their class level whereas a magic user can only prepare spells that are already in their spell book.

Spell Preparation

Each morning through meditation (cleric), or study (magic-user), a caster prepares the spells they plan to cast that day. The total number of spells that can be prepared is the spell casters level + their casting stat modifier.

E.g. For Clerics this is Wisdom and magic-users it is Intelligence. So a 4th-level Cleric with 16 Wisdom (+3) can prepare a total of 4+3=7 spells each day.

Spell Slots

A spell caster's level determines both the quantity and level of spells that they can cast. As they progress in levels, so do their abilities.

Spells are cast using slots, so a 3rd level caster has 4 first-level slots and 2 second-level slots. A first-level spell fits into a first-level slot but can also fit into a higher-level slot, but the reverse does not apply.

A higher-level spell can not be cast using a lower level slot. You can picture the spells needing slightly larger slots as they increase levels. Once that spell slot is expended a caster requires a short rest before they can use it again.

Level	1st	2nd	3rd	4th	5th	6th
1st	2	-	-	-	-	-
2nd	3	-	-	-	-	-
3rd	4	2	-	-	-	-
4th	4	3	-	-	-	-
5th	4	3	2	-	-	-
6th	4	3	3	-	-	-
7th	4	3	3	1	-	-
8th	4	3	3	2	-	-
9th	4	3	3	3	1	-
10th	4	3	3	3	2	-
11th	4	3	3	3	2	1
12th	4	3	3	3	2	1

Casting with Armor

Spells cannot be cast whilst wearing armor unless the caster has taken the Armored Caster Feat

Spellbook

A magic user's spell book is the center of their world. It's where they store all of the arcane knowledge they have collected and must be studied daily to prepare spells.

Spells can be added to the spell book as you gain levels or "acquire" other magic-users spell books. You can even copy scrolls into your book, which expends the scroll but leaves that spell accessible to you.
Copying a new spell into your book is an in-depth process, requiring the finest inks and large amounts of practice as you decipher the spell and recreate it with your own unique notation. It takes 1 day for every level of the spell and costs 500gp per day.

Because spell books are so valuable, magic-users often spend some downtime making a copy for safekeeping. As these spells are already known to you and in your own notation it's a much easier process, and only takes 1 hour per level of spell and costs 100gp per level.

Cantrips

Cantrips are essentially level 0 spells and can be cast at will by magic-users only. The two cantrips available in this game are wizards bolt and prestidigitation.

Spellcasting Focus

To cast spells you must channel your magic through a focus. For magic users it's an arcane focus and for clerics it's a holy symbol. This focus must be held firmly in hand whilst casting.

Casting a Spell

Each spell description begins with a block of information, including the spell's name, level, casting time, range, components, and duration. The rest of a spell entry describes the spell's effect.

Casting Time

Most spells require a single action to cast, but some spells require more time to cast. If a spell requires more time then you must maintain concentration while doing so (see "Concentration" below)

Components

A spell's components are the physical requirements you must meet in order to cast it. Each spell's description indicates whether it requires verbal (V) or somatic (S) components.

Verbal (V) this requires the caster to be able to speak freely and be heard - so an area of silence would make it impossible to cast a spell with this component.

Somatic (S) Require Spellcasting gestures that require at least one hand to be free. These gestures are obvious and easily identified as casting a spell.

Concentration

If a spell requires concentration, it is still possible to move, perform actions and even attack an opponent.
You can only concentrate on one spell at a time
If you take damage, you must make a Normal (DC 12) Constitution saving throw. If you fail you lose concentration and the spell dissipates.
If you are incapacitated or killed your spell dissipates
The referee might decide that other environmental phenomena may require a constitution saving throw like being hit by a wave on a ship. The dc of the check will be set by the referee.

Targets

To target a person or point you must have a clear path to the Target. If the spell is an area of effect you only have to have a clear path to the original point from which the spell erupts. So, a fireball's area of effect can expand to areas not in your line of sight.

Saving Throws

If a spell requires a saving throw, the DC to resist equals 8 + your spellcasting ability modifier + your proficiency bonus + any special modifiers.

Attack Rolls

Some spells require the caster to make an attack roll to determine whether the spell effect hits the intended target. Your attack bonus with a spell attack equals your spellcasting ability modifier + your proficiency bonus.

Combining Magical Effects

The effects of different spells add together while the durations of those spells overlap. The effects of the same spell cast multiple times do not combine, however. Instead, the most potent effect (such as the highest bonus) from those castings applies while their durations overlap.

> *For example, if two clerics cast bless on the same target, that character gains the spell's benefit only once; he or she doesn't get to add two +1's to attack rolls.*

Cleric Spell List

1st level
Cure/Cause Light Wounds *
Detect Evil
Detect Magic
Light
Protection from Evil
Purify Food & Water

2nd level
Bless
Find Traps
Hold Person
Silence
Snake Charm
Speak with Animals

3rd level
Continual Light
Cure/Cause Disease *
Locate Object
Prayer
Remove/Cause Curse *
Speak with Dead

4th level
Create Water
Cure/Cause Serious Wounds *
Neutralize Poison
Protection from Evil, Near
Speak with Plants
Turn Sticks to Snakes

5th level
Commune
Create Food
Dispel Evil
Insect Plague
Quest
Raise Dead

6th level
Animate Object
Blade Barrier
Conjure Animals
Find the Path
Speak with Monsters
Word of Recall

* Some Spells are reversible but this is dependent on the cleric's deity. A god of light and goodness might not allow one of their clerics to create disease or cause wounds to an innocent. This would be left up to the referee.
When preparing a spell the cleric must decide what form of the spell they are preparing.

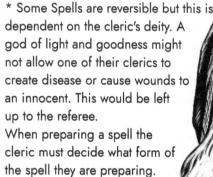

Magic-User Spell List

Cantrips
Prestidigitation
Wizards Bolt

1st level
Charm Person
Detect Magic
Hold Portal
Light
Magic Missile
Protection from Evil
Read Languages
Read Magic
Shield
Sleep

2nd level
Continual Light
Darkness
Detect Evil
Detect Invisible
ESP
Invisibility
Knock
Levitate
Locate Object
Magic Mouth
Mirror Image
Phantasmal Forces
Pyrotechnics
Strength
Web
Wizards Lock

3rd level
Clairaudience
Clairvoyance
Darkvision
Dispel Magic
Explosive Runes
Fireball
Fly
Haste
Hold Person
Invisibility, Close radius
Lightning Bolt
Monster Summoning I
Protection from Evil, Near
Protection from Normal Missiles
Rope Trick
Slow
Suggestion
Water Breathing

4th level
Charm Monster
Confusion
Dimension Door
Extension I
Fear
Hallucinatory Terrain
Ice Storm
Massmorph
Monster Summoning II
Plant Growth
Polymorph Others
Polymorph Self
Remove Curse
Wall of Ice
Wall of Fire
Wizard Eye

5th level

Animal Growth
Animate Dead
Cloudkill
Conjure Elemental
Contact Higher Plane
Extension II
Feeblemind
Hold Monster
Magic Jar
Monster Summoning III
Passwall
Telekinesis
Teleport
Transmute Rock to Mud
Wall of Iron
Wall of Stone

6th level

Anti-Magic Shell
Control Weather
Death Spell
Disintegrate
Enchant Item
Extension III
Geas
Invisible Stalker
Legend Lore
Lower Water
Monster Summoning IV
Move Earth
Part Water
Project Image
Reincarnation
Repulsion
Stone to Flesh

Animal Growth

5th-level magic-user spell
Casting Time: 1 action
Range: Far
Components: V, S
Duration: 2 hours

This spell causes 1d6 normal creatures to grow immediately to giant size. While the spell lasts, the affected creatures can attack as per a giant version of themselves.

Animate Dead

5th-level magic-user spell
Casting Time: 1 action
Range: Far
Components: V, S
Duration: Permanent

This spell animates skeletons or zombies from dead bodies. 1d6 undead are animated per level of the caster above 8th. The corpses remain animated until slain.

Animate Object

6th Level cleric spell
Casting Time: 1 action
Range: Far
Components: V, S
Duration: 1 hour

The Cleric "brings to life" inanimate objects such as statues, chairs, carpets, and tables. The objects follow the Cleric's commands, attacking foes or performing other actions on the caster's behalf. The Referee must determine the combat attributes of the objects (such as armor class, speed, hit dice, and to-hit bonuses) on the spur of the moment. A stone statue, as a basic example, might have AC of 18, attack as a creature with 7-9 HD, and inflict 2d8 points of damage. Wooden furniture would be considerably less dangerous.

Anti-Magic Shell

6th Level magic-user spell
Casting Time: 1 action
Range: Self
Components: V, S
Duration: 2 hours

An invisible bubble of force surrounds the caster, impenetrable to magic. Spells and other magical effects cannot pass into or out of the shell. The shell is ten feet in radius.

Blade Barrier

6th Level cleric spell
Casting Time: 1 action
Range: Far
Components: V, S
Duration: 12 turns

Mystical blades, whirling and thrusting, form a lethal circle around the spell's recipient, at a radius of 15 feet. The barrier inflicts 7d10 points of damage to anyone trying to pass through.

Bless

2nd-level cleric spell
Casting Time: 1 action
Range: Near
Components: V
Duration: 1 hour

This spell grants its recipient a +1 to attack rolls and saving throws.

Charm Monster

4th-level magic-user spell
Casting Time: 1 action
Range: Near
Components: V
Duration: see below

This spell operates in the same manner as Charm Person, but can affect any one living creature, including powerful monsters.

For monsters of fewer than 3 hit dice, up to 3d6 can be affected. Monsters can break free of the charm, (one chance per week) by making a successful CHA saving throw.

Charm Person

1st-level magic-user spell
Casting Time: 1 action
Range: Near
Components: V, S
Duration: Until dispelled

This spell affects living bipeds of human size or smaller, such as goblins or dryads. If the spell succeeds (CHA saving throw allowed), the unfortunate creature falls under the caster's influence. Every month a charmed creature is allowed a CHA saving throw, but if the creatures HD is greater than the casters level then the save can be performed once a week.

Clairaudience

3rd-level magic-user spell
Casting Time: 1 action
Range: Near
Components: V, S
Duration: 2 hours

Clairaudience allows the caster to hear through solid stone (limiting range to 2 feet or so), and other obstacles, any sounds within a range of Near. The spell's effect cannot pass through even a thin sheeting of lead for this metal blocks it utterly.

The spell can be cast through a crystal ball.

Clairvoyance

3rd-level magic-user spell
Casting Time: 1 action
Range: Near
Components: V, S
Duration: 2 hours

Clairvoyance allows the caster to see through solid stone (limiting range to 2 feet or so), and other obstacles, anything within a range of Near. The spell's effect cannot pass through even a thin sheeting of lead, however, for this metal blocks it completely.

Cloudkill

5th-level magic-user spell
Casting Time: 1 action
Range: Moves 6ft. per minute
Components: V, S
Duration: 1 hour

Foul and poisonous vapors boil from the thin air, forming a cloud 15 feet in radius at any target point within Far. The cloud moves directly forward at a rate of 6 feet per minute unless its direction or speed is affected by winds. Unusually strong gusts can dissipate and destroy the cloud.

Poison-laden, the horrid mist is heavier than air, and thus sinks down any pits or stairs in its path. For any creature with fewer than 5HD, touching the cloud (much less breathing it) requires a CON saving throw to avoid immediate death.

Commune

5th-level cleric spell
Casting Time: 1 action
Range: Self
Components: V, S
Duration: 3 Questions

Higher powers grant an answer to three questions the caster poses to them. Higher powers do not like being constantly interrogated by mere mortals, so use of the spell should be limited to once per week or so by the Referee.

Confusion

4th-level magic-user spell
Casting Time: 1 action
Range: Far
Components: V
Duration: 2 hours

This spell confuses people and monsters, making them act randomly. On a roll of 2d6, the creatures will do the following:

- » 2-5 Attack Caster & His Allies
- » 6-8 Stand Baffled and Inactive
- » 9-12 Attack Each Other

The effects of the confusion may shift every ten minutes or so, and the dice are once again rolled.

The spell affects 2d6 creatures, plus an additional creature for every caster level above 8th. Creatures of 3 hit dice or fewer are automatically affected by the spell, and it takes effect instantly. Creatures of 4 hit dice or more initially automatically overcome the confusion effect but as it builds up they must make a save 1d12 + creatures HD minutes later.

Eventually, these creatures are likely to succumb to the confusion, for they must continue to make another saving throw every 10 minutes until the spell's two-hour duration has run its course.

Conjure Animals

6th Level cleric spell
Casting Time: 1 action
Range: Far
Components: V, S
Duration: 1 hour

The Cleric conjures up normal animals to serve as allies: 1 creature larger than a man (such as an elephant or bear), 3 animals the size of a man or horse (such as a lion), or 6 animals smaller than a man (such as a wolf). The animals obey the caster's commands.

Conjure Elemental

5th-level magic-user spell
Casting Time: 1 action
Range: Far
Components: V, S
Duration: Concentration, or until dispelled or slain

The caster summons a 16 HD elemental (any kind) from the elemental planes of existence, and binds it to follow commands.

The elemental obeys the caster only for as long as the caster concentrates on it; and when the caster ceases to concentrate, even for a moment, the elemental is released and will attack its former master.

Contact Higher Plane

5th-level magic-user spell Casting
Time: 1 action
Range: Self
Components: V
Duration: Instantaneous

The caster creates a mental contact with the planes, forces, powers, and geometries of the beyond, in order to gain affirmative or negative answers to the questions they contemplate. The spell's effects depend upon how deep the caster quests into the various planes of existence. The caster must decide how "far" into the planes of existence they wish to make contact. The number of planes in "depth" that they choose will affect the number of yes or no questions they can ask, the chance that the knowledge is available at that level, the chance of receiving a wrong answer, and the chance that they will become temporarily insane from the experience. Temporary insanity lasts for as many weeks as the "number" of the plane where the caster's sanity failed (or was deliberately removed).

Contact Higher Plane Table

Plane	Max # of Questions	Available Knowledge	Wrong Result	Temporary Insanity
3rd	3	25%	70%	1%
4th	4	30%	60%	10%
5th	5	40%	50%	20%
6th	6	50%	40%	30%
7th	7	60%	30%	40%
8th	8	70%	25%	45%
9th	9	80%	20%	55%
10th	10	85%	15%	65%
11th	11	90%	10%	75%
12th	12	95%	1%	85%

Continual Light

2nd-level magic-user, 3rd-level cleric spell
Casting Time: 1 action
Range: Far
Components: V, S
Duration: Permanent unless dispelled

The targeted person or object produces light as bright as sunlight (and with the same effects as sunlight), to a radius of Far.

Control Weather

6th Level magic-user spell
Casting Time: 1 action
Range: Referee's discretion
Components: V, S
Duration: Referee's discretion

The caster can summon or stop rainfall, create unusually high or low temperatures, summon or disperse a tornado, clear the sky of clouds, or summon clouds into being.

Create Food

5th-level cleric spell
Casting Time: 1 action
Range: Close
Components: V, S
Duration: Instantaneous

This spell creates a one-day supply of food for 24 humans (or the like). At 10th level the amount of food doubles.

Create Water

4th-level cleric spell
Casting Time: 1 action
Range: Close
Components: V, S
Duration: Instantaneous

This spell creates a one-day supply of drinking water for 24 people (or, for game purposes, horses). At 9th level the amount of water doubles, and it doubles again at every level thereafter.

Cure/Cause Disease

3rd-level cleric spell
Casting Time: 1 action
Range: Touch
Components: V, S
Duration: Instantaneous

Cures or causes the spell's recipient of any diseases, including magically inflicted ones. An evil reversal of this spell allows a Cleric to cause disease.

Cure/Cause Light Wounds

1st-level cleric spell
Casting Time: 1 action
Range: Touch
Components: V, S
Duration: Instantaneous

Cures 1d6+1 hit points of damage. A reversal of this spell allows a Cleric to cause light wounds rather than curing them.

Cure/Cause Serious Wounds

4th-level cleric spell
Casting Time: 1 action
Range: Touch
Components: V, S
Duration: Instantaneous

Cures 2d6+2 hit points of damage. An evil reversal of this spell allows a Cleric to cause serious wounds.

Darkness

2nd-level magic-user spell
Casting Time: 1 action
Range: Far
Components: V, S
Duration: 1 hour

Darkness falls within a Near radius of the target point, impenetrable even to darkvision. A Light spell or Dispel Magic can be used to counteract the darkness.

Darkvision

3rd-level magic-user spell
Casting Time: 1 action
Range: Touch
Components: V
Duration: 1 day

The recipient of the spell can see in total darkness out to Near for 24 hours.

Death Spell

6th-level magic-user spell
Casting Time: 1 action
Range: Far
Components: V, S
Duration: Causes normal death

Within a 30-foot radius, up to 2d8 creatures, with fewer than 7 hit dice each, perish.

Detect Evil

1st-level cleric, 2nd-level magic-user spell
Casting Time: 1 action
Range: Far
Components: V, S
Duration: 1 hour

The caster detects any evil enchantments, evil intentions, evil thoughts, or evil auras within the spell's range of Far. Poison is not inherently evil and cannot be detected by means of this spell.

Detect Invisible

2nd-level magic-user spell
Casting Time: 1 action
Range: Near
Components: V, S
Duration: 1 hour

The caster can perceive invisible objects and creatures, even those lurking in the Astral or Ethereal planes of existence.

Detect Magic

1st-level cleric or magic-user spell
Casting Time: 1 action
Range: Self, Near area
Components: V, S
Duration: 20 min.

The caster can perceive, in places, people, or things, the presence of a magical spell or enchantment out to Near. For example, magical items may be discovered in this fashion, as can the presence of a charm secretly laid upon a person.

Dimension Door

4th-level magic-user spell
Casting Time: 1 action
Range: Far
Components: V, S
Duration: 1 hour

Dimension Door is a weak form of teleportation, a spell that can be managed by lesser magicians who cannot yet manage the Teleport spell. The caster can teleport themself, an object, or another willing person, with perfect accuracy to the stated location, as long as it is within the spell's range.

Disintegrate

6th-level magic-user spell
Casting Time: 1 action
Range: Near
Components: V
Duration: Permanent-cannot be dispelled

The caster defines one specific target such as a door, a peasant, or a statue, and it disintegrates into dust. Magical materials are not disintegrated, and living creatures (such as the aforementioned peasant) are permitted a saving throw.

Dispel Evil

5th-level cleric spell
Casting Time: 1 action
Range: Near
Components: V, S
Duration: Instantaneous or 10 minutes against an item This spell is similar to the Magic-User spell Dispel Magic but affects only evil magic. Also, unlike the Dispel Magic spell, Dispel Evil functions (temporarily) against evil "sendings", possibly including dreams or supernatural hunting beasts.
The power of an evil magic item is held in abeyance for 10 minutes rather than being permanently dispelled. Evil spells are completely destroyed.
As with Dispel Magic, the chance of successfully dispelling evil is a percentage based on the ratio of the level of the dispelling caster over the level of the original caster (or HD of the monster). Thus, a 5th-level Cleric attempting to dispel an evil charm cast by a 10th-level Cleric has a 50% chance of success (5/10 = .50, or 50%). If a 10th-level Cleric was dispelling a 9th-level Cleric's charm, success would be certain (10/9 = 1.11, or 111%).

Dispel Magic

3rd-level magic-user spell
Casting Time: 1 action
Range: Far
Components: V, S
Duration: Instantaneous or 10 minutes against an item

Dispel Magic, although not powerful enough to permanently disenchant a magic item (nullifies for 10 minutes), can be used to completely dispel most other spells and enchantments.

The chance of successfully dispelling magic is a percentage based on the ratio of the level of the dispelling caster over the level of the original caster (or HD of the monster). Thus, a 5th-level Magic-User attempting to dispel a charm cast by a 10th-level Magic-User has a 50% chance of success (6/12 =.50, or 50%). If the 10th-level Magic-User was dispelling the 5th-level Magic-User's charm, success would be certain (10/5 = 2.00, or 200%).

Enchant Item

6th-level magic-user spell
Casting Time: Referee's discretion
Range: Touch
Components: V
Duration: Permanent

This spell is used in the creation of a magical item, in addition to whatever research, special ingredients, or other efforts the Referee may determine are necessary for the task.

ESP

2nd-level magic-user spell
Casting Time: 1 turn
Range: Near
Components: V
Duration: 2 hours

The caster can detect the thoughts of other beings at a distance of Near. The caster must pick a direction and if there are multiple creatures the caster must make an intelligence check to make sense of the noise. The spell cannot penetrate more than two feet of stone and is blocked by even a thin sheet of lead.

Explosive Runes

3rd-level magic-user spell
Casting Time: 1 action
Range: Written on Parchment
Components: V, S
Duration: Permanent

The Magic-User scribes a rune onto parchment, vellum, or paper as a deadly trap. If anyone other than the caster reads the rune, the sigil explodes into fire, automatically dealing 4d6 points of damage to anyone directly in front of it.

The parchment or book upon which the rune was scribed will also be destroyed. An explosive rune can be detected, bypassed, and even removed by a higher-level Magic-User. Any Magic-User at least two levels higher than the rune's creator has a 60% chance to detect it, a 75%

chance to bypass it (if it is detected), and a 100% chance to remove it (if it is successfully detected and bypassed).

Extension I

4th-level magic-user spell
Casting Time: Instant (no action)
Range: Self
Components: V, S
Duration: see below

Extension I lengthens the duration of another of the caster's spells by 50%. Only spells of levels 1-3 can be affected by Extension I.

Extension II

5th-level magic-user spell
Casting Time: Instant (no action)
Range: Self
Components: V, S
Duration: see below

Extension II lengthens the duration of another of the caster's spells by 50%. Only spells of levels 1-4 can be affected by Extension II.

Extension III

6th-level magic-user spell
Casting Time: Instant (no action)
Range: Self
Components: V, S
Duration: See below

Extension III doubles the duration of another of the caster's spells. Spells of levels 1-5 can be affected by Extension III.

Fear

4th-level magic-user spell
Casting Time: 1 action
Range: Cone to Far
Components: V, S
Duration: 1 hour

This spell causes the creatures in its cone-shaped path to flee in horror if they fail a CHA saving throw. If they fail the save they must make a WIS saving throw or drop whatever they are holding. The cone extends to Far from the caster.

Feeblemind

5th-level magic-user spell
Casting Time: 1 action
Range: Near
Components: V
Duration: Permanent until dispelled

Feeblemind is a spell that affects only Magic-Users. The INT saving throw against the spell is made at a disadvantage, and if the saving throw fails, the targeted Magic-User's intelligence drops to 1 and they become feeble of mind and unable to cast spells until the magic is dispelled.

Find the Path

6th-level cleric spell
Casting Time: 1 action
Range: Self
Components: V
Duration: 1 hour +10 minutes/level; 1 day outdoors

The caster perceives the fastest way out of an area, even if the area is designed to be difficult to navigate, such as a labyrinth. Outdoors the spell has greater power, lasting a full day.

Find Traps

2nd-level cleric spell
Casting Time: 1 action
Range: Near
Components: V, S
Duration: 20 minutes

The caster can perceive both magical and non-magical traps at a distance of Near.

Fireball

3rd-level magic-user spell
Casting Time: 1 action
Range: Far
Components: V, S
Duration: Instantaneous

A bead-like missile shoots from the caster's finger, to explode, at the targeted location, in a furnace-like blast of fire. The burst radius is an area of Near from the target point, and damage is 1d6 per level of the caster (i.e. an 8th level magic-user casts an 8d6 fireball). A successful DEX saving throw means that the target takes only half damage.

Fly

3rd-level magic-user spell
Casting Time: 1 action
Range: Self
Components: V, S
Duration: 10 minutes per caster level + 1d6x10 minutes

This spell imbibes the Magic-User with the power of flight, with a movement rate of Fast per round. The Referee secretly rolls the 1d6 x 10 additional minutes; the player does not know exactly how long the power of flight will last.

Geas

6th-level magic-user spell
Casting Time: 1 action
Range: Near
Components: V, S
Duration: Until task is completed

If the spell succeeds (saving throw cancels), the caster may set a task for the spell's victim. If the victim does not diligently work at performing the task, the refusal will cause weakness (50% reduction in strength), and trying to ignore the geas eventually causes death.

Hallucinatory Terrain

4th-level magic-user spell
Casting Time: 1 action
Range: Within Eyesight
Components: V, S
Duration: Until touched (other than by ally) or dispelled

This spell changes the appearance of the terrain into the semblance of what the caster desires. A hill can be made to disappear, or it could be replaced with an illusory forest, for example.

Haste

3rd-level magic-user spell
Casting Time: 1 action
Range: Far
Components: V, S
Duration: 30 minutes

In an area with a radius of Near feet around the point where the spell is targeted, as many as 24 creatures become able to move and attack at double normal speed.

Hold Monster

5th-level magic-user spell
Casting Time: 1 action
Range: Near
Components: V, S
Duration: 1 hour + 10 min. per caster level

The caster targets 1d4 creatures, which are completely immobilized (WIS saving throw applies). The caster may also target a single creature, in which case the WIS saving throw is made at disadvantage.

Hold Person

2nd-level cleric spell, 3rd-level magic-user spell
Casting Time: 1 action
Range: Far
Components: V, S
Duration: 90 minutes

The caster targets 1d4 persons (according to the same parameters as the Charm Person spell), who are completely immobilized (WIS saving throw applies). The caster may also target a single person, in which case the saving throw is made with disadvantage.

Hold Portal

1st-level magic-user spell
Casting Time: 1 action
Range: Touch
Components: V, S
Duration: 2d6 x 10 minutes

This spell holds a door closed for the spell's duration or until dispelled (see Dispel Magic p.73). Creatures with magic resistance can shatter the spell without effort. This arcane lock lasts for 2d6 x 10 minutes.

This spell requires 25 gp in gold dust, which the spell casting consumes.

Ice Storm

4th-level magic-user spell
Casting Time: 1 action
Range: Far
Components: V, S
Duration: 1 round

A whirling vortex of ice, snow, and hail forms with a diameter of Near (30ft) from the target point. Massive hailstones inflict 3d10 hit points of damage (no saving throw applies) to all within the area.

Insect Plague

5th-level cleric spell
Casting Time: 1 action
Range: Within eyesight
Components: V, S
Duration: 24 hours

This spell works only outdoors. A storm of insects gathers and goes wherever the caster directs. The cloud covers approximately 400 square feet (20 feet by 20 feet, with roughly corresponding height). Any creature of 2 HD or fewer that is exposed to the cloud of insects flees in terror (no saving throw).

Invisibility

2nd-level magic-user spell
Casting Time: 1 action
Range: Far
Components: V, S
Duration: Until dispelled or an attack is made

The object of this spell, whether a person or a thing, becomes invisible to both normal sight and darkvision. The result is that an invisible creature cannot be attacked unless its approximate location is known, and all attacks are made at disadvantage to hit. If the invisible creature makes an attack, the spell is broken. Otherwise, it lasts until dispelled or removed by the caster.

Invisibility, Close

3rd-level magic-user spell
Casting Time: 1 action
Range: Far
Components: V, S
Duration: Concentration, or until dispelled or an attack is made

Like the Invisibility spell, Invisibility, Close makes the target creature or object invisible to normal sight and darkvision. It also, however, throws a 10-foot radius of invisibility around the recipient, which moves with it/them. Nothing inside the radius of invisibility can be attacked unless its approximate location is known, and all attacks are made at disadvantage to hit.

If an invisible creature makes an attack, the spell is broken. Otherwise, it lasts until concentration ends, dispelled or removed by the caster.

Invisible Stalker

6th-level magic-user spell
Casting Time: 1 action
Range: Close
Components: V, S
Duration: Until mission is completed

This spell summons (or perhaps creates) an invisible stalker, an invisible being with 8 HD. (See Monsters p.143) The stalker will perform one task as commanded by the caster, regardless of how long the task may take or how far the stalker may have to travel. The stalker cannot be banished by means of Dispel Magic; it must be killed in order to deter it from its mission.

Knock

2nd-level magic-user spell
Casting Time: 1 action
Range: Near
Components: V, S
Duration: Instantaneous

This spell unlocks and unbars all doors, gates, and portals within its range, including those held or locked by normal magic.

Legend Lore

6th-level magic-user spell
Casting Time: 1 action
Range: Self
Components: V
Duration: See below

Over the course of long and arduous magical efforts (1d100 days), the caster gains knowledge about some legendary person, place, or thing. The spell's final result may be no more than a cryptic phrase or riddle, or it might be quite specific.

Levitate

2nd-level magic-user spell
Casting Time: 1 action
Range: Self
Components: V, S
Duration: 10 min. per caster level

This spell allows the Magic-User to levitate themself, moving vertically up or down, but the spell itself provides no assistance with lateral movement. A wall, cliffside, or ceiling could, of course, be used to pull along hand over hand.

Levitation allows up or downward movement at a rate of up to 6 feet per minute (60 feet per 10 min.), and the caster cannot levitate more than 20 feet per level from the ground level where the spell was cast. (Such range is applied both to movement into the air and to downward movement into a pit or chasm.)

Light

1st-level cleric or magic-user spell
Casting Time: 1 action
Range: Touch
Components: V, S
Duration: 2 hours

The target person or object produces light about as bright as a torch, to a radius of Near for the duration.

Lightning Bolt

3rd-level magic-user spell
Casting Time: 1 action
Range: Self, out to Far
Components: V, S
Duration: Instantaneous

A bolt of lighting extends out to Far from the caster, almost ten feet wide. Anyone in its path suffers 1d6 points of damage per level of the caster (half with a successful DEX saving throw). The bolt always extends to Far, this means that it ricochets backward from something that blocks its path.

Locate Object

3rd-level cleric, 2nd -level magic-user spell
Casting Time: 1 action
Range: Near
Components: V, S
Duration: 1 round per caster level

Within the spell's range, the caster perceives the correct direction (as the crow flies) toward an object the caster specifies by description in the spell.

The object must be something the caster has seen, although the spell can detect an object in a general class of items known to the caster: stairs, gold, etc.

Lower Water

6th-level magic-user spell
Casting Time: 1 action
Range: 2 x Far
Components: V, S
Duration: 2 hours
This spell lowers the depth and water level of lakes, rivers, wells, and other bodies of water to one-half normal.

Magic Jar

5th-level magic-user spell
Casting Time: 1 action
Range: See below
Components: V, S
Duration: See below

This spell relocates the caster's life essence, intelligence, and soul into an object of virtually any kind. The 'jar' must be within Near of the caster's body for the transition to succeed. Once within the magic jar, the caster can possess the bodies of other creatures and people, provided that they are within Far of the jar and fail a CHA saving throw.

The caster can return their soul to the magic jar at any time; if a body the caster controls is slain, the soul returns to the jar immediately. The Magic-User can return from the jar to their original body whenever desired, thus ending the spell. If the caster's body is destroyed while their soul is in the magic jar, the soul no longer has a home other than within the magic jar, although the disembodied magic-user can still possess other bodies as before. If the jar itself is destroyed while the Magic-User's soul is within, the soul is lost.

Magic Missile

1st-level magic-user spell
Casting Time: 1 action
Range: Far
Components: V,S
Duration: Instantaneous

A magical missile flies where the caster directs, within a distance of Far. The missile hits automatically, doing 1d4+1 points of damage.
The magic-user casts an additional two missiles for every 5 levels of experience. Thus, at 5th level, the caster is able to hurl 3 magic missiles for 3d4+3 damage and 5 missiles at 10th level for 5d4+5 damage.

Magic Mouth

2nd-level magic-user spell
Casting Time: 1 action
Range: Touch
Components: V, S
Duration: Permanent or until triggered or dispelled

This enchantment is set upon an object, and the magic is triggered when certain conditions established by the caster are met.

When that happens, a mouth appears on the object and speaks the message it has been commanded to speak. The message may be up to thirty words long.

Massmorph

4th-level magic-user spell
Casting Time: 1 action
Range: Far
Components: V, S
Duration: Concentration or until dispelled

One hundred or fewer man, or horse-sized creatures are changed to appear like innocent trees. The illusion is so perfect that creatures moving through the 'forest' will not detect the deception.

Mirror Image

2nd-level magic-user spell
Casting Time: 1 action
Range: Self
Components: V, S
Duration: 1 hour or until destroyed

The spell creates 1d4 images of the caster, acting in perfect synchronization with them like mirror images. Attackers cannot distinguish the images from the caster and may attack one of the images instead of the caster themself (determined randomly). When a hit is scored upon one of the images, it disappears.

Monster Summoning I

3rd-level magic-user spell
Casting Time: 1 action
Range: n/a
Components: V, S
Duration: 2d6 rounds

The caster summons allies, who serves them until slain (or until the duration of the spell expires). The allies appear immediately.

D6 Roll	Summoned
1	1d6 giant rats
2	1d3 goblins
3	1d3 hobgoblins
4	1d6 kobolds
5	1d3 orcs
6	1d3 skeletons

Monster Summoning II

4th-level magic-user spell
Casting Time: 1 action
Range: n/a
Components: V, S
Duration: 2d6 rounds

The caster summons allies, who serves them until slain (or until the duration of the spell expires). The allies appear immediately.

D6 Roll	Summoned
1	1d2 hobgoblins
2	1d2 zombies
3	1d2 gnolls
4	1d2 bugbears
5	1d6 orcs
6	1d6 skeletons

Monster Summoning III

5th-level magic-user spell
Casting Time: 1 action
Range: n/a
Components: V, S
Duration: 2d6 rounds

The caster summons allies, who serves them until slain (or until the duration of the spell expires). The allies appear immediately.

D6 Roll	Summoned
1	1d4 bugbears
2	1d2 harpies
3	1d2 ochre jellies
4	1d2 wererats
5	1d2 wights
6	1d2 wild boar

Monster Summoning IV

6th-level magic-user spell
Casting Time: 1 action
Range: n/a
Components: V, S
Duration: 2d6 rounds

The caster summons allies, who serves them until slain (or until the duration of the spell expires). The allies appear immediately.

D6 Roll	Summoned
1	1 Gargoyle
2	1 Ogre
3	1 Owlbear
4	1 Shadow
5	1 Werewolf
6	1 Wraith

Move Earth

6th-level magic-user spell
Casting Time: 1 action
Range: 2 x Far
Components: V, S
Duration: 1 hour; effects permanent

This spell can only be used above ground. It allows the caster to move hills and other raised land or stone at a rate of 6 feet per minute (60 feet per turn).

Neutralize Poison

4th-level cleric spell
Casting Time: 1 action
Range: Touch
Components: V, S
Duration: Instantaneous

This spell counteracts poison if used promptly, but cannot be used to bring the dead back to life later.

Part Water (Magic-User)

6th-level magic-user spell
Casting Time: 1 action
Range: Far
Components: V, S
Duration: 1 hour

This spell creates a gap through water, but only to a depth of 10 feet. If cast underwater it produces a cylinder of air.

Passwall

5th-level magic-user spell
Casting Time: 1 action
Range: Near
Components: V, S
Duration: 30 minutes

This spell creates a hole through solid rock, about 7 feet high, 10 feet wide, and 10 feet deep (possibly deeper at the discretion of the Referee). The hole closes again at the end of the spell's duration.

Phantasmal Forces

2nd-level magic-user spell
Casting Time: 1 action
Range: Far
Components: V, S
Duration: Concentration

This spell creates an illusion that seems realistic to all who view it. The illusion disappears when it is touched, but if the viewer believes the illusion is real, it can cause damage.

Unless the Referee rules otherwise, victims of the spell are permitted an INT saving throw, and the illusion cannot cause more than 2d6 points of damage per victim. This will depend on circumstances; a truly brilliant use of the spell can be quite devastating, and a poorly thought-out illusion might cause almost immediate disbelief.

Plant Growth

4th-level magic-user spell
Casting Time: 1 action
Range: Far
Components: V, S
Duration: Permanent until dispelled

Undergrowth in the area suddenly grows into an impassable forest of thorns and vines. A radius out to Far can be affected by this spell and the caster can decide the shape of the area to be enchanted.

Polymorph Others

4th-level magic-user spell
Casting Time: 1 action
Range: Touch
Components: V, S
Duration: Permanent until dispelled

This spell allows the caster to turn another being into a different type of creature, such as a dragon, a garden slug, or of course, a frog or newt. The polymorphed creature gains all the abilities of the new form, but retains its own mind and hit points. Unwilling targets get a WIS saving throw. If the HD of the new creature is more than double the originals then the spell fails.

Polymorph Self

4th-level magic-user spell
Casting Time: 1 action
Range: Self
Components: V, S
Duration: 1 hour or Referee's Discretion

The caster assumes the form of any object or creature, gaining the new form's attributes (the use of wings, for example), but not its hit points or combat abilities. The Referee might allow the benefit of the new form's armor class if it is due to heavily armored skin. A great deal of the spell's effect is left to the Referee to decide.

Prayer

3rd-level cleric spell
Casting Time: 1 action
Range: Near
Components: V
Duration: 1 round

The Prayer spell seeks short-term favor from the gods to help some other spell or attack to succeed. Prayer affects a Near area, causing all creatures in that area to have disadvantage on their saving throws.
The penalty lasts for one full round.

Prestidigitation

Cantrip magic-user
Casting Time: 1 action
Range: Close
Components: V, S
Duration: Up to 1 hour

The rudimentary prestidigitation spell is a building block for arcane study and enables you to perform a variety of simple magical effects. This spell can clean, soil, or alter the color of items in a 1-foot cube. It can chill, warm, or flavor 1 pound of non-living material. It can move up to 1 pound of matter. It can create effects like a puff of smoke, very minor illusions, sound effects or temporary change in color. This spell can never inflict damage or disrupt the casting of other spellcasters. Prestidigitation lacks the power to duplicate any other spell effects. Any actual change to an object (beyond just moving, cleaning or soiling it) persists for only 1 hour.

Project Image

6th-level magic-user
Casting Time: 1 action
Range: 2 x Far
Components: V
Duration: Instantaneous

The caster projects an image of themself, to a maximum range of 240 feet. Not only does the projected image mimic the caster's sounds and gestures, but also any spells being cast will appear to originate from the image.

Protection from Evil

1st-level cleric or magic-user spell
Casting Time: 1 action
Range: Self
Components: V, S
Duration: 1 hour

Creates a magical field of protection immediately around the caster, blocking out aberrations, evil elementals, undead, and fiends. These monsters suffer a disadvantage penalty to hit the caster and the caster has advantage on saving throws against them. You can also not be charmed, frightened, or possessed by such a creature.

Protection from Evil, Near

3rd-level cleric & 4th-level magic-user spell
Casting Time: 1 action
Range: Self, Near radius around self
Components: V, S
Duration: 1 hour

Creates a magical field of protection around the caster in a Near radius. Blocking out aberrations, evil elementals, undead, and fiends. These monsters suffer a disadvantage penalty to hit the caster and the caster has advantage on saving throws against them. You can also not be charmed, frightened or possessed by such a creature.

Protection from Normal Missiles

3rd-level magic-user spell
Casting Time: 1 action
Range: Self
Components: V, S
Duration: 2 hours

The caster becomes invulnerable to non-magical missiles, although larger missiles such as boulders will overcome the spell's magic.

Purify Food & Water

1st-level cleric spell
Casting Time: 1 action
Range: Touch/Close (Referee's discretion)
Components: V, S
Duration: Instantaneous

Enough food and water for up to a dozen people is made pure, removing spoilage and poisons.

Pyrotechnics

2nd-level magic-user spell
Casting Time: 1 action
Range: Far
Components: V, S
Duration: 1 Hour

The caster creates either fireworks, or blinding smoke from a normal fire source such as a torch or campfire. The Referee will decide exactly how much smoke (or fireworks) is produced, what effect it has, and what happens to it as it is produced, but the amount of smoke will definitely be more than a Near radius.

Quest

5th-level cleric spell
Casting Time: 1 action
Range: Near
Components: V, S
Duration: Until completed

If the spell succeeds (WIS saving throw applies), the caster may set a task for the spell's victim. If the victim does not diligently work at performing the task, a deadly weakness will set in (50% reduction in Strength), and an attempt to entirely abandon the quest incurs a curse set by the caster in the wording of the original Quest. The details, of course, must be approved by the Referee.

Raise Dead

5th-level cleric spell
Casting Time: 1 action
Range: Touch/Close (Referee's discretion)
Components: V, S
Duration: Instantaneous

Raise Dead allows the Cleric to raise a corpse from the dead, provided it has not been dead too long. The normal time limit is 5 days, but for every caster level higher than 8th, the time limit extends another 5 days.

The dead must make a successful NORMAL (DC 12) CON saving throw to be brought back to life (failing this saving throw the same cleric may not attempt to raise this particular dead again). This spell functions only on 'human-like' races, that is, ones that can be used for player characters.

Read Languages

1st-level magic-user spell
Casting Time: 1 action
Range: Normal Reading Distance
Components: V
Duration: Instantaneous

This spell allows the caster to decipher directions, instructions, and formulas in languages unknown to the caster. This can be particularly useful for treasure maps, but it does not solve any codes.

Read Magic

1st-level magic-user spell
Casting Time: 1 action
Range: Self
Components: V
Duration: 1 or 2 scrolls or other magical writings

This spell allows the caster to read the magical writings, including scrolls or other magic-users spellbooks. Without the use of this spell, magical writing cannot be read even by a Magic-User.

Reincarnation

6th-level magic-user spell
Casting Time: 1 action
Range: Touch
Components: V, S
Duration: Instantaneous

This spell brings a dead character's soul back from the dead, but the soul reappears in a newly formed body. If the resulting creature is a normal character race, roll 1d6 to determine the character's new level.

Die Roll	Reincarnated as...
1	Bugbear
2	Centaur
3	Dog, Cat, or Wolf
4	Dwarf
5	Elf
6	Gnoll
7	Goblin
8	Half-orc
9	Harpy
10	Hobgoblin
11	Human
12	Kobold
13	Lizard man
14	Lycanthrope (Werewolf or other)
15	Minotaur
16	Ogre
17	Ogre Mage
18	Orc
19	Troll
20	Wyvern

Remove Curse

3rd-level cleric,
4th-level magic-user spell
Casting Time: 1 action
Range: Touch
Components: V, S
Duration: Instantaneous

This spell removes one curse from a person or object.

Repulsion

6th-level magic-user spell
Casting Time: 1 action
Range: Far
Components: V, S
Duration: 1 hour

Any creature trying to move toward the caster finds itself moving away, instead.

Rope Trick

3rd-level magic-user spell
Casting Time: 1 action
Range: Touch
Components: V, S
Duration: 1 hour + 10 minutes per caster level

This spell enables the user to cause a length of rope (6' to 24') to stand upright by itself, and when they (and up to three others) climbs to its summit, disappears into another dimension. The rope is simply tossed into the air and climbed.

If undisturbed the rope remains in place for the duration of the spell, but it can be removed, and if it is, the persons coming back from the other dimension will fall the distance they climbed to the top of the rope.

Shield

1st-level magic-user spell
Casting Time: 1 action
Range: Self
Components: V, S
Duration: 20 minutes

The caster conjures up an invisible shield that interposes itself in front of attacks. The shield improves the caster's armor class to AC 16. If the caster's armor class is already better than the spell would grant, the spell has no effect.

Silence

2nd-level cleric spell
Casting Time: 1 action
Range: Far
Components: V, S
Duration: 2 hours

Magical silence falls in an area with a Near diameter around the targeted creature or object, and moves with it. Nothing from this area, no matter how loud, can be heard outside the radius.

Sleep

1st-level magic-user spell
Casting Time: 1 action
Range: Far
Components: V, S
Duration: 1 Hour

This spell puts enemies into an enchanted slumber (no saving throw is permitted). It affects creatures based on their hit dice.

Victims HD	Number Affected
Less than 1d8	4d4
1d8 to 2d8	2d6
3d8	1d6
4d8	1

Slow

3rd-level magic-user spell
Casting Time: 1 action
Range: Far
Components: V, S
Duration: 30 minutes

In an area with a radius of Near around the point where the spell is targeted, as many as 24 creatures failing a WIS saving throw can move and attack only at half speed.

Snake Charm

2nd-level cleric spell
Casting Time: 1 action
Range: Near
Components: V, S
Duration: 1d4 x 10 plus 20 minutes

One hit die (1 HD) of snakes can be charmed per level of the caster. The snakes obey the caster's commands.

Speak with Dead

3rd-level cleric spell
Casting Time: 1 action
Range: Touch
Components: V
Duration: 3 Questions

The caster can ask three questions of a corpse, and it will answer, although the answers might be cryptic. Only higher-level Clerics have enough spiritual power to command answers from long-dead corpses.

Clerics lower than 8th level can gain answers only from bodies that have been dead 1d4 days. Clerics levels 8+ can speak to corpses that have been dead for 1d4 months.

Note * A die roll is involved here: for example, a seventh-level Cleric attempting to speak with a two- day-old corpse might still fail-the d4 roll might indicate that only a one-day-old corpse can be reached with this particular attempt at the spell.*

Speak with Animals

2nd-level cleric spell
Casting Time: 1 action
Range: Self
Components: V
Duration: 1 hour

The caster can speak with normal animals. There is a good chance that the animals will provide reasonable assistance if requested, and they will not attack - unless the caster uses the spell to say something particularly offensive.

Speak with Monsters

6th-level cleric spell
Casting Time: 1 action
Range: Speaking range
Components: V
Duration: 3d4 Questions

The caster can speak with any type of monster, for the duration of a certain number of questions. The monster is not forced to answer.

Speak with Plants

4th-level cleric spell
Casting Time: 1 action
Range: Speaking range
Components: V, S
Duration: 1 hour

The caster can speak and understand the speech of plants. Plants smaller than trees will obey commands,

moving aside when requested, etc.

Stone to Flesh

6th-level magic-user spell
Casting Time: 1 action
Range: Far
Components: V, S
Duration: Permanent until reversed

This spell can be used to counteract the negative effects of monsters who petrify their victims. It can also be reversed to turn flesh into stone, as desired by the caster. A saving throw is permitted to avoid being turned to stone, but if the spell succeeds the victim is transformed into a statue; the stone-to-flesh version of the spell will restore the victim to normal.

Strength

2nd-level magic-user spell
Casting Time: 1 action
Range: Touch
Components: V, S
Duration: 8 hours

This spell may be cast upon a Fighter or a Cleric.

For the duration of the spell, a Fighter gains 2d4 points of Strength, and a Cleric gains 1d6 points of Strength. Strength cannot exceed 20.

Suggestion

3rd-level magic-user spell
Casting Time: 1 action
Range: Shouting distance
Components: V, S
Duration: 1 week

A spell that works on the principle of hypnosis. If the creature which it is thrown at fails to make a Wisdom saving throw it will carry out the suggestion, immediately or deferred according to the wish of the magic-user. Self-destruction is 99% unlikely, but carefully worded suggestions can, at the referee's option, alter this probability.

Suggestions must be simple and relatively short, i.e. a sentence or two.

Telekinesis

5th-level magic-user spell
Casting Time: 1 action
Range: Far
Components: V, S
Duration: 1 hour

The caster can move objects using mental power alone. The amount of weight that can be lifted and moved is 20 pounds per caster level. It is up to the Referee's interpretation of the spell whether the objects can be thrown, and at what speed.

Teleport

5th-level magic-user spell
Casting Time: 1 action
Range: Touch
Components: V, S
Duration: Instantaneous

This spell transports the caster or another person to a destination that the caster knows, or at least knows what it looks like from a picture or a map. Success depends on how well the caster knows the targeted location, as follows:

If the caster has only seen the location in a picture or through a map (so that knowledge is not based on direct experience), there is only a 25% chance of success, and failure means death, for the traveler's soul is lost in the spaces between realities.

If the caster has seen but not studied the location, there is a 20% chance of error. In the case of an error, there is a 50% chance that the traveler arrives low, 1d10x10 feet below the intended location (with death resulting from arrival within a solid substance). If the error is high (over the 50% chance for a "low" arrival), the traveler arrives 1d10x10 feet above the targeted location-likely resulting in a deadly fall. If the caster is well familiar with the location or has studied it carefully, there is only a 5% chance of error. On a 1 in 6 (roll 1d6) the teleport is low, otherwise, it is high. In either case, the arrival is 1d4x10 feet high or low.

Transmute Rock to Mud

5th-level magic-user spell
Casting Time: 1 action
Range: Far
Components: V, S
Duration: 3d6 day unless reversed

This spell transmutes rock (and any other form of earth, including sand) into mud. An area of roughly 300 x 300 feet becomes a deep mire, making it Difficult Terrain.

Turn Sticks to Snakes

4th-level cleric spell
Casting Time: 1 action
Range: Far
Components: V, S
Duration: 1 hour

The caster may turn as many as 2d8 normal sticks into snakes, each one having a 50% chance of being venomous. The snakes follow commands but turn back into sticks at the end of the spell, or when killed.

Wall of Fire

4th-level magic-user spell
Casting Time: 1 action
Range: Near
Components: V, S
Duration: Concentration

A wall of fire flares into being and burns for as long as the caster concentrates upon it.

Creatures with 3 or fewer hit dice cannot pass through it, and no creature can see through it to the other side.

Passing through the fire inflicts 1d6 hit points of damage (no saving throw) and undead creatures sustain twice the normal damage. The caster may choose to create a straight wall 60 feet long and 20 feet high, or a circular wall with a 15-foot radius, also 20 feet high.

Wall of Ice

4th-level magic-user spell
Casting Time: 1 action
Range: Near
Components: V, S
Duration: Concentration

The caster conjures up a wall of ice, six feet thick and non-transparent. The caster may choose to create a straight wall 60 feet long and 20 feet high, or a circular wall with a 15-foot radius, also 20 feet high.

Creatures with 3 or fewer hit dice cannot affect the wall, but creatures of 4+ hit dice are able to smash through it, taking 1d6 points of damage in the process.

Creatures with fire-based metabolisms take 2d6 instead of the normal 1d6. Fire spells and magical effects are negated in the vicinity of the wall.

Wall of Iron

5th-level magic-user spell
Casting Time: 1 action
Range: Near
Components: V, S
Duration: 2 hours

The caster conjures an iron wall from thin air. The wall is 3 feet thick, 50 feet tall, and 50 feet long.

Wall of Stone

5th-level magic-user spell
Casting Time: 1 action
Range: Near
Components: V, S
Duration: Permanent until dispelled

The wall of stone conjured by this spell is two feet thick, with a surface area of 1,000 square feet. The caster might choose to make the wall 50 feet long (in which case it would be 20 feet tall), or 100 feet long (in which case it would be only 10 feet tall).

Water Breathing

3rd-level magic-user spell
Casting Time: 1 action
Range: Touch
Components: V Duration: 2 hours

The recipient of the spell is able to breathe underwater until the spell's duration expires.

Web

2nd-level magic-user spell
Casting Time: 1 action
Range: Far
Components: V, S
Duration: 8 hours

Fibrous, sticky webs fill an area up to Near radius from the target point. It is extremely difficult to get through the mass of strands - it takes 10 minutes if a torch and sword (or a flaming sword) are used, and creatures larger than a horse can break through in 20 minutes. Humans alone take more time to break through-perhaps 30-40 minutes or longer at the Referee's discretion.

Wizard Eye

4th-level magic-user spell
Casting Time: 1 action
Range: Far
Components: V, S
Duration: 1 hour

The caster conjures up an invisible, magical "eye" through which they can see, that can move a maximum of Far range from its creator. It floats along as directed by the caster, and has a movement rate of Normal

Wizards Bolt

Cantrip magic-user
Casting Time: 1 action
Range: Near
Components: V, S
Duration: Instantaneous

You hurl a bolt of magical energy at a creature or object within range. Make a ranged spell attack against the target. On a hit, the target takes 1d3 force damage.

Wizards Lock

2nd-level magic-user spell
Casting Time: 1 action
Range: Touch
Components: V
Duration: Permanent unless dispelled

As with a Hold Portal spell, Wizard Lock holds a door closed, but it is permanent until dispelled.

Creatures with magic resistance can shatter the spell without effort. Any magic-user at least three levels higher than the caster can open the portal, and a Knock spell will open it as well, although the spell is not permanently destroyed in these cases.

Word of Recall

6th-level cleric spell
Casting Time: 1 action
Range: Indefinite
Components: V, S
Duration: Immediate

The Cleric teleports without error back to a prepared sanctuary.

As with most Tabletop RPG games, rolling dice determines whether a player fails or succeeds.

In Olde Swords Reign there are a few basics to cover before we get into the nitty-gritty.

Specific Beats General

When you put these many rules together, sometimes they clash. In these cases, employ common sense but, if you need more, a specific rule trumps a general rule.

An example would be that generally magic users can use only daggers and staffs as weapons, but elven weapon training specifically grants proficiency in long bows, thus allowing an elven magic-user to add their proficiency bonus to longbows.

Round Down

Whenever you divide a number in the game, if you end up with a fraction, then round down, even if the fraction is one-half or greater.

Difficulty

Olde Swords uses a simplified difficulty system to speed up the running of the game and make rulings easier. This is the target number or Difficulty Class (DC) that players have to meet or beat to perform tasks, or save.

Obviously, feel free to use any DC's of your choice but there is very little in the game that can't be covered by either EASY, NORMAL, or HARD.

Using these in the game makes both running and playing feels a little more intuitive.

Difficulty	DC
VERY EASY	4
EASY	8
NORMAL	12
HARD	16
VERY HARD	20

Advantage and Disadvantage

Sometimes a special ability, spell, or situation gives you advantage or disadvantage on a d20 dice roll.
When that happens, you roll a second d20. For advantage, you take the higher of the two results, for disadvantage you take the lower.

If multiple situations affect a roll, you do not roll more than one additional d20. In circumstances where you have both advantage and disadvantage, they cancel each other out.

There are many situations where the referee might declare that someone has advantage/disadvantage. It could be taking the high ground/having a huge tactical advantage in combat or a player assisting another on a single task.

EG. 2 players trying to break a door down together would result in one player making a single roll with advantage

Inspiration

Inspiration allows you to have advantage on a check, attack, or saving throw. You can decide to use it after your initial role has failed.

Gaining Inspiration

It's up to your Referee how inspiration is awarded but, typically, it happens if your character does something epic, or plays their character in a way that is true to their story.

Your Referee will tell you how you can earn inspiration in the game. You either have inspiration or you don't—you can't stockpile multiple "inspirations" for later use unless you have the feat Blessed by the Gods.

You can also give your inspiration to another character who fails their roll, if you wish.

Inspiration, however, cannot be used on Death Saving Throws.

Contests

Sometimes players or monsters may directly oppose one another and, when this happens, you must make a contested roll.

The two characters make rolls, adding the attribute bonus of their relevant stat, and whoever rolls the highest wins.

This does not necessarily need to be the same attribute rolled against each other. If a player was trying to sneak past someone actively looking for them it could be the player's Dex rolled against the NPC's wisdom.

Passive Checks

A passive check may be used when an ability check has not been called for.

To determine a character's total for a passive check:

10 + ability score modifier + proficiency bonus(if applicable) = passive score

EG. If a monster is hiding in a bush, and the party is not actively looking for it, the referee would compare the player's passive Wisdom score to the Dexterity roll of the monster to see if they spot it. If there was a player with a hunter background, the referee would add their proficiency bonus to their score.

Group Checks

When a number of individuals are trying to accomplish something as a group, the Referee might ask for a group ability check.

In such a situation, the characters who are skilled at a particular task help cover those who aren't.

To make a group ability check, everyone in the group makes the ability check and, if at least half the group succeeds, the whole group succeeds. Otherwise, the group fails.

Failed Check

If a check is failed, generally players should not be able to keep on trying until they succeed. They need a change of circumstances to have another try.

So, if someone fails to pick a lock, maybe that lock is currently above their abilities or rusted shut. If a door is stuck then they are not strong enough to break it open, maybe they need to use something as a ram to break it down.

Saves, Time & Movement

Saving Throws

A saving throw—also called a save—represents an attempt to resist a spell, trap, poison, disease, or a similar threat. You don't normally decide to make a saving throw; you are forced to make one because your character or monster is at risk of harm.

To make a saving throw, roll a d20 and add the appropriate ability modifier. Your class will grant you proficiency in two saving throws and, if you're human, you will get to pick another. This will allow you to add your proficiency bonus to the save.

A successful save generally means the harm or effect is reduced or nullified.

Time

Time is a tool used to add tension to a campaign, drive decisions, and force players to make meaningful choices. Characters can do anything, but you can't do everything.

In Olde Swords Reign we have 4 main time segments that tend to apply to different situations.

Time	Typical Use
Round - 6 Seconds	Combat
Turn - 10 Minutes	Dungeon exploration
Watch - 4 Hours	Wilderness exploration and resting
Day	Downtime, recover and longer travel

As you work through combat, exploration, and recovery, you can see how these can be easily applied to gameplay.

> *"YOU CAN NOT HAVE A MEANINGFUL CAMPAIGN IF STRICT TIME RECORDS ARE NOT KEPT."*
> **Gary Gygax**

Speed

The distance a player or monster can travel is determined by their speed, which is the distance they can walk in 1 round. This number assumes short bursts of energetic movement in the midst of a life-threatening situation.

The speeds in Olde Swords Reign are purposefully vague Slow (roughly 15 ft), Normal (roughly 30ft), and Fast (roughly 45ft). When you combine these speeds with the ranges, it allows you to run tactical combats efficiently without getting caught up in the minutia.

Turn speed is how far that character or monster can travel in a dungeon while taking reasonable care, taking in their surroundings, watching their feet, making an acceptable amount of noise, etc. This turn speed is 3 x their base speed.

Watch speed is the distance a character or monster can reasonably travel at a march, with gear, in a 4-hour period. The speed they can travel may be affected by the weather conditions or terrain over which they are traveling (see Wilderness Adventuring p.111).

Speed	Rounds (yards)	Turn (yards)	Watch (miles)
Slow	15	45	4.5
Normal	30	90	9
Fast	45	135	13.5

Ranges

Ranges can become important. Olde Swords Reign uses a simple and freeform range system but for those using grid-based play on a table or VTT the following increments can be used:

Range	Distance	Use
CLOSE	within 5 feet	Striking distance for melee weapons and close enough to whisper to someone
NEAR	within 30 feet	Within distance of all ranged weapons. Someone with normal movement can travel this distance and still take an action during combat. A normal voice would need to be used.
FAR	from NEAR to 120 feet	Distance of more powerful ranged weapons. At this distance you would need to shout
VERY FAR	beyond 120 feet	Often puts combatants out of eyesight and/or far out of striking range of each other

Climbing, Swimming, and Crawling

While climbing or swimming, movement is reduced to one step (from Fast to Normal, Normal to Slow, etc.), unless a creature has a climbing or swimming speed. Climbing a slippery vertical surface, or one with few handholds, requires a successful Strength check the DC of which will be decided by the GM. Similarly, gaining any distance in rough water might require a successful Strength check.

Jumping

You can Long Jump at a distance equal to your Strength score in feet, as long as you have a 10-foot run-up. This assumes the height of your jump doesn't matter.

If the jump has factors that make it more difficult, like a slippy landing, your Referee may require an appropriate check.

You can High Jump a distance equal to 1/2 your Strength score if you have a 10-foot run-up. If it is a standing high jump you can only jump 1/4 of your Strength score.

In some circumstances, your Referee might allow you to make a Strength check (EASY, NORMAL, or HARD) to jump higher than you normally can.

Encumbrance

Encumbrance in Olde Swords Reign is very simple, a character can carry their Strength ability score in armor, weapons, and items, plus an additional 10 items with a backpack. If they exceed their limit they are encumbered and their speed drops to Slow (15ft). If they exceed their limit by more than their strength score their speed drops to 0 and they'll need to drop some items.

Some larger items, like heavy weapons or plate armor, take up 2 inventory slots. Encumbrance can be increased with sacks (see sacks in the adventuring gear section p.54). Every 100 coins count as 1 item. This minimizes bookkeeping but lets you still benefit from having it in your game.

Unfortunately, encumbrance gets hand-waved in too many games, which is a shame. Managing resources means players have to overcome constraints. They have to plan and interact with the world, maybe hire some people or buy some animals. They have to make hard choices when undertaking a mission, and hard choices are a good thing.

The Environment

Falling

If a player falls they take 1d6 cumulative damage for every 10 feet they fall and they land prone.
I.e. 10ft = 1d6 damage, 30ft = 1d6+2d6+3d6 = 6d6 damage.

Suffocating

A creature can hold its breath for a number of minutes equal to 1 + it's Constitution modifier (minimum of 30 seconds).

When they run out of breath they can survive for a number of rounds equal to its Constitution modifier (minimum of 1 round). At the start of their next turn, they drop to 0 hit points and are dying, and can't regain hit points or be stabilized until they can breathe again.

Vision and Light

Vision can be heavily or lightly obscured.

Heavily obscured would be in complete darkness or heavy fog, and the creature would be effectively blinded (See Blinded Condition p.233).

Lightly obscured would be in dim light, or light fog, and all wisdom checks that rely on vision would be at disadvantage.

Blindsight

A creature with blindsight can perceive its surroundings without relying on sight, within a Near radius.

Darkvision

If a creature has darkvision they can see in darkness within Near 30ft as if the darkness were dim light, but they can't discern color in darkness, only shades of gray.

Truesight

A creature with truesight can, out to Near, see in normal and magical darkness, see invisible creatures and objects, automatically detect visual illusions, succeed on saving throws against them, and perceive the original form of a shapechanger (or a creature that is transformed by magic).

Rests

There are three types of Rests in Olde swords Reign; Breathers, Short Rests, & Long Rests.

Breather

Immediately after combat, characters can take a Breather, which is a short, ten-minute rest period where they bandage wounds, sip some water, and get their wits about them again.

As long as the Breather is uninterrupted, each character uses one Provision and regains 1d4 plus (or minus) their Constitution modifier in hit points, with a minimum of 1 hit point healed.

If the characters have no Provisions they only heal their Constitution modifier in hit points or a minimum of 1 hit point.

Only one Breather can be taken after combat, and the damage healed during a Breather can only be from the combat preceding it. Breathers cannot restore temporary hit points or more hit points than the character's maximum.

Short Rest

A short rest is a period of downtime, at least 8 hours long, during which a character does nothing more strenuous than sleeping, eating, drinking, reading, keeping watch, and tending to wounds.

The rest cannot be interrupted by a period of strenuous activity, and provisions must be expended for eating and drinking (see provisions p.112) at least 1 hour of walking, fighting, casting spells, or similar adventuring activity— or the characters must begin the rest again to gain any benefits.

Once complete, a character regains hitpoints by spending one or more of their Hit Dice, up to the character's maximum number of Hit Dice, which is equal to the character's level. For each Hit Die spent in this way, the player rolls the die and adds the character's Constitution modifier to it. The character regains hit points equal to the total.

The player can decide to spend an additional Hit Die after each roll. These hit die can only be regained by completing a long rest.

If the characters do not eat or drink expending provisions, then hit dice rolls are at disadvantage.

Spellcasting characters regain all Spell Slots after a Short Rest.

Long Rest

A long rest is a period of extended downtime, 1d4+1 days long in a safe and non-strenuous place, such as a village, castle, town, or city. If the rest is interrupted by any long combats or strenuous activity they cannot gain the benefits of a long rest.

Long rests are often done in between adventures but, on the rare occasion characters wish to take one during an adventure, they can do so if they can find a safe place, and the Referee allows it.

At the end of a long rest, a character regains all lost hit points. The character also regains spent Hit Dice, up to a number of dice equal to half of the character's total number of them (minimum of one die). For example, if a character has eight Hit Dice, he or she can regain four spent Hit Dice upon finishing a long rest.

Characters can take two back-to-back long rests (an Extended Rest) between adventures to regain ALL of their Hit Dice.

Dungeon Adventuring

Dungeon crawling was always a game of attrition. The procedures from older editions were designed to add tension, make time matter, run-down resources, and as a result challenge the players to make hard decisions.

Do we go on? Do we turn back? Should we parlay? Can we trade?

Turn Sequence

1. **Marching Order** - Deciding who is at the front and back will have an impact on random encounters and traps.

2. **Random Encounters** - Every 2 turns GM rolls to see if there is a random encounter

3. **Players Declare their Actions** - The referee can determine the DC of any actions that require a roll

4. **Make Rolls and GM describes the outcomes** - Once the rolls have been made the GM describes the outcomes and the new situation

5. **End of turn** - The GM marks the time and players mark the use of torches/lanterns.

Random Encounters

Generally, in a dungeon, random encounters are rolled every 2 turns. You roll a d6 and, on a 1, you then roll on your random encounters table (see Monsters p.143).

The purpose of random encounters is to make the dungeon feel alive, it's not just full of static monsters waiting for you to find them. They also provide a sense of danger and urgency to the players. Waiting around, dilly-dallying, and indecision become potentially dangerous options.

Spending a lot of time in one place can be dangerous, so finding safe havens and securing them becomes ever more important. If players make a lot of noise, then feel free to roll for a random encounter as well. This tension really adds to the game and again helps players to make harder decisions.

Light

Light is one of the most precious resources in the dungeon. A torch lasts for 6 turns (60 minutes) whilst a lantern burns out in 6 hours. Each turn player should mark down a tick representing 10 minutes of use.

Dungeon Doors

Dungeons are riddled with doors. Some are easily opened, others are locked and some are stuck. Most actions take 1 turn.

Stuck Door: A stuck door can be opened with a successful Strength check. Easy, Normal, or Hard depending on door condition material and condition. If another player is assisting, the check can be made with advantage. If failed then that door cannot currently be opened without changing the situation.

Locked Door: Can be picked by someone with the right skills and tools.

Listen at Door: You can spend a turn listening at the door to determine if something is on the other side. Wisdom check. Easy, Normal or Hard depending on what is on the other side.

Secret Doors: Secret doors can only be spotted if characters are specifically looking for them. The player must be looking in the right location. Elves are an exception (see Elves p.12).

Chopping Down Doors: Doors can be chopped down with a wood axe. This action is noisy and will result in a wandering monster check. If a battle axe is used it can become blunt. Roll an Easy (DC8) check for the axe, on a fail, the axe has become blunt and damage is rolled at disadvantage until the owner spends a turn sharpening their axe.

Swinging Shut: Doors that have been opened have a habit of swinging closed. This can be stopped by the use of wedges, iron spikes, or whatever the players can reasonably come up with.

My players have a running joke that doors are their worst enemies. Not being able to open one, being worried about what's behind or even having them shut by monsters when someone goes in has led to some pretty fantastic war stories.

Searching

Dungeons often include hidden features such as secret doors and traps. Adventurers can spot these by searching a specific area. The DC will be determined by the GM.

If a character does not have a specific skill, searches for traps are rolled with disadvantage.

Traps

Most traps are old and have seen better days so they do not always trigger.

If a player performs an action that would trigger the trap, there is a 2 in 6 chance the trap will trigger. If it's a weight-based trap, the pc is small, then the chance is 1 in 6. This way the player at the front is not always the victim.

If a character is not skilled in searching for traps, searches are performed with disadvantage.

Trap damage: Damage inflicted by a triggered trap is usually automatic, without an attack roll.

Surprise

When surprise is a possibility each player rolls a Normal (DC12) wisdom check to see if they are surprised. If surprised they do not act in the first round of combat.

It is possible for only some members of the party to be surprised.

Wilderness Adventuring

To tame the wilds, wilderness exploration needs structure. As the world's favorite roleplaying game has progressed the structure found in earlier versions has been slowly abandoned. We need to bring a little back to make the wilderness truly come alive.

The following section should allow you to inject some of the unexpectedness found in nature, helping to create a little more emergent story. It's also an opportunity to really make some players' backgrounds sing.

Provisions

Provisions are an amalgamation of food, water, and first aid supplies. This allows you to simplify book-keeping but still keep the tension that tracking supplies can provide. When exploring new areas, having a party member that can hunt, forage, or fish can make a huge difference.

Each day a person must consume two provisions, one for food and the other for water. If water is found (see Find Water p.115) by a member of the party, then it can supply the entire party for that day.

When the group is successful at foraging, hunting, or fishing (see p.114) they get to add the newly acquired provision to their inventories.

Provisions are also consumed when taking a breather, representing bandages, herbs, and poultices from a first aid kit.

1 provision costs 1gp
10 provisions take up one inventory slot.

You can optionally expand this in principle to other items. Eg. you could spend a turn using 1 provision to create 10 torches. This could be thought of as using animal fat or fungus that had been gathered to fuel the torch.

When expanding, ask a few questions; Is it reasonable that this resource could be resupplied from provisions? What is the cost of this in civilization? Use that cost to help decide how many provisions it would take.

Watch.

When we zoom out to wilderness adventuring, we look at time in 4-hour watches. This lets us break the day into 6 usable segments.

Watch Sequence

1. **Position** - Players decide where they will be positioned, for marching it will be who is at the front and back.

2. **Random Encounters** - The GM rolls to see if there is a random encounter. This may be once a day or more often dependent on terrain.

3. **Players Declare their Actions** - The referee can determine the DC of any actions that require a roll

4. **Rolls and outcomes** - Once the rolls have been made the GM describes the outcomes and the new situation

5. **End of watch** - The GM marks the time, distance traveled and location

Watch Actions

There are several actions that characters can take during a watch

Investigate
This can be to find out more about the current area or even to find a good, easily defensible campsite. If specifically to find a good campsite, then any lookout checks made that evening will be made with advantage.

Travel
Each watch, the party can cover the distance of the slowest PC. They can travel for 2 watches (8 hours) a day without difficulty. If they wish to push on for a third, all characters must make a Normal (DC12) constitution check every hour or receive one level of exhaustion.

Navigate
Whoever is leading the party will perform a Wisdom check to ensure the party does not lose its way. The DC is based on the terrain table (see p116).

Getting Lost

If you fail your check, you can potentially veer off course. The GM rolls a d10 on a 5-6 you are lucky enough to keep in the right direction, otherwise, you head in the direction shown.

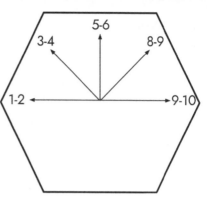

The image shows this on a hex where 5-6 is the direction you were traveling in but the principle same applies to any navigation.

Hunt

A player can choose to hunt, which takes at least 2 watches. A player can attempt to shorten this to 1 watch but all rolls will be at disadvantage. This can not be done while traveling. The process is as follows and DC is based on the terrain table.

Locate the prey: Wisdom check
Prey size: 1d6 + 1d6 for every 3 points the initial check beat the target by. This determines how many provisions can be harvested with a successful kill.
Roll an attack: based on the terrain table DC.
Success: Prey brought down and provisions harvested.
Failure: Prey gets away.

> E.g. If a player rolled a 13 for the wisdom check-in a forest where the target was Easy(8) they would have located prey that could provide 2d6 worth of provision. If they then succeed on their attack roll they take down the prey and harvest the provisions.

Forage

A player can choose to forage for a watch. This cannot be done while traveling, and the check DC is based on the terrain table. On a successful Wisdom check, the player can collect provisions 1d2 + 1d2 for every 3 points the check exceeds the DC.

Fish

If a suitable water source is near, and a player has the correct equipment, they can attempt to fish. A player makes a Dex check and, on a success, they catch 1d4 provisions of fish. If they succeed they can make another check (max 4 checks per watch).

Find Water

Roll an intelligence check vs DC. On a success, the party does not need to consume a provision to represent water that evening.

Eat, Drink and Sleep

For a player to get the benefits of a short rest they must spend two watches eating sleeping, and resting. They may however spend 2 hours on lookout whilst the rest of the party is sleeping.

Players only receive the benefit of a short rest if they consume 2 provisions (1 x food, 1 x water) and rest for 8 full hours. If they do not sleep they must make a Normal (DC12) Constitution save or receive a level of exhaustion. For every additional day, the DC increases by 3.

Craft/Repair

If an item is damaged, or something needs to be made, then a player can spend a watch performing that action, providing they have the correct skills and equipment. The referee will decide the duration and DC for the action.

You can see a full example of exploration in Appendix B

DC for Checks based on terrain

Here is a list of sample DC's for checks. Feel free to change them to fit your game:

Terrain	Speed	Nav	Water	Hunt	Forage	Fish
Arctic	Slow	Normal	Easy	Hard	Hard	Normal
Coast	Normal	Easy	Normal	Normal	Easy	Easy
Desert	Slow	Normal	Hard	Hard	Hard	
Forest	Slow	Hard	Easy	Easy	Easy	Normal
Grassland	Normal	Normal	Easy	Easy	Easy	Normal
Sea		Normal				Easy
Mountain	Slow	Normal	Normal	Hard	Hard	Hard
Swamp	Slow	Hard	Easy	Normal	Normal	Easy
Plains	Normal	Normal	Normal	Normal	Normal	Hard
Underground	Slow	Hard		Hard	Normal	Normal
Urban	Normal	Easy	Easy	Hard	Hard	Hard

Proficiency: If a pc is skilled in that area, then standard checks will have proficiency bonuses added. Eg. barbarian hunting for food.

Disadvantage or impossible: If a pc is unskilled, or does not have the correct equipment, then checks are either at disadvantage or impossible at the referee's discretion.

   Eg. Ice fishing without a drill - impossible. Fishing with a rod but without a suitable background - disadvantage. Finding water in the artic - Easy if you have the means to melt the ice.

Advantage: If a pc is particularly familiar with the environment or circumstances are particularly favorable. Eg. barbarian hunting on their native plains.

Weather

You can use a weather table to impact the game. Powerful storms might make travel impossible, Normal storms can half travel speed, and rain can obscure vision making it harder to see.

Don't be afraid to adjust the DC of other checks based on the current weather conditions.

Weather Table

d20	Weather	Cold Climate	Temperate Climate	Desert
1	Powerful storm	Blizzard	Windstorm, blizzard, hurricane, tornado	Downpour
2-3	Storm	Snowstorm	Thunderstorm, snowstorm	Duststorm
4-5	Inclement weather	Precipitation (snow)	Precipitation (normal for season)	Hot, windy
6-7	Abnormal weather	Heatwave or cold snap	Heatwave or cold snap	Hot, windy
8-20	Normal weather	Cold, calm	Normal for season	Hot, calm

I haven't included every possible combination of terrain, speed, and weather or the list would be exhaustive and bore you to tears. But trust your instincts, bump the travel speed, or difficulty, up or down a level, according to what feels right. Hunting is harder in the rain as finding tracks is nearly impossible, but you might not need to check for water.

Downtime

Recuperating

You can use downtime between adventures to recover from a debilitating injury, disease, or poison.

After three days of downtime spent recuperating, you can make a NORMAL (DC 12) Constitution saving throw. On a successful save, you can choose one of the following results:
End one effect on you that prevents you from regaining hit points.
For the next 24 hours, gain advantage on saving throws against one disease or poison currently affecting you.

Training

You can spend time between adventures learning a new language, or training with a weapon, or a set of tools. Your Referee might allow additional training options.

First, you must find an instructor willing to teach you.

The Referee determines how long it takes, and whether one or more ability checks are required.
Training typically lasts for 250 days and costs 1 gp per day.

After you spend the requisite amount of time and money, you learn the new language or gain proficiency with a new tool or weapon.

Lifestyle Expenses

Between adventures, you choose a particular quality of life and pay the cost of maintaining that lifestyle.

The lifestyle you live can affect the way other individuals and groups react to you. For example, when you lead an aristocratic lifestyle, it might be easier for you to influence the nobles of the city likewise, living frugally might keep you under the radar but you are unlikely to make powerful connections.

Lifestyle Expenses Table

Lifestyle	Description	Daily Price	Consequences (optional)
Wretched	Inhumane conditions, sneaking into barns and begging for food	-	Weekly Hard Con Check or catch a disease, 30% chance of being robbed
Squalid	Vermin infested boarding house	1 sp	Weekly Easy Con Check or catch a disease, 10% chance of being robbed
Poor	Flop house or common room in a cheap tavern. Threadbare clothes	2 sp	Monthly Easy Con Check or catch a disease, 10% chance of being robbed
Modest	Rent a room, don't go hungry	1 gp	
Comfortable	Small cottage, nice neighborhood	2 gp	Associate with merchants, skilled tradespeople and military officers
Wealthy	Respectable, suite at a nice inn, spacious home	4 gp	Associate with highly successful merchant, business owners
Aristocratic	Townhouse, dine at finest inns. Fashionable clothes	10 gp min	Invites to social gatherings, mix with high priests, leaders, politicians

COMBAT RULES

The Order of Combat

1. Determine surprise.

2. Roll initiative.

3. Take turns. Each participant in the combat takes a turn in the initiative order.

4. Begin the next round. Return to step 3 until the combat has ended.

Surprise

The Referee determines who might be surprised. Sometimes it's an easy decision if one side is making a lot of noise, for example. If a side tries to be stealthy, the Referee compares the Dexterity checks of anyone hiding with the passive Wisdom score of each creature on the opposing side to see if they notice.

If you're surprised, you can't move or take an action on your first turn of the combat. A member of a group can be surprised even if the other members aren't.

Initiative

Initiative determines the order of turns during combat.

When combat starts, each player rolls a d20 modified by their Dex. The referee rolls for the monsters, usually as groups. The order of combat is in order of these rolls, from highest to lowest.

Your Turn

On your turn, you can move a distance up to your speed and take one action. You decide whether to move first or take your action first. For most characters, their speed is Normal (30ft).

The most common actions you can take are described in the "Actions in Combat" section.

The "Movement and Position" section gives the rules for your move.

You can forgo moving, taking an action, or doing anything at all on your turn. If you can't decide what to do on your turn, consider taking the Dodge or Ready action, as described in "Actions in Combat."

Movement & Position

Movement Rates

As mentioned in the speed section there are 3 movement rates in Olde Swords Reign

- » Slow (15ft)
- » Normal (30ft)
- » Fast (45 ft).

A creature's speed is determined by several factors including encumbrance but, generally, a player's speed is Normal.

Breaking Up Your Move

You can break up your movement on your turn, using some of your speed before and after your action. For example, if you have a speed of Normal, you can move 10 feet, take your action, and then move 20 feet.

Difficult Terrain

If the referee decides the terrain is difficult - a boulder-strewn cavern, briar-choked forest, or a treacherous staircase, then every foot of movement in difficult terrain costs 1 extra foot. This rule is true even if multiple things in a space count as difficult terrain.

Being Prone

Combatants often find themselves lying on the ground, either because they are knocked down or because they throw themselves down. In the game, they are prone, a condition described in appendix A.

You can drop prone without using any of your speed. Standing takes more effort and costs half your speed.

For example, if your speed is Normal, you must spend 15 feet of movement to stand up.

Moving while prone is difficult, and crawling costs an extra foot of movement for every foot crawled. Crawling 1 foot in difficult terrain, therefore, costs 3 feet of movement.

Interacting with Objects Around You

Here are a few examples of the sorts of things you can do in tandem with your movement and action:

- » draw or sheathe a sword
- » open or close a door
- » withdraw a potion from your backpack
- » pick up a dropped axe
- » take a bauble from a table
- » remove a ring from your finger
- » stuff some food into your mouth
- » plant a banner in the ground
- » fish a few coins from your belt pouch
- » drink all the ale in a flagon
- » throw a lever or a switch
- » pull a torch from a sconce
- » take a book from a shelf you can reach
- » extinguish a small flame
- » don a mask
- » pull the hood of your cloak up and over your head
- » put your ear to a door
- » kick a small stone
- » turn a key in a lock
- » tap the floor with a 10-foot pole
- » hand an item to another character

Moving Around Other Creatures

You can move through a non-hostile creature's space. By contrast, though, you can only move through a hostile creature's space if the creature is at least two sizes larger or smaller than you.

Remember that another creature's space is difficult terrain for you.

Whether a creature is a friend or an enemy, you can't willingly end your move in its space.

Opportunity Attack

If you leave a hostile creature's reach during your move, you provoke an opportunity attack. A creature can only take an opportunity to attack if they are not in melee combat with another creature.

An opportunity attack is essentially a bonus single attack and does not impact the creature's next turn. A creature can only perform one opportunity attack per round.

Flying Movement

If a flying creature is knocked prone, has its speed reduced to 0 or is otherwise deprived of the ability to move, the creature falls unless it has the ability to hover or it is being held aloft by magic, such as by the fly spell.

Creature Size

Each creature takes up a different amount of space.

The Size Categories table shows how much space a creature of a particular size controls in combat:

Space

A creature's space is the area, in feet, that it effectively controls in combat, rather than an expression of its physical dimensions. A typical Medium creature isn't 5 feet wide, for example, but it does control a space that wide.
If a Medium hobgoblin stands in a 5-foot-wide doorway, other creatures can't get through unless the hobgoblin lets them.

Size Categories

A creature's space also reflects the area it needs to fight effectively. For that reason, there's a limit to the number of creatures that can surround another creature in combat.

Assuming Medium combatants, eight creatures can fit in a 5-foot radius around another one.

Squeezing into a Smaller Space

A creature can squeeze through a space that is large enough for a creature one size smaller than it. Thus, a Large creature can squeeze through a passage that's only 5 feet wide.

While squeezing through a space, a creature must spend 1 extra foot for every foot it moves there, and it has disadvantage on attack rolls and Dexterity saving throws. Attack rolls against the creature have advantage while it's in the smaller space.

Size	Space
Tiny	2 1/2 x 2 1/2 ft.
Small	5 x 5 ft.
Medium	5 x 5 ft.
Large	10 x 10 ft.
Huge	15 x 15 ft.
Gargantuan	20 x 20 ft. or larger

ACTIONS IN COMBAT

Attack

With this action, you make one melee or ranged attack. See the "Making an Attack".

Certain features, such as the Multiple Attacks feature of the fighter, allow you to make more than one attack with this action.

Cast a Spell

Spellcasters can cast a spell.

Each spell has a casting time, which specifies whether the caster must use an action, minutes, or even hours to cast the spell. Casting a spell is, therefore, not necessarily an action, but most spells do have a casting time of 1 action.

Dash

When you take the Dash action, you can move again doubling your movement.

Disengage

If you take the Disengage action, your movement doesn't provoke opportunity attacks for the rest of the turn. You can also Dash after Disengaging to flee danger or retreat.

Dodge

When you take the Dodge action, any attack made against you, that you are aware of, has disadvantage, and you make Dexterity saving throws with advantage.

So, if a hidden attacker fires at you from the shadows, you are unable to dodge.

You lose this benefit if you are incapacitated (as explained in appendix A), or if your speed drops to 0.

Help

To perform the help action you must come up with a reasonable way you could help a creature, then that creature gains advantage for their next ability check or attack.

Ready

When you take the ready action on your turn, you prepare an action to take place on a specific trigger.

If an enemy comes within 5 feet, I'll strike with my sword. If an enemy stands on the trapdoor, I'll pull the lever.

If you ready a spell, you cast it as normal, expending that spell slot but holding on to its energy, which you release on your trigger. This takes concentration (see Magic p.57) but, if your concentration is broken, or the action isn't triggered, the spell dissipates without taking effect and the spell slot is expended.

Hide

To hide, you make a Dexterity check against the creature's passive perception, at which point the creature no longer knows where you are. You must break the line of sight in order to hide. If you succeed you gain benefits (see Unseen Attackers p.129).

Search

If you search for something, the referee will tell what you have found if it's obvious, or your description of where/how you were searching would have led to you discovering what you were searching for, or they might have you make a Wisdom check, or an Intelligence check.

Use an Object

When an object requires your action for its use, you take the Use an Object action.

MAKING AN ATTACK

Choose a target.

- » Declare who you want to attack and how.
- » The referee will tell you if any modifiers like cover apply
- » Make the attack roll if you meet or beat their AC roll damage.

Critical Hits and Failures

If the d20 roll for an attack is a 20, the attack hits regardless of any modifiers or the target's AC. This is called a critical hit. You also roll the damage twice and then add any damage modifiers.

If the d20 roll for an attack is a 1, the attack misses regardless of any modifiers or the target's AC. This is called a critical fail. Often referees will apply some type of consequence like your weapon breaks or you hit a close ally.

Attack Rolls

To attack, you roll a d20 and add appropriate modifiers. If it's equal to or exceeds the target's AC, the attack hits.

Modifiers to the Roll

Generally for melee attacks you use your strength modifier and, for ranged attacks, you use your dexterity modifier.

There are some specific exceptions.

If the melee weapon has the finesse property, you can choose whether to use your dexterity or strength to attack.

If you throw a melee weapon that uses your strength modifier to attack then you use the same modifier for the thrown attack.

Some spells also require an attack roll. The ability modifier used for a spell attack depends on the spellcasting ability of the spellcaster.

Unseen Attackers and Targets

When you attack a target that you can't see, you have disadvantage on the attack roll. The referee might declare a miss regardless of your roll, if you are swinging in entirely the wrong area.

When a creature can't see you, you have advantage on attack rolls against it. If you are hidden-both unseen and unheard-when you make an attack, you give away your location when the attack hits or misses.

Ranged Attacks

Range

You can make ranged attacks only against targets within a specified range. Each weapon or spell has a range of Near or Far.

Your attack roll has disadvantage when your target is beyond that range, and you can't attack a target at all beyond double that range.

Ranged Attacks in Close Combat

If you try to make a ranged attack while CLOSE, you have disadvantage on the attack roll.

Cover

Cover is greatly simplified in Olde Swords Reign. If you have partial cover attacks against you have disadvantage. If you are completely shielded by an object then you can not be directly hit although an area of effect spell might include your location. The referee will determine what counts as cover.

Firing into Melee

If a target is in melee they are classed as having partial cover unless your angle lets you see the entire target. If you miss roll again to see if you strike the object that was granting the cover.

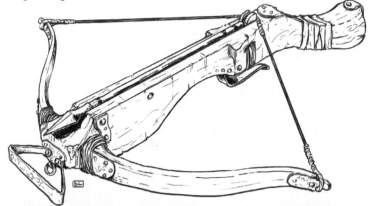

Melee Attacks

Most creatures have a 5-foot reach and can thus attack targets within 5 feet of them. Some creatures and weapons allow melee attacks beyond this range.

Unarmed attack

You can use an unarmed strike: a punch, kick, head-butt, or similar forceful blow. On a hit, an unarmed strike deals bludgeoning damage equal to 1 + your Strength modifier. You are proficient with your unarmed strikes.

Two-Weapon Fighting

If you are attacking with a light melee weapon in one hand, you can use the same action to attack with a different light melee weapon that you're holding in the other hand.

You don't add your ability modifier to the damage of the second attack unless that modifier is negative and the off-hand attack is rolled with disadvantage.

If either weapon has the thrown property, you can throw the weapon, instead of making a melee attack with it.

Grappling

The target of your grapple must be no more than one size larger than you and must be within your reach.

Using at least one free hand, you try to seize the target by making a grapple check instead of an attack roll: a Strength check contested by the target's Strength or Dexterity check (the target chooses the ability to use). If you succeed, the target is grappled and their speed becomes 0 (see Grappled Condition p.233). You can release the target whenever you like (no action required).

Escaping a Grapple. A grappled creature can use its action to escape. To do so, it must succeed on a Strength or Dexterity check contested by the grappler's Strength check.

Moving a Grappled Creature. When you move, you can drag or carry the grappled creature with you, but your speed is halved unless the creature is two or more sizes smaller than you.

Pushing a Creature

Using the Attack action, you can make a special melee attack to shove a creature, either to knock it prone or push it away from you. If you're able to make multiple attacks with the Attack action, this attack replaces one of them.

The target must be no more than one size larger than you and must be within your reach. Instead of making an attack roll, you make a Strength check contested by the target's Strength or Dexterity check (the target chooses the ability to use). If you win the contest, you either knock the target prone or push it 5 feet away from you.

DAMAGE & HEALING

Hit Points

Hit points represent a combination of physical and mental durability, the will to live, and luck.

Creatures with more hit points are more difficult to kill. Those with fewer hit points are more fragile.

Whenever a creature takes damage, that damage is subtracted from its hit points. The loss of hit points has no effect on a creature's capabilities until the creature drops to 0 hit points.

Damage Rolls

When you roll damage you add the stat modifier that you rolled the attack with to the damage and any other modifiers (like a +2 magic sword). With a penalty, it is possible to deal 0 damage, but never negative damage.

If a spell or other effect deals damage to more than one target at the same time, roll the damage once for all of them. For example, when a magic-user casts fireball, the spell's damage is rolled once for all creatures caught in the blast.

Healing

When a creature receives healing of any kind, hit points regained are added to its current hit points. A creature's hit points can't exceed its hit point maximum, so any hit points regained in excess of this number are lost.

A creature that has died can't regain hit points until magic such as the *Raise the Dead* spell has restored it to life.

Dropping to 0 Hit Points: When you drop to 0 hit points, you either die outright or fall unconscious, as explained in the following sections:

Instant Death

Massive damage can kill you instantly.

When damage reduces you to 0 hit points and there is damage remaining, this becomes negative hit points. If your negative hit points equal or exceed your hit point maximum you die instantly.
For example, if a wizard with 5 max hit points takes 10 damage they are instantly dead.

Falling Unconscious

If damage reduces you to 0 hit points and fails to kill you, you fall unconscious (see Unconscious Condition p.235). This unconsciousness ends if you regain any hit points.

Death Saving Throws

Whenever you start your turn with 0 hit points, you must make a special saving throw, called a death saving throw.

Roll a d20. If the roll is 10 or higher, you succeed. Otherwise, you fail. A success or failure has no effect by itself.

On your third success, you become stable (see below). On your third failure, you die. The successes and failures don't need to be consecutive; keep track of both until you collect three of a kind. The number of both is reset to zero when you regain any hit points or become stable.

Rolling 1 or 20: When you make a death saving throw and roll a 1 on the d20, it counts as two failures. If you roll a 20 on the d20, you become conscious and regain 1 hit point.

Optional: When you roll 1 on a death save, you die instantly.
This statistically makes very little difference, but really ratchets up the tension. It completely changes how people aproach combat and once someone drops makes every decision matter.

Damage at 0 Hit Points: If you take any damage while you have 0 hit points, you suffer a death-saving throw failure. If that damage is from a melee attack from within 5ft, it counts as a critical hit and you suffer two failures instead. If the damage, when added to your negative hit points equals or exceeds your hit point maximum, you suffer instant death.

Stabilizing a Creature

The best way to save a creature with 0 hit points is to heal it. If healing is unavailable, the creature can at least be stabilized by another player making a NORMAL (DC 12) Wisdom check to stench the flow of blood.

A stable creature doesn't make death-saving throws, even though it has 0 hit points, but it does remain unconscious. The creature stops being stable and must start making death-saving throws again if it takes any damage. A stable creature that isn't healed regains 1 hit point after 1d4 hours.

Monsters and Death

Most Referees have a monster die the instant it drops to 0 hit points, rather than having it fall unconscious and make death-saving throws.

Mighty villains and special non-player characters are common exceptions; the Referee might have them fall unconscious and follow the same rules as player characters.

Knocking a Creature Out

Sometimes an attacker wants to incapacitate a foe, rather than deal a killing blow. The player must declare they are trying to knock the creature out before making the blow. When the creature drops to 0hp it is then unconscious, rather than dead, providing it hasn't taken enough damage to instantly kill it.

Temporary Hit Points

Temporary hit points aren't actual hit points; they are a buffer against damage, a pool of hit points that protect you from injury.

When you have temporary hit points and take damage, the temporary hit points are lost first, and any leftover damage carries over to your normal hit points. Because temporary hit points are separate from your actual hit points, they can exceed your hit point maximum. A character can, therefore, be at full hit points and receive temporary hit points.

Healing can't restore temporary hit points and temporary hit points can not be added together. If you have temporary hit points and receive more of them, you decide whether to keep the ones you have or to gain the new ones.

If you have 0 hit points, receiving temporary hit points doesn't restore you to consciousness or stabilize you. They can still absorb damage directed at you while you're in that state, but only true healing can save you.

Underwater Combat

When making a melee weapon attack underwater, a creature that doesn't have a swimming speed (either natural or granted by magic) has disadvantage on the attack roll unless the weapon is a dagger, shortsword, or spear.

A ranged weapon attack automatically misses a target beyond the weapon's normal range. Even against a target within normal range, the attack roll has disadvantage unless the weapon is a crossbow or a weapon that is thrown like a spear.

Creatures and objects that are fully immersed in water have resistance to fire damage.

Mounteò Combat

You need a willing creature that is at least one size larger than you that has appropriate anatomy that can serve as a mount.

Mounting and Dismounting

Once during your move, you can mount a creature that is within CLOSE of you or dismount. Doing so costs an amount of movement equal to half your speed. For example, if your speed is Normal, you must spend 15 feet of movement to mount a horse. Therefore, you can't mount it if you don't have 15 feet of movement left, or if your speed is 0.

If an effect moves your mount against its will while you're on it, you must succeed on a NORMAL (DC 12) Dexterity saving throw or fall off the mount, landing prone in a space within 5 feet of it. If you're knocked prone while mounted, you must make the same saving throw.

If your mount is knocked prone, you can dismount it as it falls and land on your feet. Otherwise, you are dismounted and fall prone in a space within 5 feet of it.

Controlling a Mount

While you're mounted, you have two options. You can either control the mount or allow it to act independently. Intelligent creatures, such as dragons, act independently.

You can control a mount only if it has been trained to accept a rider. Domesticated horses, donkeys, and similar creatures are assumed to have such training. The initiative of a controlled mount changes to match yours when you mount it. It moves as you direct it, and it has only three action options: Dash, Disengage, and Dodge. A controlled mount can move and act even on the turn that you mount it.

An independent mount retains its place in the initiative order. Bearing a rider puts no restrictions on the actions the mount can take, and it moves and acts as it wishes. It might flee from combat, rush to attack and devour a badly injured foe, or otherwise act against your wishes.

In either case, if the mount provokes an opportunity attack while you're on it, the attacker can target you or the mount.

Hired Help

There are 2 main types of people you can hire in the game - Professionals and Retainers. Professionals take a fixed wage for their services, and will not go adventuring with you, with the exception of a torchbearer.

Retainers, on the other hand, are would-be adventurers and are paid both a daily wage and a percentage of any treasure recovered. They are willing to put their lives on the line with you in the pursuit of glory, although they will not take unnecessary risks.

For both types of hired help, you must also consider board and upkeep. You can consult the lifestyle tables on page 120. If the employer does not own a stronghold to house servants and followers, lodging may need to be considered separately. The cost is up to the referee, but staying in an inn, even in a stable, will cost at least 1 sp per night.

Wages are per week and do not include the supplies needed for their craft. For an animal trainer, you would need to supply the animal, their feed and their upkeep An alchemist would still need a laboratory and all the necessary components needed to complete the job.

Job	Wage (gp)	Description
Alchemist	250	A laboratory and supplies need to be taken into account
Animal Trainer	50	Animal upkeep and food need to be considered. Training an exotic or dangerous animal may cost more
Assassin	2,000 per mission	You will need to be able to find a reliable assassin which may use a considerable amount of time and money.
Blacksmith	10	This does not include equipment or supplies
Retainer	14-35	See retainer section
Sage	500	Normally only found in large settlements but can find important information given enough time
Sailor	7	A ship will be needed as well as upkeep
Servant	7	They take care of most of you smaller jobs and is essential if passing as someone of import
Ship Captain	50	These may be able to supply their own crew - see sailor
Engineer	150	If you need something unusual constructed or to find out the integrity/ weaknesses of a structure.
Spy	500 per mission	Hard to find and may take some time but good information may be the difference between success and failure
Torchbearer	7	They will come with you on adventures, give you light and carry a little gear but do not expect them to fight or endanger themselves

Retainers

A retainer can be of any class, but their level can not exceed that of the hiring pc.

Daily pay 2-5gp based on experience and 10-50% share in any treasure recovered. Retainers gain XP and level up in the same manner as player characters, and can be taken on by players upon character death.

When hiring retainers, notices need to be posted, town criers paid, and tavern owner's palms greased. The more care, time, and money put into the process, the better quality of applicants.

The referee should match this with the location in which the hiring is taking place. In a small village, you might be lucky to get anything other than a torch bearer or an untrained villager.

Once the group is gathered, the hiring player makes a charisma check.

Refusal -1: The retainer has taken insult and further rolls in that town or region, will be at a penalty of -1 due to unkind words said by the NPC. This is cumulative if further failures are made in the same town.

Try again: The potential retainer is reluctant, and needs more convincing; the player character must "sweeten" the deal in order to get an additional roll, such as by offering more pay, a better share, a magic item, etc. If the player character makes no better offer, treat Try again as a Refusal result.

Loyalty

Retainer Reaction Table

Result	Reaction
1-4	Refusal, -1 on further rolls in that town
5-7	Refusal
8- 11	Try again
12-15	Acceptance
16+	Acceptance, +1 to Loyalty

Loyalty

If the retainer is put in unreasonable danger, then the hirer must make an Easy (DC8) Charisma check to see if they can convince them not to flee.

At the end of every adventure, after gold and XP have been distributed, the PC makes another Easy Charisma check to see if the retainer wishes to keep on working for them.

These rolls are modified by any loyalty bonus the retainer has and may be modified by the GM depending on the package offered to the retainer. If a Natural 20 is rolled, then any future rolls with that retainer receive a +1 loyalty modifier. This is cumulative.

Players may hire a maximum of 4 retainers + charisma modifier.

Monsters

Monsters in Olde Swords Reign are really easy to create and run. Nearly everything ties back to their Hit Die (HD). It helps you calculate their difficulty, proficiency bonuses, to hit modifier, and XP value.

Size

A monster can be Tiny, Small, Medium, Large, Huge, or Gargantuan. The Size Categories table shows how much space a creature of a particular size controls in combat.

Size	Space
Tiny	2 1/2 x 2 1/2 ft.
Small	5 x 5 ft.
Medium	5 x 5 ft.
Large	10 x 10 ft.
Huge	15 x 15 ft.
Gargantuan	20 x 20 ft. or larger

Monster Type

Monsters can be broken down into several different types. Certain spells, magic items, and features interact with different monster types in specific ways. *Eg. An arrow of dragon-slaying deals extra damage to all monsters with the type dragon.*

Type	Description
Aberrations	utterly alien beings
Beasts	nonhumanoid creatures that are a natural part of the fantasy ecology
Celestials	are creatures native to the Upper Planes.
Constructs	are made, not born. Golems are the iconic constructs
Dragons	large reptilian creatures of ancient origin
Elementals	creatures native to the elemental planes
Fey	magical creatures closely tied to the forces of nature
Fiends	creatures of wickedness that are native to the Lower Planes
Giants	tower over humans and their kind
Humanoids	main peoples of a fantasy gaming world, both civilized and savage, including humans and a tremendous variety of other species.
Monstrosities	monsters in the strictest sense
Oozes	gelatinous creatures that rarely have a fixed shape
Plants	vegetable creatures, not ordinary flora
Undead	once-living creatures brought to a horrifying state of undeath through the practice of necromantic magic or some unholy curse

Armor Class

A monster that wears armor or carries a shield has an Armor Class (AC) that takes its armor, shield, and Dexterity into account.

Otherwise, a monster's AC is based on its Dexterity and natural armor, if any.

Hit Points & Hit Dice

A monster usually dies or is destroyed, when it drops to 0 hit points.

A monster's hit points are presented both as a die expression and as an average number. For example, a monster with 2d8 hit points has 9 hit points on average (2 × 4.5) but you can roll the hit points yourself if you wish. This gives the monsters a little bit of variety and may influence how you play them. You might have an old lion that rolled low hit points or a giant orc if it rolled high.

Hit Dice (HD) are a d8, so a 3 HD Monster has 3d8 hit points. Some monsters have 1/2 HD or 1/4 HD. 1/2 HD is a 1d4 (or 1d8 divided by 2) and 1/4 HD is 1d2 (or 1d8 divided by 4).

A monsters HD determines not only its hit points but also determines its Challenge Rating and its Saving Throw DCs. See those sections for more.

A monsters Constitution bonus is added to their hit points similar to players. For each HD they have, their Constitution modifier is added.

I.e. A 3 Hit Dice monster with a +3 Constitution modifier has 3d8+9 Hit Points.

Speed

Speeds are listed as Slow, Normal, or Fast for all categories, therefore a creature with a Speed of Normal, fly (fast), can walk at a normal speed (roughly 30-ish feet), and fly at fast speed (roughly 45-ish feet).

Type	Description
Burrow	moves through sand, earth, mud, or ice
Climb	moves on vertical surfaces
Fly	use all or part of its movement to fly
Swim	doesn't need to spend extra movement to swim

Saving Throws

Monster Saving Throws are split into two categories- Physical and Mental. A monster with Physical saves gets their proficiency bonus on all Strength, Dexterity, or Constitution saving throws. A monster with Mental saves gets their proficiency bonus on all Intelligence, Wisdom, and Charisma saves. Some powerful creatures (such as most dragons) have both Physical and Mental saves.

The proficiency bonus is added to their ability score modifier to calculate the bonus.

Proficiency Bonus by Hit Dice Table

HD	Prof Bonus	HD	Prof Bonus
0-4	+2	17-20	+6
5-8	+3	21-24	+7
9-12	+4	25-28	+8
13-16	+5	29+	+9

Languages

The languages that a monster can speak are listed in alphabetical order.

Sometimes a monster can understand a language but can't speak it, and this is noted in its entry. A dash (-) indicates that a creature neither speaks nor understands any language.

Telepathy

A telepathic creature can communicate with another, even if they do not share the same language. The creature is in charge of the connection, being able to start and stop it whenever they want. Telepathy does not function in areas where magic does not work.

Senses

The Senses entry notes a monster's passive Wisdom (Perception) score, as well as any special senses the monster might have. Special senses are described below:

Category	Description
Blindsight	Perceive its surroundings without relying on sight, within a NEAR radius
Darkvision	Can see in the dark within a NEAR radius
Tremorsense	Can detect and pinpoint the origin of vibrations within a NEAR radius, provided that the monster and the source of the vibrations are in contact with the same ground or substance
Truesight	To a radius of near see in normal and magical darkness, see invisible creatures and objects, automatically detect visual illusions and succeed on saving throws against them, and perceive the original form of a shapechanger or a creature that is transformed by magic. Furthermore, the monster can see into the Ethereal Plane within the same range.

Challenge

A monster's challenge rating (CR) is directly related to its Hit Dice in Olde Swords Reign. Normally their CR is the same as their Hit Die but you can modify this for monsters that appear to be more challenging. The rough formula to use is

HD + 1 for multiple attacks + 1 for magic use + 1 for breath weapon.

Its CR determines its Experience Points (XP) value.

If you want to balance encounters, it can be done by comparing the number of characters and their level to the number of monsters and their HD, but balancing an encounter is not necessary, and it is fine to challenge your players with higher HD monsters... they have the option to retreat.

Experience Points

The number of experience points (XP) a monster is worth is based on its challenge rating. Typically, XP is awarded for defeating the monster, although the Referee may also award XP for neutralizing the threat posed by the monster in some other manner.

CR	XP	CR	XP
0	0 or 1	15	1,300
1/4	5	16	1,500
1/2	10	17	1,800
1	20	18	2,000
2	45	19	2,200
3	70	20	2,500
4	110	21	3,300
5	180	22	4,100
6	230	23	5,000
7	290	24	6,200
8	390	25	7,500
9	500	26	9,000
10	590	27	10,500
11	720	28	12,000
12	840	29	13,500
13	1,000	30	15,500
14	1,150	-	-

Actions

A monster can take all of the actions available to a player, such as Dash or Hide, but the most common combat actions are melee and ranged attacks.
Attacking

A monsters Hit Dice determines their attack bonus, therefore a monster with 8 HD gets a +8 to attack rolls.

A monster attacks in the same way as a player, rolling an attack, and if it meets or beats the target's AC then the attack hits, and the monster rolls damage.

Multi-attack

Some creatures have multiple attacks which it can take during combat. A creature can't use Multi-attack when making an opportunity attack, which must be a single melee attack.

Limited Usage

Some special abilities have restrictions on the number of times they can be used.

X/Day. The notation "X/Day" means a special ability can be used X number of times, and that a monster must finish a short rest to regain expended uses.

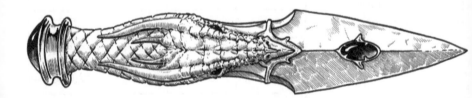

Grapple Rules for Monsters

Many monsters have special attacks that allow them to quickly grapple prey. When a monster hits with such an attack, it doesn't need to make an additional ability check to determine whether the grapple succeeds, unless the attack says otherwise.

A creature grappled by the monster can use its action to try to escape. To do so, it must succeed on a Strength or Dexterity check against the escape DC in the monster's stat block.

Monster DCs

When making saving throws versus a Monster, whether it's a spell, a breath weapon, a paralyzing gaze, etc. the DC for the saving throw is based on the Monsters HD.

Monsters HD	Save
0 to 4 HD	EASY
5 to 8 HD	NORMAL
9 + HD	HARD

Morale

Most monsters and NPC's do not wish to die. If the odds are overwhelming, a GM may decide that the monster just fleas or, alternatively, they may wish to roll a morale check. Perform a Wisdom check for the monster against an easy, normal, or hard target depending on the type of creature and circumstances.

On a success, the creature or group of creatures understands the overwhelming odds and flees or attempts to surrender. Some creatures, however, will always fight to the death

Awarding XP

How XP is awarded in a game helps to shape the type of game you are playing. In Olde Swords Reign characters are awarded experience points (XP) for killing monsters and accumulating treasure.

- » All monsters have an XP value (given in the monster's statistics)
- » Every gold piece acquired earns one point

It may seem odd to award experience for treasure, but keep in mind that Olde Swords Reign is not just about slaying monsters — it is about outwitting your foes when you can! In fact, sometimes trickery and guile are the only way to handle a powerful monster like a dragon or a demon. Skilled players avoid risking their characters' lives if there is another, smarter way to walk out of the dungeon with a backpack full of gems and loot.

Awarding Treasure

As a general guideline, the monetary value of a treasure ought to be about 2—4 times the monster's value in experience points in gold pieces.

Keep in mind that hunting and patrolling monsters likely will not be carting their treasure around with them. If the characters cannot find the monster's lair, they may get none of the treasure. Averaging the treasure out over several of the monsters in an adventure is a good way of making sure the characters get the right amount of experience points from treasure.

Some monster lairs may also have magical items or gems and other treasures (as determined by the Referee).

NOTE: Remember Olde Swords Reign is about adventurers, not superheroes, so there is no race to level up. Think about an advancement rate that suits your game and the length of the campaign, then adjust treasure accordingly. Having a rough treasure/XP per game number in your head is particularly important if you are running old-school modules as they tend to have really large quantities of treasure and need to be adjusted.

Random Encounters

For every environment type or dungeon, create a random encounter table. This does not need to be solely monsters or combat encounters. You should include NPC's, and interesting effects/noises. Be creative with this. It's well worth the investment, once you have a few you can substitute the entries in very little time.

Depending on the environment you can decide how often to roll a random encounter. Typically you roll 1d6 and if it's a 1 a random encounter happens. You then roll on the Random Encounter Table.

I'd advise adding a second column for what they are doing. Rolling a d6 for each column and figuring out how this fits with your current location will lead to far more interesting results.

These tables can be expanded to include NPC's, Locations, Non-combat encounters......
The list is endless and once prepared they save a huge amount of time.

Result	Monster	Activity
1	2d4 Hobgoblins	Just Tracks
2	3d6 Zombies	Patrolling
3	2d4 Lizards	Hunting
4	3d4 Warriors	Camped/Resting
5	1d6+3 Gnolls	Working
6	1d12+1 Berserkers	Fighting with

Monster Reactions

Result	Reaction
1-4	Attack
5-7	Unfriendly (may attack)
8- 11	Neutral (wary)
12-15	Indifferent
16+	Very Friendly

If the reaction of monsters is not obvious the first player who encounters them can make a charisma reaction roll. This may be modified by the GM depending on the type of creature and the circumstances. Again this really puts the focus on the emergent story and the fact that not every encounter is a guarantee of combat.

Monster Listings

The monsters in Olde Swords Reign have a shortened stat block. Creating new monsters is exceedingly easy and there are instructions on how to convert monsters from other editions in Appendix B

Stat Block Breakdown

HD Hit Dice   **AC** Armor Class
HP Hitpoint 5(1d8+1)
Str 10(+0) **Dex** 10(+0) **Con** 12(+1)
Int 10(+0) **Wis** 10(+0) **Cha** 10(+0)

Prof. Proficiency Bonus   **Speed** Normal
Saving Throws Phy (Physical), Men (Mental)
Senses Passive (Perception) 10
Languages Common
Challenge 1 (20 XP)

Bandit

Medium humanoid
HD 1   **AC** 12
HP 5(1d8+1)
Str 10(+0) **Dex** 10(+0) **Con** 12(+1)
Int 10(+0) **Wis** 10(+0) **Cha** 10(+0)

Prof. +2   **Speed** Normal
Saving Throws Phy
Senses Passive 10
Languages Common
Challenge 1 (20 XP)

Bandits are roving groups of thieves, sometimes organized into small armies led by more powerful bandit chiefs and captains with higher hit dice.

Actions

Attack. +1 To Hit
Sword. 3(1d6) piercing - range close
Light Crossbow. 3(1d6) piercing - range far

Basilisk

Medium monstrosity
HD 6   **AC** 15
HP 39(6d8+12)
Str 16(+3) **Dex** 8(-1)   **Con** 15(+2)
Int 2(-4)   **Wis** 8(-1)   **Cha** 7(-2)

Prof. +3   **Speed** Slow
Saving Throws Phy
Senses Passive 9, darkvision
Languages -
Challenge 7 (290 XP)

Basilisks are great multi-legged lizards whose gaze turns to stone anyone meeting its eye.

Petrifaction gaze. Anyone meeting its eye makes a NORMAL WIS save or is turned to stone. (one way of resolving this: fighting without looking incurs disadvantage on attack rolls).

Weakness. If the basilisk's own gaze is reflected back at it, it has a 10% chance to force the basilisk into a saving throw against being turned to stone itself.

Actions

Attack. +6 to hit
Bite. 5(1d10) piercing - range close

Berserker

Medium humanoid

HD 1   **AC** 12
HP 7 (1d8+3)
Str 16(+3)   **Dex** 12(+1)   **Con** 17(+3)
Int 9 (-1)   **Wis** 10(+0)   **Cha** 9(-1)

Prof. +2   **Speed** Normal
Saving Throws Phy
Senses Passive 10
Languages Common
Challenge 1 (20 XP)

Berserkers are normal humans, but they fight with astounding ferocity. A bonus of +1 is added to their attack rolls. They do not wear armor heavier than leather armor.

Actions

Attack. +2 to hit
Battle Axe. 4 (1d8) slashing - range close

Black Pudding

Large ooze

HD 10   **AC** 13
HP 75 (10d8+30)
Str 16(+3)   **Dex** 5(-3)   **Con** 16(+3)
Int 1(-5)   **Wis** 6(-2)   **Cha** 1(-5)

Prof. +4   **Speed** Slow, Climb Slow
Saving Throws Phy
Senses Passive 8, blindsight
Languages -
Challenge 10 (590 XP)

Black puddings are amorphous globs with an acidic surface. They are subterranean predators and scavengers.

Acid. Any weapon or armor contacting a black pudding will be eaten away by the acid as follows: weapon (1 hit by the weapon), chainmail or lesser armor (1 hit by pudding), plate mail (2 hits by pudding). If a weapon or armor is magical, it can take an additional hit per +1 before being dissolved.

Actions

Attack. +10 to hit
Pseudopod. 13(3d8) bludgeoning

Bugbear

Medium humanoid

HD 34 **AC** 12
HP 16(3d8+3)
Str 15(+2) **Dex** 14(+2) **Con** 13(+1)
Int 8(-1) **Wis** 10(+0) **Cha** 9(-1)

Prof. +2 **Speed** Normal
Saving Throws Phy
Senses Passive 10, darkvision
Languages Goblin
Challenge 3 (70 XP)

These large, hairy, goblin-like humanoids are stealthier than their size would suggest. Bugbears stand from 7-8 ft. in height.

Stealthy. Bugbear roll any DEX checks related to stealth or hiding with advantage.

Actions

Attack. +3 to hit
Morningstar. 4(1d8) piercing - range close
Spear. 4(1d8) piercing - range close, thrown - near

Centaur

Large monstrosity

HD 4 **AC** 12
HP 26(4d8+8)
Str 18(+4) **Dex** 14(+2) **Con** 14(+2)
Int 9(-1) **Wis** 13(+1) **Cha** 11(+0)

Prof. +2 **Speed** Fast
Saving Throws Phy
Senses Passive 11
Languages Sylvan
Challenge 5 (180 XP)

Half man, half horse, centaurs are fierce warriors and well-known creatures of mythology. The referee may choose any "version" of the centaur from myth or folklore: some are evil, some aloof, and some are soothsayers.

Actions

Attack. +4 to hit
Multiattack. The centaur makes three attacks: one with its pike and two with its hooves.
Pike. 4 (1d8) piercing - range 10ft
Hooves. 3 (1d6) bludgeoning - range near.

Chimera

Large monstrosity

HD 9   **AC** 15

HP 49(9d8+9)

Str 15(+2)   **Dex** 14(+2)   **Con** 13(+1)

Int 8(-1)   **Wis** 10(+0)   **Cha** 9(-1)

Prof. +4   **Speed** Normal, Fly Fast

Saving Throws Phy

Senses Passive 12

Languages Understands Draconic but can't speak

Challenge 10 (590 XP)

The chimera has three heads; one is the head of a goat, one the head of a lion, and one the head of a dragon. Great wings rise from its lion-like body.

Actions

Attack. +9 to hit

Multiattack. The chimera makes three attacks: one with its bite, one with its horns, and one with its claws. When its fire breath is available, it can use the breath in place of its bite or horns.

Lion Bite. 5 (2d4) piercing

Goat Horns. 2 (1d4) bludgeoning

Dragon Bite. 7 (3d4) piercing

Fire Breath (3 times daily). The dragon head exhales fire in a Near cone. Each creature in that area must make a Hard (DC 16) DEX saving throw, taking 13 (3d8) fire damage on a failed save, or half as much damage on a successful one.

_____

Cockatrice

Small monstrosity

HD 5   **AC** 13

HP 27(5d8+5)

Str 6(-2)   **Dex** 12(+1)   **Con** 12(+1)

Int 2(-4)   **Wis** 13(+1)   **Cha** 5(-5)

Prof. +2   **Speed** Slow, Fly Normal

Saving Throws Phy

Senses Passive 11

Languages -

Challenge 6 (230 XP)

A cockatrice resembles a bat-winged rooster with a long, serpentine tail. Turn to Stone. When bitten must succeed on a NORMAL (DC12) Wisdom saving throw or be turned to stone.

Actions

Attack. +5 to hit

Bite. 3 (1d6) piercing and possible Turn to Stone.

_____

Crab, Giant

Medium beast

HD 3   **AC** 16

HP 13(3d8)

Str 13(+1)   **Dex** 15(+2)   **Con** 11(+0)

Int 1(-5)   **Wis** 9(-1)   **Cha** 3(+4)

Prof. +2   **Speed** Normal, Swim Normal

Saving Throws Phy

Senses Passive 9 blindsight

Languages -

Challenge 4 (110 XP)

Larger specimens of giant crabs might move more slowly — these stats are for a crab about 5-ft. in diameter.

Actions

Attack. +3 to hit

Multiattack. Giant crab makes two claw attacks.

Claw. 7 (2d6) bludgeoning

Crocodile

Large beast

HD 3   **AC** 15

HP 16(3d8+3)

Str 15(+2)   **Dex** 10(+0)   **Con** 13(+1)

Int 2(-4)   **Wis** 10(+0)   **Cha** 5(-3)

Prof. +2   **Speed** Normal, Swim Normal

Saving Throws Phy

Senses Passive 10

Languages -

Challenge 3 (70 XP)

Some normal crocodiles are man-eaters; all are dangerous and can conceal themselves well. Normal crocodiles can grow to be as long as 15 ft.

Actions

Attack. +3 to hit

Bite. 7 (3d4) piercing

Dire Wolf

Large beast

HD 4   **AC** 14

HP 26(4d8+8)

Str 17(+3)   **Dex** 15(+2)   **Con** 15(+2)

Int 5(-3)   **Wis** 12(+1)   **Cha** 7(-2)

Prof. +2   **Speed** Fast

Saving Throws Phy

Senses Passive 13

Languages -

Challenge 4 (110 XP)

Dire Wolves are large, more intelligent wolves.

Actions

Attack. +4 to hit

Bite. 4 (1d8) piercing

Djínn

Large elemental

HD 7 **AC** 14

HP 73(7d8+42)

Str 21(+5) **Dex** 15(+2) **Con** 22(+6)
Int 15(+2) **Wis** 16(+3) **Cha** 22(+6)

Prof. +4 **Speed** Normal, fly fast
Saving Throws Phy, Men
Senses Passive 13, darkvision
Languages Auran
Challenge 7 (290 XP)

Djinn are one of the genies of folklore, creatures of the air (and possibly of the elemental planes). They can carry 700 pounds of weight, and have a number of magical powers.

Create. A djinni can create food and water of high quality, as well as wooden and cloth objects. They can also create objects of metal (including coins), but all such magically created metals disappear in time.

Djinn can call up illusions, and although these are quite excellent they disappear when touched.

Gaseous Form / Invisibility. Djinni can turn themselves into gaseous form (cannot attack or be attacked, can enter any area that is not airtight), and can become invisible at will.

Whirlwind. Finally, a djinni can turn itself into a Huge sized whirlwind much like an air elemental, sweeping away any creature with one or fewer hit dice.

More powerful types of djinn might be capable of granting limited wishes or even true wishes.

Actions

Attack. +7 to hit

Scimitar. 9 (2d8) slashing

Dragon, Black (6-8)

Huge dragon
HD 6-8   **AC** 17
HP 67-76(6d8+30 to 8d8+40)
Str 23(+6) **Dex** 14(+2) **Con** 21(+5)
Int 14(+2) **Wis** 13(+1) **Cha** 17(+3)

Prof. +3   **Speed** Normal, fly or swim Fast
Saving Throws Phy, Men
Senses Passive 21, Blindsight, Darkvision
Languages Common, Draconic
Challenge 7-9 (290-500 XP)

Black dragons tend to be evil creatures preferring to ambush their targets, using their surroundings as cover. When fighting in heavily forested swamps and marshes, they try to stay in the water or on the ground; trees and leafy canopies limit their aerial maneuverability. **Talk/ Spellcasting.** Black dragons have a 45% chance of being able to talk; talking black dragons have a 5% chance of being able to cast 1d4 first-level Magic-User spells.

Actions
Attack. +5, +6, +7 to hit
Multiattack. The dragon makes three attacks: one with its bite and two with its claws or one Breath Weapon attack.
Bite. 10 (3d6) piercing, range 10ft.
Claw. 2 (1d4) slashing, range close.
Breath Weapon (3 times daily). The dragon exhales acid in a 5-foot wide line out to Far. Each creature in that line must make a NORMAL (DC 12) DEX saving throw, taking 21 to 28 (6d6 to 8d6) acid damage on a failed save, or half as much damage on a successful one.

Dragon, Blue (8-10)

Huge dragon
HD 8-10   **AC** 17
HP 84-105(8d8+48 to 10d8+60)
Str 25(+7) **Dex** 10(+0) **Con** 23(+6)
Int 16(+3) **Wis** 15(+2) **Cha** 19(+4)

Prof. +4   **Speed** Fast, Fly & Swim Fast
Saving Throws Phy, Men
Senses Passive 22, blindsight, darkvision
Languages Common, Draconic
Challenge 9 to 11 (500-720 XP)

Typically, blue dragons attack from above or burrow beneath the sands until opponents come within 100 feet. Older dragons use their special abilities, such as hallucinatory terrain, in concert with these tactics to mask the land and improve their chances to surprise the target. Blue dragons run from a fight only if they are severely damaged, since they view retreat as cowardly.
Talk/Spellcasting. Blue dragons have a 65% chance of being able to talk; talking blue dragons have a 15% chance of being able to cast 1d4 first-level Magic-User spells and 1d3 second-level Magic-User spells.

Actions
Attack. +8, +9, +10 to hit
Multiattack. The dragon makes three attacks: one with its bite and two with its claws or one breath weapon attack.
Bite. 13 (2d12) piercing, range 10ft.
Claw. 2 (1d4) slashing, range close.
Breath Weapon (3 times daily). The dragon exhales lightning in a 5-feet wide Line out to Far. Each creature in that line must make a NORMAL (DC 12)DEX saving throw, taking 28-35 (8d6 to 10d6) lightning damage on a failed save, or half as much damage on a successful one.

Dragon, Gold (10-12)

Huge dragon
HD 10-12 **AC** 17
HP 115-138(10d8+70 to 12d8+84)
Str 27(+8) **Dex** 14(+2) **Con** 25(+7)
Int 16(+3) **Wis** 15(+2) **Cha** 24(+7)

Prof. +5 **Speed** Fast, Fly & Swim Fast
Saving Throws Phy, Men
Senses Passive 24, blindsight, darkvision
Languages Common, Draconic
Challenge 11 to 13 (720-1000 XP)

Gold dragons usually parley before fighting and are usually considered to be good creatures. When conversing with intelligent creatures, they use Intimidate and Sense Motives to gain the upper hand. In combat, they employ bless and their luck bonus; older dragons use their luck bonus at the start of each day. They make heavy use of spells in combat. Among their favorites are cloudkill, fireball, wall of fire, hallucinatory terrain, sleep, slow, and suggestion.
Talk/ Spellcasting. Gold dragons have a 100% chance of being able to talk and a 25% chance of being able to cast Magic-User spells: 1d4 first-level, 1d3 second-level, 1d2 third-level, and 1 fourth-level spell.
Change Shape. Gold dragons often appear as human or in some other guise.

Actions
Attack. +10, +11, +12 to hit
Multiattack. The dragon makes three attacks: one with its bite and two with its claws or one of its two breath weapon attack.
Bite. 19 (3d12) piercing, range 10ft.
Claw. 2 (1d4) slashing, range close.
Breath Weapons (each 3 times daily)
Fire Breath. The dragon exhales fire in a cone out to Near. Each creature in that area must make a HARD(DC 16) DEX saving throw, taking 45 (10d8 to 12d8) fire damage on a failed save, or half as much damage on a successful one.
Weakening Breath. The dragon exhales gas in a cone out to Near. Each creature in that area must succeed on a HARD (DC 16) STR saving throw or have disadvantage on Strength-based attack rolls, Strength checks, and Strength saving throws for 2d4 x 10 minutes.

Dragon, Green (7-9)

Huge dragon
HD 7-9   **AC** 17
HP 67-86(7d8+35 to 9d8+45)
Str 23(+6) **Dex** 12(+1) **Con** 21(+5)
Int 18(+4) **Wis** 15(+2) **Cha** 17(+3)

Prof. +3   **Speed** Fast, Fly & Swim Fast
Saving Throws Phy, Men
Senses Passive 22, blindsight, darkvision
Languages Common, Draconic
Challenge 8 to 10 (390-590 XP)

Green dragons initiate fights with little or no provocation, picking on creatures of any size. If the target is intriguing or seems formidable, the dragon stalks the creature to determine the best time to strike and the most appropriate tactics to use. If the target appears weak, the dragon makes its presence known quickly—it enjoys evoking terror. Sometimes the dragon elects to control a humanoid creature through intimidation and suggestion. Green dragons especially like to question adventurers to learn more about their society and abilities, what is going on in the countryside, and if there is treasure nearby.

Talk/ Spellcasting. Green dragons have a 55% chance of being able to talk; talking green dragons have a 10% chance of being able to cast 1d4 first-level Magic-User spells and 1d2 second-level Magic-User spells.

Actions

Multiattack. The dragon makes three attacks: one with its bite and two with its claws or a Breath Weapon attack.
Bite. 11 (2d10) piercing, range 10ft.
Claw. 2 (1d4) slashing, range close.
Breath Weapon (3 times daily). The dragon exhales a cone out to Near. Each creature in that area must make a NORMAL (DC 12) CON saving throw, taking 24-31 (7d6 to 9d6) poison damage on a failed save, or half as much damage on a successful one.

Dragon, Red (9-11)

Huge dragon
HD 9-11   **AC** 17
HP 104-127(9d8+63 to 11d8+77)
Str 27(+8) **Dex** 10(+0) **Con** 25(+5)
Int 16(+3) **Wis** 13(+1) **Cha** 21(+5)

Prof. +4/5 **Speed** Fast, Fly & Swim Fast
Saving Throws Phy, Men
Senses Passive 23, blindsight, darkvision
Languages Common, Draconic
Challenge 10 to 12 (590-840 XP)

Because red dragons are so confident, they seldom pause to appraise an adversary. On spotting a target, they make a snap decision whether to attack, using one of many strategies worked out ahead of time. A red dragon lands to attack small, weak creatures with its claws and bite rather than obliterating them with its breath weapon, so as not to destroy any treasure they might be carrying.

Talk/ Spellcasting. Red dragons have a 75% chance of being able to talk; talking red dragons have a 20% chance of being able to cast 1d4 first level Magic-User spells, 1d3 second level Magic-User spells, and 1d2 third level Magic-User spells.

Actions

Multiattack. The dragon makes three attacks: one with its bite and two with its claws or uses its Breath Weapon.
Bite. 16 (3d10) piercing + 7 (2d6) fire , range 10ft.

Claw. 2 (1d4) slashing, range close.
Breath Weapon (3 times daily). The dragon exhales fire in a cone out to Near. Each creature in that area must make a HARD (DC 16) DEX saving throw, taking 31-38 (9d6 to 11d6) fire damage on a failed save, or half as much damage on a successful one.

Dragon, White (5-7)

Huge dragon

HD 5-7   **AC** 17
HP 53-74(5d8+30 to 7d8+42)
Str 22(+6) **Dex** 10(+0) **Con** 22(+6)
Int 8(-1) **Wis** 12(+1) **Cha** 12(+1)

Prof. +3   **Speed** Fast, Fly & Swim Fast
Saving Throws Phy, Men
Senses Passive 21 blindsight, darkvision

Languages Common, Draconic
Challenge 6 to 8 (230-390 XP)

White dragons are usually found in cold regions, where they camouflage themselves in ice and snow, lying in wait for prey. White dragons are not able to talk or cast spells.

Actions

Multiattack. The dragon makes three attacks: one with its bite and two with its claws or it makes a single Breath Weapon attack.
Bite. 9 (2d8) piercing, range 10ft.
Claw. 2 (1d4) slashing, range close.
Breath Weapon. They breathe a cone of intensely cold air and frost out to Near. Each creature in that area must make a NORMAL (DC 12) Dexterity saving throw, taking 16-24 (5d6 to 7d6) cold damage on a failed save, or half as much damage on a successful one.

Dryad

Medium fey
HD 2   **AC** 10
HP 53-74(5d8+30 to 7d8+42)
Str 10(+0) **Dex** 12(+1) **Con** 11(+0)
Int 14(+2) **Wis** 15(+2) **Cha** 18(+4)

Prof. +2   **Speed** Normal
Saving Throws Men
Senses Passive 14, darkvision
Languages Sylvan
Challenge 2 (45XP)

Dryads are beautiful female tree spirits who do not venture far from their home trees.
Charm. They can cast (as a native magical power) a strong charm that operates as a Charm Person spell with disadvantage to the EASY (DC 8) CHA saving throw. Those who are charmed seldom return, or might be kept for a hundred years and a day within the dryad's tree.

Actions
Attack. +2 to hit
Wooden Dagger. 2 (1d4) piercing, range close.

Efreet

Large elemental
HD 10   **AC** 17
HP 115(10d8+70)
Str 22(+6) **Dex** 12(+1) **Con** 24(+7)
Int 16(+3) **Wis** 15(+2) **Cha** 16(+3)

Prof. +4   **Speed** Normal
Saving Throws Men
Senses Passive 14, darkvision
Languages Ignan
Challenge 10 (590XP)

Efreet are a type of genie, associated with fire (in contrast to the djinn, who have powers over the air). Efreet can carry up to 1000 pounds of weight, and under the right circumstances, they can be forced to serve as a slave until they figure out how to free themselves. An efreeti can create a wall of fire (per the spell). They appear as giant humans with cruel features, their skin flickering with flames.

Actions
Attack. +10 to hit
Scimitar. 13 (3d8) slashing

Elementals

Elementals are living manifestations of the basic forms of matter: earth, air, fire, and water. They are usually summoned from their native planes of existence to do the bidding of a powerful wizard. These beings can also be "chained" within objects or structures to give the objects magical properties. Elementals are barely intelligent at all, but they are as powerful as the forces of nature that they actually are.

Elemental, Air (8HD)

Large elemental
HD 8   **HP** 52(8d8+16)
Prof. +4
Challenge 8 (390XP)

Elemental, Air (12HD)

Large elemental
HD 12   **HP** 78(12d8+24)
Prof. +5
Challenge 12 (840XP)

Elemental, Air (16HD)

Large elemental
HD 12   **HP** 104(16d8+32)
Prof. +6
Challenge 16 (1500XP)

AC 17
Str 14(+2) **Dex** 20(+5) **Con** 14(+2)
Int 6(-2) **Wis** 10(+0) **Cha** 6(-2)

Speed Fly Fast, Hover
Saving Throws Phy
Senses Passive 10, darkvision
Languages Auran

Whirlwind. Air elementals can turn into a whirlwind of air with a diameter of Huge hurling any creature of 1 HD or less for great distances (and almost certainly killing them). These elemental whirlwinds are approximately 100 ft. in height.

Actions
Attack
8HD.   +8 to hit
12HD.   +12 to hit,
16HD.   +16 to hit
Damage. 9 (2d8) bludgeoning

Elemental, Earth (8HD)

Large elemental
HD 8   **HP** 76(8d8+40)
Prof. +4
Challenge 8 (390XP)

Elemental, Earth (12HD)

Large elemental
HD 12   **HP** 114(12d8+60)
Prof. +5
Challenge 12 (840XP)

Elemental, Earth (16HD)

Large elemental
HD 16   **HP** 152(16d8+80)
Prof. +6
Challenge 16 (1,500XP)

AC 17
Str 20(+5) **Dex** 8(-1)   **Con** 20(+5)
Int 5(-3) **Wis** 10(+0) **Cha** 5(-3)

Speed Normal, Burrow
Saving Throws Phy
Senses Passive 10, darkvision, tremorsense
Languages Terran

Earth elementals are hulking man-shapes of rock and earth. They batter opponents with their great fists, although damage is reduced by 1d6 if the opponent is not standing upon earth or rock. Earth elementals can tear apart a castle wall in 1d4+4 rounds or could rip down the entire castle within 1 hour if not prevented or distracted.

Actions
Attack
8HD.   +8 to hit
12HD.   +12 to hit,
16HD.   +16 to hit
Slam. 18 (4d8) bludgeoning

Elemental, Fire (8HD)

Large elemental
HD 8   **HP** 60(8d8+24)
Prof. +4
Challenge 8 (390XP)

Elemental, Fire (12HD)

Large elemental
HD 12   **HP** 80(12d8+36)
Prof. +5
Challenge 12 (840XP)

Elemental, Fire (16HD)

Large elemental
HD 16   **HP** 120(16d8+48)
Prof. +6
Challenge 16 (1,500XP)

AC 17
Str 10(+0) **Dex** 17(+3) **Con** 16(+3)
Int 6(-2)   **Wis** 10(+0) **Cha** 7(-2)

Speed Fast
Saving Throws Phy
Senses Passive 10 darkvision
Languages Ignan

Fire elementals are formless masses of flame, perhaps with a vaguely human shape. Their attacks cause flammable materials (including wood) to ignite if the material fails a saving throw (as determined by the Referee).
Actions
Attack
8HD.   +8 to hit
12HD.   +12 to hit,
16HD.   +16 to hit
Damage. 16 (4d8) fire

Elemental, Water (8HD)

Large elemental
HD 8   **HP** 68(8d8+32)
Prof. +4
Challenge 8 (390XP)

Elemental, Water (12HD)

Large elemental
HD 12   **HP** 102(12d8+48)
Prof. +5
Challenge 12 (840XP)

Elemental, Water (16HD)

Large elemental
HD 16   **HP** 136(16d8+64)
Prof. +6
Challenge 16 (1,500XP)

AC 17
Str 18(+4) **Dex** 14(+2) **Con** 18(+4)
Int 5(-3)   **Wis** 10(+0) **Cha** 8(-1)

Speed Swim Fast
Saving Throws Phy
Senses Passive 10 darkvision
Languages Aquan

Water elementals cannot move more than Far from a large body of water, and their damage is reduced by 1d6 if the opponent is not standing in water (or swimming, etc). These powerful beings can overturn a ship if given 1d4+4 rounds to work at it. On water they can attack ships, battering them to pieces within 1 hour if not prevented or distracted.
Actions
Attack
8HD.   +8 to hit
12HD.   +12 to hit,
16HD.   +16 to hit
Damage. 18 (3d10) bludgeoning

Gargoyle

Medium elemental

HD 4   **AC** 14

HP 30(4d8+12)

Str 15(+2)   **Dex** 11(+0)   **Con** 16(+3)

Int 6(-2)   **Wis** 11(+0)   **Cha** 7(-2)

Prof. +3   **Speed** Normal, Fly Fast

Saving Throws Phy

Senses Passive 10, darkvision

Languages Terran

Challenge 5 (180XP)

Gargoyles are winged beings resembling the carven monstrosities that bedeck the walls of cathedrals and many subterranean dungeons. They are terribly vicious predators.

Immune to non-magical weapons.

Actions

Attack. +4 to hit

Multiattack. The gargoyle makes four attacks: one with its bite, one with its horns, and two with its claws.

Bite. 3 (1d6) piercing

Claws. 2 (1d3) slashing

Horns. 2 (1d4) piercing

Ghoul

Medium undead

HD 2 **AC** 13
HP 9(2d8)
Str 13(+1) **Dex** 15(+2) **Con** 10(+0)
Int 7(-2) **Wis** 10(+0) **Cha** 6(-2)

Prof. +2 **Speed** Normal
Saving Throws Men
Senses Passive 10, darkvision
Languages -
Challenge 3 (110XP)

Ghouls are pack-hunting undead corpse eaters.

Immune. Ghouls are immune, like most undead, to charms and sleep spells.

Paralyzing Touch. On a successful claw attack, the target (other than an elf or undead) must succeed on an EASY (DC 8) Strength saving throw or be paralyzed for 3d6 x 10 minutes.

Actions

Attack. +2 to hit
Multiattack: Ghouls make 2 claw attacks and one bite attack each round.
Bite. 2 (1d4) piercing
Claws. 2 (1d3) slashing and Paralyzing Touch (see above).

Gelatinous Cube

Large ooze

HD 4 **AC** 11
HP 38(4d8+20)
Str 14(+2) **Dex** 3(-4) **Con** 20(+5)
Int 1(-5) **Wis** 6(-2) **Cha** 1(-5)

Prof. +3 **Speed** Slow
Saving Throws Phy
Senses Passive 8, blindsight
Languages -
Challenge 5 (180XP)

Gelatinous cubes are semi-transparent cubes that slosh through subterranean passages, engulfing debris and carrion to digest.

Acid. Their entire substance is acidic; if the cube hits successfully, the victim must make an EASY Strength saving throw or become paralyzed (60 minutes) while the cube devours them. Most gelatinous cubes contain various metallic treasures or gems that they have engulfed but not yet digested.

Actions

Attack. +4 to hit
Pseudopod. 5 (2d4) acid + paralyze (see above).

Giant, Cloud

Huge giant

HD 12   **AC** 15

HP 126(12d8+72)

Str 27(+8) **Dex** 10(+0) **Con** 22(+6)

Int 12(+1) **Wis** 16(+3) **Cha** 16(+3)

Prof. +5   **Speed** Fast

Saving Throws Phy

Senses Passive 10, darkvision

Languages Giant

Challenge 12 (840XP)

Cloud giants are cunning beasts, often living in cloud-castles in the sky (hence their name). Cloud giants are famous for their ability to smell out food, enemies, and Englishmen.
Keen sense of smell.

Actions

Attack. +12 to hit

Morningstar. 21 (6d6) piercing

Rock. 21 (6d6) bludgeoning range Far

Giant, Fire

Huge giant

HD 11   **AC** 15

HP 115(11d8+66)

Str 25(+7) **Dex** 9(-1) **Con** 23(+6)

Int 10(+0) **Wis** 14(+2) **Cha** 13(+1)

Prof. +4   **Speed** Normal

Saving Throws Phy

Senses Passive 16

Languages Giant

Challenge 11 (720XP)

Fire giants are usually found near volcanic mountains, in great castles of basalt or even iron.
Immune to fire.

Actions

Attack. +11 to hit

Greatsword. 17 (5d6) slashing, reach 10 ft

Rock. 17 (5d6) bludgeoning, range Far

Giant, Frost

Huge giant

HD 10   **AC** 15

HP 95(10d8+50)

Str 23(+6) **Dex** 9(-1) **Con** 21(+5)

Int 9(-1) **Wis** 10(+0) **Cha** 12(+1)

Prof. +4   **Speed** Normal

Saving Throws Phy

Senses Passive 13

Languages Giant

Challenge 10 (590XP)

Frost giants dwell in cold regions, where they build (or conquer) castles in remote places of ice and snow.
Immune to Cold.

Actions

Attack. +11 to hit

Greataxe. 14 (4d6) slashing

Rock. 14 (4d6) bludgeoning, range Far

Giant, Hill

Huge giant

HD 8   **AC** 15
HP 68(8d8+32)
Str 21(+5)   **Dex** 8(-1)   **Con** 19(+4)
Int 5(-3)   **Wis** 9(-1)   **Cha** 6(-2)

Prof. +3   **Speed** Normal
Saving Throws Phy
Senses Passive 12
Languages Giant
Challenge 8 (390XP)

Hill giants are the least of the giant races; most are brutish cave-dwellers who dress in pelts and uncured hides.

Actions

Attack. +11 to hit
Greatclub. 9 (2d8) bludgeoning, reach 10 ft.
Rock. 9 (2d8) bludgeoning, range Near

Giant, Stone

Huge giant

HD 9   **AC** 15
HP 85(9d8+45)
Str 23(+6)   **Dex** 15(+2)   **Con** 20(+5)
Int 10(+0)   **Wis** 12(+1)   **Cha** 9(-1)

Prof. +4   **Speed** Normal
Saving Throws Phy
Senses Passive 14
Languages Giant
Challenge 9 (500XP)

Stone giants dwell in caves, isolated in the mountain fastnesses. They can be quite crafty in setting up ambushes in their native mountains. Travelers who wander into the territory of stone giants seldom return.

Actions

Attack. +9 to hit
Greatclub. 10 (3d6) bludgeoning, reach 15 ft.
Rock. 10 (3d6) bludgeoning, range Far.

Gnoll

Medium humanoid

HD 2   **AC** 14
HP 9(2d8)
Str 14(+2)   **Dex** 12(+1)   **Con** 11(+0)
Int 6(-2)   **Wis** 10(+0)   **Cha** 7(-2)

Prof. +3   **Speed** Normal
Saving Throws Phy
Senses Passive 10 darkvision
Languages Gnoll
Challenge 2 (45XP)

Gnolls are tall humanoids with hyena-like heads. They may be found both above ground and in subterranean caverns. They form into loosely organized clans, often ranging far from home in order to steal and kill with rapacious ferocity.

Actions
Attack. +2 to hit
Bite. 2 (1d4) piercing.
Spear. 3 (1d6) piercing, range close or thrown near.
Longbow. 5 (1d8) piercing, range far

Goblin

Small humanoid
HD 1/2   **AC** 15
HP 2(1d4)
Str 8(-1)   **Dex** 14(+2)   **Con** 10(+0)
Int 10(+10) **Wis** 8(-1)   **Cha** 8(-1)

Prof. +2   **Speed** Normal
Saving Throws Phy
Senses Passive 8, darkvision
Languages Goblin
Challenge 1/2 (10XP)

Goblins are small creatures (4 ft tall or so) that inhabit dark woods, underground caverns, and (possibly) the otherworldly realms of the fey.
Sunlight Sensitivity. While in sunlight, the goblin has disadvantage on attack rolls, as well as on Wisdom checks that rely on sight.

Actions
Attack. +1 to hit
Bite or Claw. 2 (1d4) piercing.
Goblin Scimitar. 3 (1d6) slashing
Goblin Shortbow. 3 (1d6) piercing, range far

Golem, Flesh

Medium construct

HD 8 **AC** 10

HP 68(8d8+32)

Str 19(+4) **Dex** 9(-1) **Con** 18(+4)

Int 6(-2) **Wis** 10(+0) **Cha** 5(-3)

Prof. +4 **Speed** Normal

Saving Throws Phy

Senses Passive 10, darkvision

Languages Understands the language of its creator but can't speak.

Challenge 8 (390XP)

Golems are man-shaped creatures built to serve their masters, usually powerful wizards or high priests. They are often used as guardians.

Immune to nonmagical weapons and spells. Golems cannot be hit with non-magical weapons and are unaffected by most spells.

A creation stitched together from human limbs and other parts, a flesh golem is similar to Frankenstein's monster. Only +1 or better magic weapons can harm a flesh golem, and it is slowed by fire and cold spells. Lightning heals the golem for the number of points of damage that it would normally inflict. No other type of spell affects a flesh golem.

Actions

Attack. +8 to hit

Fist. 9 (2d8) bludgeoning

Golem, Iron

Large construct

HD 16 **AC** 14

HP 152(16d8+80)

Str 24(+7) **Dex** 9(-1) **Con** 20(+5)

Int 3(-4) **Wis** 11(+0) **Cha** 1(-5)

Prof. +6 **Speed** Normal

Saving Throws Phy

Senses Passive 10, darkvision

Languages Understands the language of its creator but can't speak.

Challenge 16 (1500XP)

Golems are man-shaped creatures built to serve their masters, usually powerful wizards or high priests. They are often used as guardians.

Immune to nonmagical weapons and spells. Golems cannot be hit with non-magical weapons and are unaffected by most spells.

Iron golems are huge moving statues of iron. They can breathe a NEAR radius cloud of poison gas as well as attack with great power. Weapons of +2 or less do not affect iron golems. These hulking statues are slowed by lightning spells, but fire-based spells actually restore hit points to them. No other type of spell affects them.

Actions

Attack. +16 to hit

Fist. 17 (4d8) bludgeoning

Golem, Stone

Large construct,
HD 12   **AC** 14
HP 114(14d8+60)
Str 22(+6) **Dex** 9(-1)   **Con** 20(+5)
Int 3(-4)   **Wis** 11(+0)   **Cha** 1(-5)

Prof. +5   **Speed** Normal
Saving Throws Phy
Senses Passive 10, darkvision
Languages Understands the language
of its creator but can't speak.
Challenge 12 (840XP)

*Golems are man-shaped creatures built
to serve their masters, usually powerful
wizards or high priests. They are often
used as guardians.*

Immune to nonmagical weapons and
spells. Golems cannot be hit with non-
magical weapons and are unaffected
by most spells.

Stone golems are massive stone
statues animated by very powerful
magics (much more than just animate
object, in other words). They are
slowed by fire spells, damaged by
rock-to-mud spells, and healed by the
reverse. Spells that affect rock, and fire
spells, are the only ones that affect
stone golems. They can only be hit by
+2 or better weapons.

Actions
Attack. +12 to hit
Fist. 13 (3d8) bludgeoning

Gorgon

Large monstrosity

HD 8   **AC** 17
HP 78(8d8+32)

Str 20(+5)   **Dex** 11(+0)   **Con** 18(+4)
Int 2(-4)   **Wis** 12(+1)   **Cha** 7(-2)

Prof. +3   **Speed** Fast
Saving Throws Phy
Senses Passive 14, darkvision
Languages -
Challenge 9 (500XP)

Gorgons are bull-like creatures with dragon-like scales.
Breath Weapon. Their breath turns people to stone (NEAR range, NORMAL (DC12) CON saving throw applies).

Actions
Attack. +8 to hit
Gore. 7 (2d6) piercing

———————

Gray Ooze

Medium ooze

HD 3   **AC** 11
HP 22(3d8+9)

Str 12(+1)   **Dex** 6(-2)   **Con** 16(+3)
Int 1(-5)   **Wis** 6(-2)   **Cha** 2(-4)

Prof. +2   **Speed** Normal
Saving Throws Phy
Senses Passive 8, blindsight
Languages -
Challenge 3 (70XP)

Gray ooze is almost identical in appearance to wet rock, but it is a slimy, formless substance that devours prey and carrion with its acidic secretions, lashing out to strike enemies.
Immune. Gray ooze is immune to spells, heat, and cold damage.
Acid. Metal (but not stone or wood) must make an EASY CON saving throw when exposed to gray ooze or be rotted through. When the gray ooze hits a character in metal armor, the armor must make an item saving throw.
Immune to bludgeoning. Only cutting and piercing damage a grey ooze—it is impervious to blunt or crushing attacks.

Actions
Attack. +3 to hit
Pseudopod. 9 (2d8) bludgeoning and acid.

———————

Green Slime

Medium ooze

HD 2   **AC** 14

HP 13(2d8+4)

Str 1(-5)   **Dex** 1(-5)   **Con** 13(+2)

Int 1(-5)   **Wis** 1(-5)   **Cha** 1(-5)

Prof. +2   **Speed** None

Saving Throws Phy

Senses Passive 5

Languages Terran

Challenge 2 (45XP)

Green slime isn't technically a monster, just an extremely dangerous hazard in underground tombs and other such places.

Any metal or organic substance it touches begins to turn to green slime (EASY CON saving throw). It can be killed with fire or extreme cold, and the transformation process can be arrested by the use of a cure disease spell.

Griffon

Large monstrosity

HD 7   **AC** 16

HP 52(7d8+21)

Str 18(+4)   **Dex** 15(+2)   **Con** 16(+3)

Int 2(-4)   **Wis** 13(+1)   **Cha** 8(-1)

Prof. +3   **Speed** Normal, Fly Fast

Saving Throws Phy

Senses Passive 15, darkvision

Languages -

Challenge 8 (390XP)

Griffons have the body of a lion, with the head, fore-claws, and wings of an eagle. These creatures can be tamed and ridden as mounts. They usually nest in high mountain aeries, where they lay their eggs and hunt their prey. Because the fledglings can be tamed, young griffons and griffon eggs command a very high price in the marketplaces of the great cities, or to noble lords and wizards.

Actions

Attack. +3 to hit

Multiattack. The griffon makes three attacks: one with its beak and two with its claws.

Beak. 9 (2d8) piercing

Claws. 2 (1d4) slashing

_____

Harpy

Medium monstrosity

HD 3   **AC** 12

HP 16(3d8+3)

Str 12(+1)   **Dex** 13(+1)   **Con** 12(+1)

Int 7(-2)   **Wis** 10(+0)   **Cha** 13(+1)

Prof. +2   **Speed** Normal, Fly Normal

Saving Throws Phy

Senses Passive 10

Languages Common

Challenge 4 (110XP)

Harpies have the upper body of a human female and the lower body and wings of a vulture.

Song. Their song is a charm that draws its victims to the harpy (EASY CHA saving throw applies).

Touch. The harpy's touch casts the equivalent of a charm person spell (again, EASY CHA saving throw applies).

Actions

Attack. +3 to hit

Multiattack. The harpy makes three attacks: two with its claws and one with its club.

Claws. 2 (1d3) slashing

Club. 3 (1d6) bludgeoning

Hellhound

Medium fiend

HD 4-7   **AC** 15

HP 26-45(4d8+8 to 7d8+14)

Str 17(+3)   **Dex** 12(+1)   **Con** 14(+2)

Int 6(-2)   **Wis** 13(+1)   **Cha** 6(-2)

Prof. +2,3   **Speed** Normal

Saving Throws Phy

Senses Passive 15, darkvision

Languages Understands Infernal but cannot speak

Challenge 5-8 (180-390XP)

Hell hounds are fire-breathing dogs of the underworlds or lower planes.

Actions

Attack. +4, +5, +6, +7 to hit

Bite. 3 (1d6) piercing

Fire Breath. 8-14 (4d4 to 7d4) fire damage, range Near one target.

Hippogriff

Large monstrosity

HD 3   **AC** 14

HP 16(3d8+3)

Str 17(+3)   **Dex** 13(+1)   **Con** 13(+1)

Int 2(-4)   **Wis** 12(+1)   **Cha** 8(-1)

Prof. +2   **Speed** Normal, Fly Fast
Saving Throws Phy
Senses Passive 11
Languages -
Challenge 4 (110XP)

The hippogriff is similar to a griffon, having the head, foreclaws, and wings of an eagle, but instead of the body of a lion, it has the body of a horse.

Actions

Attack. +3 to hit
Multiattack. The hippogriff makes three attacks: one with its beak and two with its claws.
Beak. 5 (1d10) piercing
Claws. 3 (1d6) slashing

Hobgoblin

Medium humanoid
HD 1   **AC** 14
HP 14(1d8+1)
Str 13(+1) **Dex** 12(+1) **Con** 12(+1)
Int 10(+0) **Wis** 10(+0) **Cha** 9(-1)

Prof. +2   **Speed** Normal
Saving Throws Phy
Senses Passive 10, darkvision
Languages Goblin
Challenge 1 (20XP)

Hobgoblins are simply large goblins, possibly a separate breed living apart from their smaller cousins, or perhaps not, as the Referee decides.

Actions

Attack. +1 to hit
Sword. 4 (1d8) slashing
Longbow. 3 (1d8) piercing, Range Far.

Homunculus

Tiny monstrosity
HD 2   **AC** 13
HP 9(2d8)
Str 4(-3)   **Dex** 15(+2) **Con** 11(+0)
Int 10(+0) **Wis** 10(+0) **Cha** 7(-2)

Prof. +2   **Speed** Slow, Fly Normal
Saving Throws Phy
Senses Passive 10, darkvision
Languages Understands the language of its creator but cannot speak
Challenge 2 (45XP)

A homunculus is a living, man-like creature created by a powerful magic-user as a servant. The precise abilities of a homunculus depend upon the spells and procedures used in its creation), although virtually all are created with wings of some kind.
Sleep Bite. The most common homunculus has a sleep-inducing bite (EASY CON saving throw).
Other Bites. Other homunculus might be created with a poison bite, or might have unusual powers of perception instead (such as the ability to detect magic, evil, spells, etc).

Actions

Attack. +2 to hit
Bite. 2 (1d3) piercing

Horse, Riding

Large beast
HD 2   **AC** 12
HP 9(2d8)
Str 16(+3) **Dex** 12(+1) **Con** 10(+0)
Int 2(-4)   **Wis** 11(+0) **Cha** 7(-2)

Prof. +2   **Speed** Fast
Saving Throws Phy
Senses Passive 10
Languages -
Challenge 2 (45XP)
Actions
Attack. +2 to hit
Hooves. 2 (1d4) bludgeoning

Horse, War

Large beast
HD 3   **AC** 12
HP 19(3d8+6)
Str 18(+4) **Dex** 12(+1) **Con** 14(+2)
Int 2(-4)   **Wis** 12(+1) **Cha** 7(-2)

Prof. +2   **Speed** Fast
Saving Throws Phy
Senses Passive 11
Languages -
Challenge 3 (70XP)
Actions
Attack. +3 to hit
Hooves. 4 (1d8) bludgeoning

Human Commoner

Medium humanoid
HD -   **AC** 10
HP 3(1d6)
Str 10(+0) **Dex** 10(+0) **Con** 10(+0)
Int 10(+0) **Wis** 10(+0) **Cha** 10(+10)
Prof. +2   **Speed** Normal
Saving Throws Phy
Senses Passive 10
Languages -
Challenge 1/4 (5XP)

Humans are such a versatile race that any number of "monsters" and NPCs can be made from them.
Berserker warriors, tribesmen, cavemen, princesses, evil high priests, captains of the guard, foot-soldiers, and tavern-keepers are all different human "monsters." Don't try to build your non-player characters according to the rules for player characters. Just make up their stats and abilities as you see fit.
Actions
Attack. +0 to hit
Club. 2 (1d4) bludgeoning

Hydra, 5 to 12 Headed

Huge monstrosity
HD 5-12   **AC** 14
HP 47-114(5d8+25 to 12d8+60)
Str 20(+5) **Dex** 12(+1) **Con** 20(+5)
Int 2(-4)   **Wis** 10(+0) **Cha** 7(-2)

Prof. +2,4 **Speed** Normal, Swim Normal
Saving Throws Phy
Senses Passive 10
Languages -
Challenge 6 to 13 (230XP to 1000XP

Hydrae are great lizard-like or snake-like creatures with multiple heads.

Actions
Attack. +5 to +12 to hit
Multiattack. The hydra makes as many bite attacks as it has heads.
Bite. 3 (1d6) piercing, range 10 ft

Invisible Stalker

Medium elemental

HD 8   **AC** 16
HP 52(8d8+16)
Str 16(+3)   **Dex** 19(+4)   **Con** 14(+2)
Int 10(+0)   **Wis** 15(+2)   **Cha** 10(+0)

Prof. +4   **Speed** Fast, Fly Fast
Saving Throws Men
Senses Passive 18
Languages -
Challenge 8 (390XP)

Invisible stalkers are generally found only as a result of the spell Invisible Stalker. They are invisible flying beings created to follow a single command made by the caster.

Actions
Attack. +8 to hit
Weapon. 10 (4d4) bludgeoning

Kobold

Small humanoid

HD 1/2   **AC** 12
HP 1(1d4-1)
Str 7(-2)   **Dex** 15(+2)   **Con** 9(-1)
Int 8(-1)   **Wis** 7(+2)   **Cha** 8(-1)

Prof. +2   **Speed** Normal

Saving Throws Phy
Senses Passive 8, darkvision
Languages Draconic
Challenge 1/2 (10XP)
Languages Draconic
Challenge 1/2 (10 XP)

Kobolds are subterranean, vaguely goblin-like humanoids.

Sunlight Sensitivity. While in sunlight, the kobold has disadvantage on attack rolls, as well as on Wisdom checks that rely on sight.

Actions
Attack. +1 to hit
Dagger. 3 (1d4) piercing
Sling. 3 (1d4) bludgeoning, Range Near.

Lammasu

Large monstrosity

HD 6   **AC** 13
HP 45(6d8+18)
Str 21(+5)   **Dex** 10(+0)   **Con** 17(+3)
Int 16(+3)   **Wis** 17(+3)   **Cha** 14(+2)

Prof. +3   **Speed** Normal, Fly Fast
Saving Throws Phy, Men
Senses Passive 19
Languages Common, Draconic, Celestial & More
Challenge 8 (390XP)

Lammasu are akin to angels; they are human-headed, winged lions that often serve as temple guardians and agents of divine Law. Lammasu tend to be defenders of Law, temples, and civilization rather than being active against the forces of Chaos. If the need arises, of course, a lammasu is quite capable of taking the offensive against threats to its wards — but because they are often pledged to guard particular places, people, or objects, they will often engage other servants of Law to pursue such threats. This being the case, a high level party of Lawful characters might very well be contacted by a lammasu with a request for assistance. The lammasu are usually generous with their rewards to those who are effective allies in the battle against Chaos.

Spells & Powers. Lammasu are able to

1) Become invisible;
2) Cast Dimension Door;
3) Use Cleric spells as if they were of 6th-level Cleric status;
4) continually emanate a Protection From Evil, Near Radius.

They speak all human languages.

Actions

Attack. +6 to hit
Multiattack. The lammasu makes two claw attacks.
Claw. 3 (1d6) slashing

Lich

Medium undead

HD 12-18   **AC** 19
HP 90-135(12d8+36 to 18d8+54)
Str 11(+0)   **Dex** 16(+3)   **Con** 16(+3)
Int 20(+5)   **Wis** 14(+2)   **Cha** 16(+3)

Prof. +5,7 **Speed** Normal
Saving Throws Phy
Senses Passive 19, darkvision
Languages Common, plus up to 5 more
Challenge 13 to 19 (1000XP to 2,200XP)

Liches are the undead remnants of wizards, either made undead by their own deliberate acts during life, or as the result of other magical forces (possibly including their own magics gone awry).

Spells. A lich can cast as a 12th level magic-user.

Lich Touch. A lich's touch causes paralysis with no saving throw.

Fear. The very sight of one of these dread creatures causes any being of 4 HD or below to flee in abject terror. Liches are highly intelligent and totally malign.

Actions

Attack. +12 to +18 to hit
Paralyzing Touch. 5 (1d10) cold damage + paralyzed.

Lion

Large beast
HD 5   **AC** 13
HP 27(5d8+5)
Str 17(+3)   **Dex** 14(+2)   **Con** 13(+1)
Int 3(-4)   **Wis** 12(+1)   **Cha** 8(-1)

Prof. +3   **Speed** Fast
Saving Throws Phy
Senses Passive 10
Languages -
Challenge 5 (180XP)

The first lion encountered will be male; all the rest in the encounter will be lionesses.

Actions

Attack. +5 to hit
Multiattack. Lions make two claw attacks and one bite attack.
Bite. 5 (1d10) piercing
Claw. 2 (1d3) slashing

Lizard, Giant

Large beast
HD 3   **AC** 14
HP 16(3d8+3)
Str 15(+2)   **Dex** 12(+1)   **Con** 13(+1)
Int 2(-4)   **Wis** 10(+0)   **Cha** 5(-3)

Prof. +2   **Speed** Normal, Climb Normal

Saving Throws Phy
Senses Passive 10
Languages -
Challenge 3 (70XP)

Giant lizards (the ones described here, in any case) are about 4ft tall at the shoulder (not quite large enough to ride). Larger specimens could certainly be found — perhaps they continue to grow throughout their long lives, leading to giant lizards of close to saurian dimensions.

Actions

Attack. +3 to hit
Bite. 5 (2d4) piercing

Lizardman

Medium humanoid
HD 2   **AC** 14
HP 11(2d8+2)
Str 15(+2)   **Dex** 10(+0)   **Con** 13(+1)
Int 7(-2)   **Wis** 12(+1)   **Cha** 7(-2)

Prof. +2   **Speed** Fast
Saving Throws Phy
Senses Passive 11, darkvision
Languages Lizardfolk
Challenge 3 (70XP)

Lizardmen are reptilian humanoids, both male and female, usually living in tribal villages in the depths of fetid swamps. Some can hold their breath for long durations (an hour or more), while others can actually breathe underwater.

Actions

Attack. +2 to hit
Multiattack. The lizardfolk makes three melee attacks, two claws, and one bite, or can make one weapon attack.
Claws. 2 (1d3) slashing
Bite. 4 (1d8) piercing
Heavy Club. 4 (1d8) bludgeoning

Lycanthrope, Werebear

Medium humanoid
HD 6   **AC** 14
HP 45(6d8+18)
Str 19(+4)   **Dex** 10(+0)   **Con** 17(+3)
Int 11(+0)   **Wis** 12(+1)   **Cha** 12(+1)

Prof. +3   **Speed** Normal, Fast in bear form
Saving Throws Phy
Senses Passive 15
Languages Common (can't speak in bear form)
Challenge 7 (290XP)

Werebears are often found in temperate forests and tend to take the role of guardian instead of ravenger.
Immune. They cannot be hit by normal weapons: only silver and magical weapons affect them.
Curse of Lycanthropy. If anyone is attacked and brought below 50% hit points by a lycanthrope, the person will become a lycanthrope themself.

Actions

Attack. +6 to hit
Multiattack. A werebear makes two claw and one bite attack.
Bite. 5 (2d4) piercing
Claw (Bear or Hybrid Form Only). 2 (1d3) slashing
Hug. On an attack roll of 18+ (natural roll) with both its claws, the werebear grabs its victim and hugs it for an additional 2d8 points of damage.

Lycanthrope, Wereboar

Medium humanoid

HD 4   **AC** 14

HP 26(4d8+8)

Str 17(+3)   **Dex** 10(+0)   **Con** 15(+2)
Int 10(+0)   **Wis** 11(+0)   **Cha** 8(-1)

Prof. +2   **Speed** Normal, Fast in boar form

Saving Throws Phy

Senses Passive 14

Languages Common (can't speak in boar form)

Challenge 4 (110XP)

Wereboars are often found in the remote wilderness.
They can take the form of a bear, a human, or a boar-like biped.

Immune. They cannot be hit by normal weapons: only silver and magical weapons affect them.

Curse of Lycanthropy. If anyone is attacked and brought below 50% hit points by a lycanthrope, the person will become a lycanthrope themself.

Actions

Attack. +4 to hit

Bite. 7 (2d6) piercing

Lycanthrope, Wererat

Medium humanoid

HD 3   **AC** 13

HP 16(3d8+3)

Str 10(+0)   **Dex** 15(+2)   **Con** 12(+1)
Int 11(+0)   **Wis** 10(+0)   **Cha** 8(-1)

Prof. +2   **Speed** Normal, Fast in rat form

Saving Throws Phy

Senses Passive 14, darkvision

Languages Common (can't speak in rat form)

Challenge 4 (110XP)

Wererats are often found in cities, lurking in shadowy alleyways.

Rat Control. Wererats can control rats.

Stealth. Wererats are extremely stealthy, rolling with advantage on any surprise, stealth, or hiding checks.

Immune. They cannot be hit by normal weapons: only silver and magical weapons affect them.

Curse of Lycanthropy. If anyone is attacked and brought below 50% hit points by a lycanthrope, the person will become a lycanthrope themself.

Actions

Attack. +3 to hit

Multiattack. The wererat makes two attacks, only one of which can be a bite.

Bite. 2 (1d3) piercing

Club. 4 (1d6) piercing

Lycanthrope, Weretiger

Medium humanoid

HD 6   **AC** 14
HP 45(6d8+18)
Str 17(+3) **Dex** 15(+2) **Con** 16(+3)
Int 10(+0) **Wis** 13(+1) **Cha** 11(+0)

Prof. +2   **Speed** Normal, Fast in tiger form
Saving Throws Phy
Senses Passive 15
Languages Common (can't speak in tiger form)
Challenge 7 (290XP)

Weretigers are often found in tropical cities and ancient jungle ruins but will appear in more temperate climates as well if tigers live in the surrounding wilderness. These lycanthropes can assume the form of a tiger, a human, or a bipedal, tiger-like hybrid of the two forms.

Immune. They cannot be hit by normal weapons: only silver and magical weapons affect them.

Curse of Lycanthropy. If anyone is attacked and brought below 50% hit points by a lycanthrope, the person will become a lycanthrope themself.

Actions

Attack. +6 to hit
Multiattack. A weretiger makes two claw and one bite attack.
Bite. 5 (1d10) piercing
Claw (Tiger or Hybrid Form Only). 2 (1d4) slashing

Lycanthrope, Werewolf

Medium humanoid

HD 4   **AC** 14
HP 26(4d8+8)
Str 15(+2) **Dex** 13(+1) **Con** 14(+2)
Int 10(+0) **Wis** 11(+0) **Cha** 10(+0)

Prof. +2   **Speed** Normal, Fast in wolf form
Saving Throws Phy
Senses Passive 14, darkvision
Languages Common (can't speak in wolf form)
Challenge 4 (110XP)

Werewolves are the traditional Lycanthropes seen in horror movies. They can turn into a wolf or into a wolf-man.

Immune. They cannot be hit by normal weapons: only silver and magical weapons affect them.

Curse of Lycanthropy. If anyone is attacked and brought below 50% hit points by a lycanthrope, the person will become a lycanthrope themself.

Weakness. Wolfsbane keeps them at bay.

Actions

Attack. +4 to hit
Bite. 5 (2d4) piercing

Manticore

Large monstrosity

HD 6   **AC** 10

HP 55(6d8+18)

Str 17(+3)   **Dex** 16(+3)   **Con** 17(+3)

Int 7(-2)   **Wis** 12(+1)   **Cha** 7(-2)

Prof. +3   **Speed** Normal, Fly Fast

Saving Throws Phy

Senses Passive 11, darkvision

Languages Common

Challenge 7 (290XP)

This horrid monster has bat wings, the face of a feral human, the body of a lion, and a tail tipped with 24 iron spikes. The manticore can hurl up to 6 of the iron spikes from its tail per round, at a maximum range of Far.

Actions

Attack. +6 to hit

Multiattack. The manticore makes three to eight attacks each round: one with its bite and two with its claws and 1d6 tail spikes (up to 24 spikes, spikes regrow after a Long Rest).

Bite. 4 (1d8) piercing

Claw. 2 (1d3) slashing

Tail Spike. 3 (1d6) piercing, range Near

Mastadon

Huge beast

HD 12   **AC** 14

HP 114(12d8+60)

Str 24(+7)   **Dex** 9(-1)   **Con** 21(+5)

Int 3(-4)   **Wis** 11(+0)   **Cha** 6(-2)

Prof. +5   **Speed** Fast

Saving Throws Phy

Senses Passive 10

Languages -

Challenge 12 (840XP)

Mastadon are huge, shaggy precursors to elephants, larger and more feral, with great, curving tusks. They might be trained as mounts by snow-barbarians. If a lone Mastadon is encountered, there is a 50% chance that it is sick or old (no more than 4hp per HD) and a 50% chance that it is a young bull (no fewer than 4hp per HD).

Actions

Attack. +12 to hit

Multiattack. Mastadon make one gore attack and one stomp attack.

Gore. 10 (3d6) piercing, reach 10 ft.

Stomp. 7 (2d6) bludgeoning

Medusa

Medium monstrosity

HD 4   **AC** 11
HP 30(4d8+12)
Str 10(+0) **Dex** 15(+2) **Con** 16(+3)
Int 12(+1) **Wis** 13(+1) **Cha** 15(+2)

Prof. +2   **Speed** Normal
Saving Throws Phy
Senses Passive 14, darkvision
Languages Common
Challenge 5 (180XP)

The terrifying medusa has a female face but hair of writhing snakes; it has no legs, but the body of a serpent.
Gaze Turns to Stone. Avoiding the gaze of a medusa requires an EASY (DC 8) WIS saving throw. On a fail the target turns to stone in 1d4 rounds. Medusa are subject to effects of their own gaze like basilisk.
Poison. Those bitten must make an EASY (DC 8) CON saving throw or the poison drops them to 0 HP, see Death Saves.

Actions
Attack. +4 to hit
Multiattack. The medusa makes two attacks, one with its bite and one with its gaze.
Bite. 5 (1d10) piercing damage plus Poison (see above).

Merman

Medium humanoid

HD 1   **AC** 12
HP 5(1d8+1)
Str 10(+0) **Dex** 13(+1) **Con** 12(+1)
Int 11(+0) **Wis** 11(+0) **Cha** 12(+1)

Prof. +2   **Speed** Normal, Swim Fast
Saving Throws None
Senses Passive 10, darkvision
Languages Aquan
Challenge 1 (20XP)

Mermen have the torso of a human and the lower body of a fish. Although the race is called "mermen," there are female members as well.
Breath water.

Actions
Attack. +1 to hit
Spear. 3 (1d6) piercing close or thrown range Near.

___

Minotaur

Large monstrosity

HD 6   **AC** 14
HP 45(6d8+18)
Str 18(+4) **Dex** 11(+0) **Con** 16(+3)
Int 6(-2) **Wis** 16(+3) **Cha** 9(-1)

Prof. +3   **Speed** Fast
Saving Throws Phy
Senses Passive 17, darkvision
Languages Abyssal
Challenge 6 (230XP)

The minotaur is a man-eating predator, with the head of a bull and the body of a massive human, covered in shaggy

hair. Most are not particularly
intelligent.
Special: Never get lost in labyrinths.
Actions
Attack. +4 to hit
Multiattack. A minotaur makes 3
attacks each round, 1 weapon, 1 gore,
and 1 bite.
Battle Axe. 4 (1d8) slashing
Gore. 5 (2d4) piercing
Bite. 2 (1d3) piercing

Mummy
Medium undead
HD 5   **AC** 10
HP 32(5d8+10)
Str 16(+3)   **Dex** 8(-1)   **Con** 15(+2)
Int 6(-2)   **Wis** 10(+0)   **Cha** 12(+1)

Prof. +3   **Speed** Slow
Saving Throws Phy
Senses Passive 10, darkvision
Languages The languages it knew in
life
Challenge 5 (180XP)

*Mummified kings, pharaohs, priests, or
powerful than normal mummies.*
Immune. Mummies cannot be hit by
normal weapons, and even magical
weapons cause only half damage.
Mummy Rot. In addition to normal
damage, their touch also inflicts a
rotting disease that prevents magical
healing and causes wounds to heal at
one-tenth of the normal rate. A Cure
Disease spell can increase healing rate
to one-half normal, but a Remove
Curse spell is required to completely
lift the mummy's curse.
Actions
Attack. +5 to hit
Fist. 7 (1d12) bludgeoning

Nixie
Small fey
HD 1/2   **AC** 12
HP 1(1d4-1)
Str 6(-2)   **Dex** 17(+3)   **Con** 9(-1)
Int 12(+1)   **Wis** 16(+3)   **Cha** 17(+3)

Prof. +2   **Speed** Normal, Swim Fast
Saving Throws Phy
Senses Passive 17
Languages Aquan, Sylvan
Challenge 1/2 (10XP)

Nixies are weak water fey creatures.
Charm. One in ten of them has the
power to cast a powerful charm
person (disadvantage penalty to EASY
(DC 8) CHA saving throw) that causes
the victim to walk into the water and
join the nixies as their slave for a year.
Casting dispel magic against the curse
has only a 75% chance of success,
and once the victim is actually in the
water the chance drops to 25%. Nixies
are ordinarily friendly, but they are
highly capricious.
Actions
Attack. +1 to hit
Small Sword. 2 (1d4) piercing

Ochre Jelly

Large ooze
HD 5   **AC** 11
HP 32(5d8+10)
Str 15(+2)   **Dex** 6(-2)   **Con** 14(+2)
Int 2(-4)   **Wis** 6(-2)   **Cha** 1(-5)

Prof. +3   **Speed** Slow, Climb Slow
Saving Throws Phy
Senses Passive 8
Languages -
Challenge 5 (180XP)

Ochre jellies are amorphous oozes that damage opponents with their acidic surface. They dissolve any adventurers they kill, making a raise dead spell impossible. The creature divides if struck with lightning (each with half the monster's existing hit points).

Actions
Attack. +5 to hit
Pseudopod. 7 (2d6) bludgeoning

Ogre

Large giant
HD 4   **AC** 10
HP 30(4d8+12)
Str 19(+4)   **Dex** 8(-1)   **Con** 16(+3)
Int 5(-3)   **Wis** 7(-2)   **Cha** 7(-2)

Prof. +2   **Speed** Fast
Saving Throws Phy
Senses Passive 8, darkvision
Languages Giant
Challenge 4 (110XP)

Ogres are normally quite stupid, but more intelligent versions might be encountered here and there.

Actions
Attack. +4 to hit
Greatclub. 5 (1d10) bludgeoning, reach 10 ft.
Large Spear. 5 (1d10) piercing, reach 10 ft or thrown Far.

Ogre Mage

Large giant
HD 5   **AC** 15
HP 42(5d8+20)
Str 19(+4)   **Dex** 8(-1)   **Con** 18(+4)
Int 5(-3)   **Wis** 7(-2)   **Cha** 7(-2)

Prof. +3   **Speed** Fast
Saving Throws Phy
Senses Passive 8, darkvision
Languages Giant
Challenge 6 (230XP)

Magic. The ogre mage is an ogre with magic powers, based on Japanese legend. An ogre mage can fly, turn invisible (per the spell), create a 10-foot-radius circle of magical darkness, change into human form, cast Sleep and Charm Person once per day, and cast a Cone of Frost with a range of Near, causing 8d6 damage to any caught within (NORMAL DEX saving throw applies).

Actions
Attack. +5 to hit
Sword. 6 (1d12) slashing

Orc

Medium humanoid
HD 1   **AC** 13
HP 7(1d8+3)
Str 16(+3) **Dex** 12(+1) **Con** 16(+3)
Int 7(-2)   **Wis** 11(+0) **Cha** 10(+0)

Prof. +2   **Speed** Normal
Saving Throws Phy
Senses Passive 10, darkvision
Languages Orc
Challenge 1 (20XP)

Orcs are humanoids that gather in tribes of hundreds. Occasionally, war-bands or even entire tribes of orcs issue forth from their caverns to raid and pillage by night. Orcish leaders are great brutes with additional hit dice, and magic-using shamans may also be found in the larger tribes. Orcish tribes hate each other and will fight savagely unless restrained by a powerful and feared commander, such as a high priest or a sorcerer.
Sunlight Sensitivity. While in sunlight, Orcs have disadvantage on attack rolls, as well as on Wisdom checks that rely on sight.

Actions
Attack. +1 to hit
Axe. 3 (1d6) slashing
Spear. 3 (1d6) piercing

Owlbear

Large monstrosity
HD 5   **AC** 14
HP 37(5d8+15)
Str 20(+5) **Dex** 12(+1) **Con** 17(+3)
Int 3(-4)   **Wis** 12(+1) **Cha** 7(-2)

Prof. +3   **Speed** Fast
Saving Throws Phy
Senses Passive 13, darkvision
Languages -
Challenge 6 (230XP)

Owlbears have the body of a bear, but the beak of an owl (with some feathers on the head and places on the body as well).
Hug. On an attack roll of 18+ (natural roll), the owlbear grabs its victim and hugs it for an additional 2d8 points of damage.

Actions
Attack. +5 to hit
Multiattack. The owlbear makes three attacks: one with its bite and two with its claws.
Bite. 6 (1d12) piercing
Claws. 3 (1d6) slashing

Pegasus

Large celestial

HD 4 **AC** 10
HP 34(4d8+12)
Str 18(+4) **Dex** 15(+2) **Con** 16(+3)
Int 10(+0) **Wis** 15(+2) **Cha** 13(+1)

Prof. +3 **Speed** Fast, Fly Fast
Saving Throws Phy
Senses Passive 16, darkvision
Languages understands Common but can't speak
Challenge 4 (110XP)

Pegasi are winged horses. Most have feathered wings, but some might have bat wings and some might be evil—at the Referee's discretion.

Actions
Attack. +4 to hit
Multiattack. Pegasi make two attacks with their hooves.
Hooves. 4 (1d8) bludgeoning

Phase Spider

Large monstrosity
HD 2 **AC** 13
HP 13(2d8+4)
Str 15(+2) **Dex** 15(+2) **Con** 14(+2)
Int 6(-2) **Wis** 10(+0) **Cha** 6(-2)

Prof. +3 **Speed** Normal, Climb Normal
Saving Throws Phy
Senses Passive 10, darkvision
Languages -
Challenge 3 (70XP)

Phase spiders can shift out of phase with their surroundings (so they can be attacked only by ethereal creatures), only to come back into phase later for an attack.
Dimension Phasing. Phase spiders can phase in and out of the material plane.
Lethal Poison. When bit make an EASY CON saving throw, on a fail drop to 0 hit points.

Actions
Attack. +2 to hit
Bite. 7 (1d6) piercing and poison.

Pixie

Tiny fey

HD 1/2 **AC** 14
HP 2(1d6-1)
Str 2(-4) **Dex** 20(+5) **Con** 8(-1)
Int 10(+0) **Wis** 14(+2) **Cha** 15(+2)

Prof. +2   **Speed** Normal, fly (fast)
Saving Throws Men
Senses Passive 14
Languages Sylvan
Challenge 1/2 (10XP)

Pixies are nasty, treacherous creatures of the fey, resembling small, winged people.

Invisibility. They are naturally invisible and do not become visible when they attack. After one round of attacks, the general location of the pixies may be discerned while they keep fighting, and they may thus be attacked (although with disadvantage to the attacker's die rolls to hit them).

There may certainly be similar fairies that are more powerful than ordinary pixies — these might have arrows that cause sleep and attack with advantage when using arrows.

Actions
Attack. +1 to hit
Dagger. 2 (1d4) piercing

Purple Worm

Gargantuan monstrosity
HD 15   **AC** 13
HP 157(15d8+90)
Str 28(+9) **Dex** 7(-2)   **Con** 22(+6)
Int 1(-5)   **Wis** 8(-1)   **Cha** 4(-3)

Prof. +6   **Speed** Fast, Burrow Normal
Saving Throws Phy
Senses Passive 9, darkvision, tremorsense
Languages -

Challenge 17 (1800XP)

Purple worms are massive annelids that grow 40 ft and more in length, and sometimes exceed ten feet in width. They are subterranean, chewing tunnels in rock (or through sand, in deserts, where they are a tan color). Aquatic versions of the purple worm might also exist.

Swallow Whole. These beasts swallow their prey whole if their natural roll is 4 higher than the needed number to hit. They can swallow anything the size of a horse or smaller.

Poison Sting. The poison injected by the stinger is lethal if the victim fails a HARD (DC 16) CON saving throw, dropping the target to 0 hit points

Actions
Attack. +15 to hit
Multiattack. The worm makes two attacks: one with its bite and one with its stinger.
Bite. 13 (2d12) piercing, reach 10 ft.
Stinger. 4 (1d8) piercing, reach 10 ft., and see Poison Sting above.

Rat, Giant

Small beast

HD 1/2   **AC** 12

HP 2(1d4)

Str 7(-2)   **Dex** 15(+2)   **Con** 11(+0)

Int 2(-4)   **Wis** 10(+0)   **Cha** 7(-2)

Prof. +2   **Speed** Normal

Saving Throws Phy

Senses Passive 10, darkvision

Languages -

Challenge 1/2 (10XP)

Giant rats are often found in dungeons and are about the size of a cat, or perhaps a lynx. The bite of some (1 in 20) giant rats causes disease. A saving throw (EASY CON) is allowed. The effects of the disease are decided by the Referee.

Actions

Attack. +1 to hit

Bite. 2 (1d3) piercing

Roc

Gargantuan monstrosity

HD 12   **AC** 15

HP 114(12d8+60)

Str 28(+9) **Dex** 10(+0) **Con** 20(+5)

Int 3(-4)   **Wis** 10(+0)   **Cha** 9(-1)

Prof. +5   **Speed** Normal, Fly Fast

Saving Throws Phy

Senses Passive 10, darkvision

Languages -

Challenge 13 (1000XP)

Rocs are the mythological great birds of legend, large enough to prey upon elephants. They can be trained as fledglings to serve as steeds, so roc eggs or fledglings would be a prize indeed, worth great sums of gold. Rocs might grow as large as 18 HD, with commensurately increased statistics.

Actions

Attack. +12 to hit

Multiattack. The roc makes three attacks: one with its beak and two with its talons.

Beak. 10 (3d6) piercing, reach 10 ft.

Talons. 7 (2d6) slashing

Rust Monster

Medium monstrosity

HD 1   **AC** 10

HP 5(1d8+1)

Str 13(+1)   **Dex** 12(+1)   **Con** 13(+1)

Int 2(-4)   **Wis** 13(+1)   **Cha** 6(-2)

Prof. +2   **Speed** Fast

Saving Throws Phy

Senses Passive 11, darkvision

Languages -

Challenge 1 (20XP)

These bizarre creatures are about man-size, and look vaguely like an armadillo; they have armored hide, two antennae, and a long tail with a flanged growth at the end. Rust monsters do not attack people — they turn metal into rust and eat the rust — but they just can't resist trying to eat delicious foods like swords and plate mail, even if they are being attacked.

Rust. A hit from a rust monster's antennae causes metal to rust into pieces, and the same is true for metal objects striking the rust monster's body.

Magical metal has a 10% cumulative chance to avoid rusting per +1 bonus of the armor or weapon.

Actions

Attack. +1 to hit

Antennae. Rust. see above.

Sabre-tooth Tiger

Large beast

HD 7   **AC** 13

HP 45(7d8+14)

Str 18(+4)   **Dex** 14(+2)   **Con** 15(+2)

Int 3(-4)   **Wis** 12(+1)   **Cha** 8(-1)

Prof. +3   **Speed** Fast

Saving Throws Phy

Senses Passive 13

Languages -

Challenge 8 (390XP)

Sabre-tooth tigers are larger than normal tigers and have huge, curving, front fangs.

Rear Claws. If they hit with both fore claws, they can pull up to rake with their rear claws (2 additional attacks).

Actions

Attack. +7 to hit

Multiattack. Saber-tooth tigers make two claw attack and one bite attack.

Bite. 7 (2d6) piercing

Claw. 3 (1d4) slashing

Salamander

Large elemental

HD 7   **AC** 14
HP 45(7d8+14)
Str 18(+4)   **Dex** 14(+2)   **Con** 15(+2)
Int 11(+0)   **Wis** 10(+0)   **Cha** 12(+1)

Prof. +3   **Speed** Normal
Saving Throws Phy
Senses Passive 10
Languages -
Challenge 8 (390XP)

*Salamanders are intelligent creatures
of the elemental planes of fire. They
have the upper body of a human and
the lower body of a snake and give off
tremendous, intense heat.*
*The very touch of a salamander deals
1d6 hit points of fire damage, and they
wrap their tails around foes to cause
an additional 2d8 points of crushing
damage per round as the victim writhes
in the deadly heat of the serpentine
coils.*
*Salamanders cannot be enslaved in the
same manner djinn and efreet might
be.*

Actions

Attack. +7 to hit
Multiattack. The salamander makes
two attacks: one with its spear and one
with its tail.
Spear. 3 (1d6) piercing plus 3 (1d6)
fire
Tail Constrict. 11 (2d8) bludgeoning
damage plus 3 (1d6) fire damage, and
the target is grappled. Reach 10 ft.

Scorpion, Giant

Large beast

HD 6   **AC** 16
HP 39(6d8+12)
Str 15(+2)   **Dex** 13(+1)   **Con** 15(+2)
Int 1(-5)   **Wis** 9(-1)   **Cha** 3(-4)

Prof. +3   **Speed** Normal
Saving Throws Phy
Senses Passive 9, blindsight
Languages -
Challenge 7 (290XP)

*Giant scorpions are the size of a
human being and are very aggressive.*
Poison. On a successful sting, the
target must make a NORMAL (DC 12)
CON saving throw or drop to 0 hit
points.

Actions

Attack. +6 to hit
Multiattack. The scorpion makes
three attacks: two with its claws and
one with its sting.
Claw. 5 (1d10) bludgeoning
Sting. 2 (1d4) piercing damage and
poison.

Sea Monster

Gargantuan monstrosity

HD 30   **AC** 17

HP 345(30d8+210)

Str 28(+9) **Dex** 18(+4) **Con** 25(+7)

Int 3(-4) **Wis** 8(-1) **Cha** 7(-2)

Prof. +9   **Speed** Swim Fast

Saving Throws Phy, Men

Senses Passive 16, blindsight

Languages -

Challenge 30 (15,500XP)

Sea monsters generally resemble bizarre fish, long-necked monsters with seal-like bodies, or massive eels, although virtually all have a hide of incredibly tough scales. In general, their appearance is quite varied, for there does not appear to be a particular "species" of sea monster.

Swallow Whole. Sea monsters swallow their prey whole, like sea serpents: if the attack roll is 10 or more over the required number (or a natural 20), the victim is swallowed, will die in an hour, and will be fully digested within a day.

Sea monsters are not generally venomous. They are generally encountered underwater; unlike sea serpents, they seldom venture to the surface.

Actions

Attack. +30 to hit

Multiattack. Sea Monsters make two attacks: one with their bite and one with their tail.

Bite. 22 (4d10) piercing, reach 20 ft.

Tail. 22 (4d10) bludgeoning, 20 ft.

Sergeant-at-Arms

Medium humanoid

HD 3   **AC** 14

HP 19(3d8+6)

Str 16(+3) **Dex** 12(+1) **Con** 14(+2)

Int 10(+0) **Wis** 10(+0) **Cha** 10(+0)

Prof. +2   **Speed** Normal

Saving Throws Phy

Senses Passive 11, darkvision

Languages Common

Challenge 3 (70XP)

Human sergeants are normally found in command of 1d6+5 human soldiers. These are the leaders of city guard units and other small military groups.

Actions

Attack. +3 to hit

Sword. 4 (1d8) slashing

_____

Shadow

Medium undead

HD 3   **AC** 12
HP 5(3d8+3)
Str 6(-2)   **Dex** 14(+2)   **Con** 13(+1)
Int 6(-2)   **Wis** 10(+0)   **Cha** 8(-1)

Prof. +2   **Speed** Fast
Saving Throws Men
Senses Passive 10, darkvision
Languages -
Challenge 3 (70XP)

Shadows are undead creatures: they are immune to Sleep and Charm, but the Referee may decide whether they are undead creatures subject to turning or whether they are some horrible "other" thing: a manifestation, perhaps, or a creature from another dimension (or gaps in the dimensions). Shadows are dark and resemble actual shadows, though they may be even darker in coloration.
Immune to nonmagical weapons. They are not corporeal, and can only be harmed with magical weapons or by spells.
Chill Touch. Their chill touch drains one point of Strength with a successful hit, and if a victim is brought to a Strength attribute of 0, they are transformed into a new shadow. If the person does not come to such a dark ending, then Strength points return after 90 minutes.

Actions
Attack. +3 to hit
Chill Touch. see Chill Touch (above)

Skeleton

Medium undead

HD 1/2   **AC** 11
HP 4(1d4+2)
Str 10(+0)   **Dex** 14(+2)   **Con** 15(+2)
Int 6(-2)   **Wis** 8(-1)   **Cha** 5(-3)

Prof. +2   **Speed** Normal
Saving Throws Phy
Senses Passive 9, darkvision
Languages -
Challenge 1/2 (10XP)

Skeletons are animated bones of the dead, usually under the control of some evil master.
Immune to sleep and charm spells. Takes half damage from piercing weapons.

Actions
Attack. +1 to hit
Sword. 3 (1d6) piercing
Shortbow. 3 (1d6) piercing, range Far

_____

Slug, Giant

Large monstrosity

HD 12   **AC** 11
HP 90(12d8+36)
Str 14(+2)   **Dex** 13(+1)   **Con** 16(+3)
Int 1(-5)   **Wis** 12(+1)   **Cha** 5(-3)

Prof. +5   **Speed** Slow, Climb Slow
Saving Throws Phy
Senses Passive 13, darkvision
Languages -
Challenge 12 (840XP)

These tremendously large masses of slimy, rubbery flesh are completely immune to blunt weapons.

Saliva. In addition to their powerful bite, giant slugs can spit their acidic saliva at one target at a time. The base range for spitting is 60 feet, and the victim must make a HARD DEX saving throw, on a fail taking 6d6 damage, and half that on a success.

Some giant slugs might have more or less virulent acidity, thus changing the damage inflicted.

Actions

Attack. +12 to hit
Bite. 7 (2d4 + 2) piercing

Snake, Giant Constrictor

Large beast

HD 6   **AC** 14
HP 33(6d8+6)
Str 19(+4) **Dex** 14(+2) **Con** 13(+1)
Int 1(-5)   **Wis** 10(+0) **Cha** 3(-4)

Prof. +3   **Speed** Normal, Swim Normal
Saving Throws Phy
Senses Passive 12, blindsight
Languages -
Challenge 6 (230XP)

Giant constrictors are twenty to thirty feet long.

Constrict. The constrictors do automatic constriction damage after hitting, and may also manage to pinion an arm or leg (1 in 6 chance).

Actions

Attack. +6 to hit
Bite. 3 (1d6) piercing, reach 10 ft.
Constrict. 5 (2d4) bludgeoning

Snake, Giant Viper

Medium beast

HD 4   **AC** 14
HP 22(4d8+4)
Str 10(+0)   **Dex** 18(+4)   **Con** 13(+1)
Int 2(-4)   **Wis** 10(+0)   **Cha** 3(-4)

Prof. +3   **Speed** Normal, Swim Normal
Saving Throws Phy
Senses Passive 10
Languages -
Challenge 4 (110XP)

Giant vipers are about ten feet long.

Poison. The bite of a giant viper causes the target to drop to 0 hit points on a failed EASY (DC 8) CON Save.

Actions

Attack. +4 to hit
Bite. 2 (1d3) piercing damage and poison, , reach 10 ft.

———————

Soldier

Medium humanoid

HD 1   **AC** 12

HP 5(1d8+1)

Str 12(+1)   **Dex** 10(+0)   **Con** 12(+1)
Int 10(+0)   **Wis** 10(+0)   **Cha** 10(+0)

Prof. +2   **Speed** Normal
Saving Throws Phy
Senses Passive 10
Languages Common
Challenge 1 (20XP)

Human soldiers serve as city guardsmen, mercenaries, and men-at-arms. They are generally armed with leather armor and a mace, sword, or spear.

Actions

Attack. +1 to hit
Sword. 4 (1d8) slashing
Mace. 3 (1d6) bludgeoning
Spear. 3 (1d6) piercing

Spectre

Medium undead

HD 6   **AC** 17

HP 27(6d8)

Str 1(-5)   **Dex** 14(+2)   **Con** 11(+0)
Int 10(+0)   **Wis** 10(+0)   **Cha** 10(+0)

Prof. +3   **Speed** Fly Fast, Hover
Saving Throws Men
Senses Passive 10, darkvision
Languages -
Challenge 7 (290XP)

Spectres are wraith-like undead creatures without corporeal bodies. Immune to non-magical weapons. Only magical weapons can damage a spectre.

Energy Drain. When a spectre hits an opponent, with either hand or weapon, the touch drains one level from the victim. Any being killed (or drained below level 0) by a spectre becomes a spectre as well, a pitiful thrall to its creator.

Mount. In some cases, these terrifying creatures may be mounted upon living beasts, if the beasts have been trained to tolerate proximity to the undead.

Actions

Attack. +6 to hit
Touch. see Energy Drain above.

Spider, Giant

Large beast

HD 4   **AC** 15
HP 26(4d8+8)
Str 14(+2)   **Dex** 16(+3)   **Con** 14(+2)
Int 2(-4)   **Wis** 11(+0)   **Cha** 4(-4)

Prof. +3   **Speed** Normal, Climb
Normal
Saving Throws Phy
Senses Passive 10
Languages -
Challenge 4 (110XP)

Giant spiders are aggressive hunters. Web. The greater giant spiders are all web builders.

Webs spun by giant spiders require an EASY (DC 8) DEX saving throw to avoid becoming stuck. Those who make a saving throw can fight in and move (5 ft per round) through the webs. The webs are flammable.

Lethal Poison. When bit by a giant spider the target must make a NORMAL (DC 12) CON saving throw, failing the save the target drops to 0 hit points.

Actions
Attack. +4 to hit
Bite. Melee 4 (1d8) piercing plus poison.

Stirge

Tiny beast

HD 1   **AC** 12
HP 5(1d8+1)
Str 4(-3)   **Dex** 16(+3)   **Con** 12(+1)
Int 2(-4)   **Wis** 8(-1)   **Cha** 4(-2)

Prof. +2   **Speed** Normal, Fly Fast
Saving Throws Phy
Senses Passive 9, darkvision
Languages -
Challenge 1 (20XP)

Resembling small, feathered, bat-winged anteaters, stirges have a proboscis which they jab into their prey to drain blood.

Blood Drain. After a stirge's first hit, it drains blood automatically at a rate of 1d4 hp per round.

Actions
Attack. +1 to hit
Blood Drain. 2 (1d3) piercing, and attaches to the target.

Titan, 17 HD

Gargantuan giant
HP 217 (17d8+136)
Prof. +6
Challenge 17 (1,800XP)

Titan, 18 HD

Gargantuan giant
HP 220 (18d8+144) Hit Dice 18
Prof. +6
Challenge 18 (2,000XP)

Titan, 19 HD

Gargantuan giant
HP 237 (19d8+152) Hit Dice 19
Prof. +7
Challenge 19 (2,200XP)

Titan, 20 HD

Gargantuan giant
HP 50 (20d8+160) Hit Dice 20
Prof. +7
Challenge 20 (2,500XP)

Titan, 21 HD

Gargantuan giant
HP 262 (21d8+168) Hit Dice 21
Prof. +7
Challenge 21 (3,300XP)

Titan, 22 HD

Gargantuan giant
HP 275 (22d8+176) Hit Dice 21
Prof. +7
Challenge 22 (4,100XP)

AC 17
Str 30(+10) **Dex** 25(+7) **Con** 27(+8)
Int 19(+4) **Wis** 22(+6) **Cha** 26(+8)

Speed Fast
Saving Throws Phy, Men
Senses Passive 21
Languages Giant, Common

Titans are mythological creatures, almost as powerful as gods. A titan has 2 Magic-User spells of each spell level from 1st-level spells to 7th-level spells and 2 Cleric spells of each spell level from 1st to 7th. The Referee might choose to substitute other magical abilities for spells—these creatures vary considerably in powers and personalities from one to the next.

One possible spell list for a titan might include the following magic-user and Cleric spells:

Magic-User: Charm Person (1), Sleep (1), Invisibility (2), Mirror Image (2), Fireball (3), Fly (3), Polymorph Other (4), Confusion (4), Conjure Elemental (5), Feeblemind (5).

Cleric: Light (1), Protection From Evil (1), Hold Person (2), Speak with Animals (2), Cure Disease (3), Dispel Magic (3), Cure Serious Wounds (4), Neutralize Poison (4), Quest (5).

Actions

Attack. +17 to +22 to hit
Greatsword. 24 (7d6) slashing, reach 10 ft.

Toad, Giant

Large beast
HD 3   **AC** 13
HP 16(3d8+3)
Str 15(+2) **Dex** 13(+1) **Con** 13(+1)
Int 2(-4) **Wis** 10(+0) **Cha** 3(-4)

Prof. +2   **Speed** Slow, Swim Normal
Saving Throws Phy
Senses Passive 10, darkvision
Languages -

Challenge 3 (70XP)

Giant toads are about the size and weight of a human. They are predators, willing to attack creatures as large as men.
Giant toads can attack at the end of a hop, which is in addition to the toad's normal move.

Actions
Attack. +3 to hit
Bite. 5 (1d10) piercing

Treant

Huge plant
HD 7-12   **AC** 17
HP 66-114(7d8+35 to 12d8+60)
Str 13(+1) **Dex** 12(+1) **Con** 13(+1)
Int 2(-4) **Wis** 13(+1) **Cha** 6(-2)

Prof. +3,4 **Speed** Normal
Saving Throws Phy
Senses Passive 13
Languages Common, Elvish, Druidic, Sylvan
Challenge 7 to 12 (290XP to 849XP)

Treants are tree-like protectors and "shepherds" of forest trees.
Depending upon their size, they have different hit dice and do different amounts of damage: treants of 7 to 8 hit dice inflict 2d6 points of damage with each strike of their branch-like hands, treants of 9—10 hit dice inflict 3d6 points, and treants of 11—12 hit dice inflict 4d6 points.
Wake Trees. All treants can "wake" trees within 60 ft, allowing them to walk at a rate of 15 ft., and possibly to attack. (No more than two trees at a time can be awake at the behest of a single treant.)

Actions
Attack. +7 to +12 to hit
Multiattack. The treant makes two strike attacks.
Strike (7-8 HD). 7 (2d6) bludgeoning
Strike (9-10 HD). 10 (3d6) bludgeoning
Strike (11-12 HD). 14 (4d6) bludgeoning

Troll

Large giant

HD 6   **AC** 12

HP 45(6d8+18)

Str 18(+4)   **Dex** 13(+1)   **Con** 20(+5)

Int 7(-2)   **Wis** 9(-1)   **Cha** 7(-2)

Prof. +3   **Speed** Normal

Saving Throws Phy

Senses Passive 12, darkvision

Languages Giant

Challenge 7 (290XP)

Trolls are as tall as ogres, and just as strong. Unlike ogres, however, they attack with claws and teeth instead of weapons

Regeneration. The troll regains 3 hit points at the start of its turn. If the troll takes acid or fire damage, this trait doesn't function at the start of the troll's next turn. The troll dies only if it starts its turn with 0 hit points and doesn't regenerate.

Actions

Attack. +6 to hit

Multiattack. The troll makes three attacks: one with its bite and two with its claws.

Bite. 4 (1d8) piercing

Claw. 2 (1d4) slashing

Tyrannosaurus Rex

Huge beast

HD 18   **AC** 15

HP 153(18d8+72)

Str 25(+7)   **Dex** 10(+0)   **Con** 19(+4)

Int 2(-4)   **Wis** 12(+1)   **Cha** 9(-1)

Prof. +6   **Speed** Fast

Saving Throws Phy

Senses Passive 14

Languages -

Challenge 18 (2,000XP)

Tyrannosaurus is a deadly carnivorous dinosaur, walking on two legs and attacking with a massively powerful bite.

Rip and Tear. When it bites prey, it grabs the victim in its jaws, shaking and chewing for 3d8 points of automatic damage in subsequent rounds. It can inflict such damage even against opponents as large as a brontosaurus. Only creatures with shells, bone frills, or spines can avoid the horrendous tearing damage a tyrannosaur can inflict (e.g., triceratops, stegosaurus, ankylosaurus).

Actions

Attack. +18 to hit

Bite. 22 (5d8) piercing, reach 10 ft.

Unicorn

Large celestial
HD 4   **AC** 10
HP 26(4d8+8)
Str 18(+4)   **Dex** 14(+2)   **Con** 15(+2)
Int 11(+0)   **Wis** 17(+3)   **Cha** 16(+3)

Prof. +3   **Speed** Fast
Saving Throws Phy
Senses Passive 13
Languages -
Challenge 4 (110XP)

Unicorns are generally shy and benevolent creatures, who will allow only a chaste maiden to approach them.
Teleport. They can teleport once per day to a distance of 360 ft, with a rider.
Horn. The unicorn's horn has healing properties, according to legend. (The details of this, if any, are left to the Referee).
Special: double damage if the unicor has room to charge.
There is considerable room to create variant sorts of unicorns: evil ones, flying ones, etc.

Actions
Attack. +4 to hit
Multiattack. The unicorn makes three attacks: two with its hooves and one with its horn.
Hooves. 4 (1d8) bludgeoning
Horn. 4 (1d8) piercing

Vampire

Medium undead
HD 7-9   **AC** 17
HP 59 to 76(7d8+28 to 9d8+36)
Str 18(+4)   **Dex** 18(+4)   **Con** 18(+4)
Int 17(+3)   **Wis** 15(+2)   **Cha** 18(+4)

Prof. +4   **Speed** Normal, Fly Fast
Saving Throws Phy, Men
Senses Passive 17, darkvision
Languages -
Challenge 8 to 10 (290XP to 590XP)

Vampires are some of the most powerful undead creatures.
Shapechanger. can turn into a gaseous form or into a giant bat at will.

Immune to non-magical weapon.
Can only be hit by magical weapons, and when "killed" in this way they turn into a gaseous form, returning to their coffins. Can only be truly killed in their coffin with a wooden stake to the heart.

Summon. Vampire can summon a horde of bats or 3d6 wolves from the night.

Charm. Looking into a vampire's eyes necessitates a saving throw, or the character is charmed (per the Charm Person spell).

Energy Drain. A vampire's bite drains two levels from the victim. Any human killed by a vampire becomes a vampire under the control of its creator.

Regenerate. 3 hp per round.

Weaknesses. They can be killed (though these are the only known methods) by immersing them in running water, exposing them to sunlight, or driving a wooden stake through the heart. They retreat from the smell of garlic, the sight of a mirror, or the sight of "good" holy symbols.

Actions

Attack. +7 to +9 to hit

Bite. 5 (1d10) piercing damage and Energy Drain.

Weasel, Giant

Medium beast

HD 3   **AC** 10
HP 16(3d8+3)
Str 11(+0)   **Dex** 16(+3)   **Con** 12(+1)
Int 4(-3)   **Wis** 12(+1)   **Cha** 5(-3)

Prof. +2   **Speed** Fast
Saving Throws Phy
Senses Passive 13, darkvision
Languages -
Challenge 3 (70XP)

These ferocious predators are often found in dungeon complexes, for they lair in caves.

Clamp. When a giant weasel hits an opponent, it clamps its jaws and sucks blood, automatically inflicting 2d6 points of damage per round.

Guard Animal. Giant weasels can be trained as guard animals; although they cannot be trained to warn of intruders, they are far more deadly than guard dogs.

Pelts. Their pelts sell for 1d6x100gp each.

Actions

Attack. +3 to hit

Bite. 5 (2d4) piercing

Wight

Medium undead

HD 3   **AC** 14

HP 22(3d8+9)

Str 15(+2)   **Dex** 14(+2)   **Con** 16(+3)

Int 10(+0)   **Wis** 13(+1)   **Cha** 15(+2)

Prof. +2   **Speed** Normal

Saving Throws Phy

Senses Passive 11, darkvision

Languages The languages they knew in life

Challenge 3 (70XP)

Wights live in tombs, graveyards, and burial mounds (barrows).

Immune to Sleep and Charm spells.

Immune to non-magical weapons besides silvered weapons.

Actions

Attack. +3 to hit

Bite. 5 (2d4) piercing

Energy Drain. drains 1 level from the target on a hit.

If completely drained of levels by a wight becomes a wight.

Will O Wisp

Tiny undead

HD 9   **AC** 27

HP 40(9d8)

Str 1(-5)   **Dex** 28(+9)   **Con** 10(+0)

Int 13(+1)   **Wis** 14(+2)   **Cha** 11(+0)

Prof. +4   **Speed** Fly Fast, Hover

Saving Throws Phy

Senses Passive 12, darkvision

Languages -

Challenge 9 (500XP)

Will o' the wisps are phantom-like shapes of eerie light, creatures that live in dangerous places and try to lure travelers into quicksand, off the edges of cliffs, etc. They usually inhabit swamps or high moors. They can brighten or dim their own luminescence, and change their shapes as well, to appear as a group of lights, a wisp of light, or in the glowing wraithlike shape of a human (often female).

They will generally depart if the attempt to lead victims into danger fails, but if they are attacked they can defend themselves with violent shocks of lightning-like power. These creatures are intelligent and can be forced to reveal the location of their treasure hoards.

Actions

Attack. +9 to hit

Shock. 7 (2d6) lightning

Wolf

Medium beast

HD 2   **AC** 12

HP 13(2d8+4)

Str 12(+1)   **Dex** 15(+2)   **Con** 14(+2)

Int 3(-4)   **Wis** 12(+1)   **Cha** 6(-2)

Prof. +2   **Speed** Fast

Saving Throws Phy

Senses Passive 13

Languages -

Challenge 2 (45XP)

Wolves are pack hunters and may be found in large numbers. Male wolves weigh from 80 to 100 pounds.

Actions
Attack. +2 to hit
Bite. 3 (1d6) piercing

Wraith

Medium undead

HD 4   **AC** 16
HP 30(4d8+12)

Str 6(-2)   **Dex** 16(+3)   **Con** 16(+3)
Int 12(+1)   **Wis** 14(+2)   **Cha** 15(+2)

Prof. +3   **Speed** Fly Fast

Saving Throws Men
Senses Passive 12, darkvision
Languages The languages it knew in life
Challenge 4 (110XP)

Wraiths are powerful wights
Immune. Wraiths are powerful wights, immune to all non-magical weapons other than silver ones (which inflict only half damage). Arrows are particularly ineffective against them, for even magical and silver arrows inflict only one hit point of damage per hit.
Mount. Wraiths can be found riding well-trained battle steeds or more unusual mounts that will tolerate their presence.

Actions
Attack. +4 to hit
Energy Drain. drains 1 level from the target on a hit.
If completely drained of levels by a wraith becomes a wight.

Wyvern

Large dragon
HD 7   **AC** 16
HP 52(7d8+21)
Str 19(+4) **Dex** 10(+0) **Con** 16(+3)
Int 5(-3)   **Wis** 12(+1) **Cha** 6(-2)

Prof. +4   **Speed** Slow, Fly Fast
Saving Throws Phy
Senses Passive 11
Languages Draconic
Challenge 8 (390XP)

A wyvern is a two-legged form of dragon. These creatures are smaller and less intelligent than true four-legged dragons, not to mention that they do not have a breath weapon.

Actions

Attack. +7 to hit
Attacks. Wyvern make one bite or 1 sting attack each round.
Bite. 9 (2d8) piercing, reach 10 ft.
Stinger. 3 (1d6) piercing, reach 10 ft. If stung the target must make a NORMAL (DC 12) CON saving throw, on a failed save the target drops to 0 hit points (see Death Saving Throws p.133).

Yellow Mold

Medium plant
HD 8   **AC** 3
HP 12(3d8)
Str 1(-5)   **Dex** 1(-5)   **Con** 10(+0)
Int 1(-5)   **Wis** 10(+0) **Cha** 1(-5)

Prof. +2   **Speed** -
Saving Throws Phy
Senses Passive 5
Languages -
Challenge 5 (180XP)

Yellow mold is a subterranean fungus; it neither moves nor attacks.
Spores. However, if it is poked or struck, it may (50% chance) release a cloud of poisonous spores, roughly 10 ft. in diameter. Failing a NORMAL (DC 10) CON saving throw against the spores means that the character drops to 0 hit points.
Poison. Touching yellow mold causes 1d6 points of acid damage.
Immune. These growths can be destroyed with fire, but are effectively immune to weapons.

Zombie

Medium undead

HD 1   **AC** 11

HP 7(1d8+3)

Str 13(+1)   **Dex** 6(-2)   **Con** 16(+3)

Int 3(-4)   **Wis** 6(-2)   **Cha** 5(-3)

Prof. +2   **Speed** Slow

Saving Throws Phy

Senses Passive 8, darkvision

Languages -

Challenge 1 (20XP)

Zombies are mindless creatures, the walking dead.

Immune to sleep and charm.

Actions

Attack. +1 to hit

Claw/Bite. 4 (1d8) slashing or piercing

Power

Finding magic items is one of the highlights of the game. All of the magic items here are based on the origin white box but feel free to add any other items you want. The rate you release magic items into your game is, as always, entirely up to you. What I've included here are some suggestions and tables if you are looking for a little guidance.

We've split the items up into 3 simple categories - Minor, Medium & Major. This rough classification will help you decide what levels you wish your player to have access to these great powers. As a guide Minor - all levels, Medium Levels 4+, Major levels 8+.

Minor Items

These items tend to be lower-powered or single-use consumables. Think +1 swords, potions, and scrolls.

Medium Items

These items pack a little more punch, +2 swords, lower-powered sentient swords, staffs and simple wands

Major Items

These items tend to kick ass and chew bubble gum. These can be the difference when coming up against the highest levels foes that on paper seem to outmatch the party. Retrieving these items can be the reason for quests instead of something that turns up randomly.

Armors

+1 Armors (Minor). These armors give a +1 bonus to a character's Armor Class.

+2 Armors (Medium). These armors give a +2 bonus to a character's Armor Class.

+2 Shield (Medium). These armors give a +2 bonus to a character's Armor Class.

+3 Armors (Major). These armors give a +3 bonus to a character's Armor Class.

+3 Shield (Major). These armors give a +3 bonus to a character's Armor Class.

Armor of Arrow Deflection (Medium). Missiles aimed at such armor have a to-hit disadvantage penalty.

Demonic Armor (Medium). The armor is possessed by a spirit or demon, with effects to be determined by the Referee. In general, such armor would provide both benefits and drawbacks.

Ethereal Armor (Major). Ethereal armor is +3 plate mail that also allows the wearer to become insubstantial and incorporeal 50 times, after which it reverts irrevocably to normal +3 plate mail. In ethereal form, the wearer can attack and be attacked only by ethereal opponents.

Fiery Armor (Medium). Fiery armor is +1 armor that is surrounded by flames. These flames deal 1d3 damage to anyone attacking the wearer with melee weapons.

Potions

In general, since potions are the product of alchemy rather than magic, they will neither be apparent to Detect Magic spells nor easily identified without tasting and experimentation. If the Referee decides that alchemy instead manipulates magic, as opposed to fantastical but otherwise natural chemistry, then detect magic and dispel magic would work upon potions.

Potions are usable by all character classes. Unless otherwise noted, potion effects have a duration of 2d6 x 10 minutes.

Clairaudience (Minor). As per the spell.

Clairvoyance (Minor). As per the spell.

Diminution (Minor). This potion causes the drinker to shrink down to six inches tall for 2d6 hours. Taking smaller doses of the potion will result in less of a reduction in size.

Dragon Control (Minor). The drinker gains the ability to control dragons of a certain type after partaking in this type of potion. 1d3 dragons of a specific type (determined randomly by the Referee) can be affected as per Charm Monster.

Ethereality (Minor). The Imbiber can move through solid objects but cannot attack. Equipment also becomes ethereal.

Extra Healing (Minor). This potion is a potent curative; it heals 3d6+3 hit points of damage (duration does not apply).

Fire Resistance (Minor). The drinker becomes immune to normal fire, gains advantage on saving throws against fire attacks, and suffers only half damage to magic fire attacks that do not permit saving throws.

Flying (Minor). As per the spell.

Frozen Concoction (Minor). These potions can be readily identified because they are often one or two degrees cooler than the surrounding temperature. The potion allows the imbiber to climb walls without falling, and not to drop held items in case of being surprised or frightened.

Gaseous Form (Minor). The user's body turns to a mist, allowing access to any place that is not airtight. Equipment is left behind; only the body becomes gaseous.

Giant Strength (Minor). The character becomes unbelievably strong for the potion duration, gaining an additional 1d8 to damage rolls and +4 to hit (in addition to any normal bonuses, including existing Strength bonuses).

Growth (Minor). The character grows to 30 feet in height.

Healing (Minor). This potion cures 1d6+1 hit points of damage.

Heroism (Minor). The imbiber gains +2 to attacks and damage.

Invisibility (Minor). As per the spell.

Invulnerability (Minor). The drinker gains a bonus of +2 on saving throws; moreover, any opponent's attack with a penalty of -2.

Levitation (Minor). As per the spell.

Poison (Minor). The drinker must make a successful NORMAL CON saving throw or die. Some poisons cause instant death; others cause death within a certain number of rounds, or even minutes. In the case of a few poisons, failing the saving throw causes damage rather than death - such weaker poisons generally also inflict a small amount of damage even if the saving throw is successful.

Slipperiness (Minor). Except for the soles of the feet and the palms of the hands, the character suddenly has a virtually frictionless surface.

Treasure Finding (Minor). A character drinking this wonderful concoction can detect hoards of treasure within 400 feet.

Undead Control (Minor). The drinker can control undead; 2d4 undead of fewer than 4 HD and 1d4 undead of 4+ hit dice fall under the imbiber's control after the potion is consumed.

Rings

No more than two magic rings may be worn at a time (one on each hand) without unpredictable and potentially dire consequences.

Djinn Summoning (Major). The wearer of the ring can summon a djinn, who will do the wearer's bidding, following instructions precisely and to the letter, no further. Such rings can be treacherous, but only for those who use them foolishly.

Fire Resistance (Medium). The wearer has advantage on saving throws vs. magical fire and is immune to normal fire.

Human Control (Medium). Such rings allow the wearer to cast charm person once per day, and to maintain the charm on up to 3 individuals at a time.

Invisibility (Major). While wearing the ring, the wearer becomes invisible.

Mammal Control (Medium). The wearer controls 1d8 mammals at a range of up to FAR. Control does not extend to people or to giant animals.

Poison Resistance (Minor). The wearer has advantage on saving throws vs. poison.

Protection, +1 (Minor). The wearer gains a bonus of +1 to armor class, and +1 on all saving throws.

Protection, +2 (Medium). The wearer gains a bonus of +2 to armor class, and +2 on all saving throws.

Regeneration (Major). The wearer regenerates one hit point per combat round, and thus cannot die unless the ring is removed or the wearer's body is burned.

Shooting Stars (Medium). Once per day, the ring can unleash 1d6 lightning bolts that inflict 3d6 hit points each (NORMAL DEX saving throw indicating half damage).

Spell Storing, Cleric (Medium). The ring contains 1d6 random Cleric spells. The wearer (if a Cleric) can cast these spells as if they were normally prepared spells. Once a spell is cast, it cannot be cast a second time until the wearer has taken a short rest.

Spell Storing, Magic-User (Medium). The ring contains 1d6 random Magic-User spells. The wearer (if a Magic-user) can cast these spells as if they were normally memorized and prepared spells. Once a spell is cast, it cannot be cast a second time until the wearer has taken a short rest.

Spell Turning (Major). Any spell (other than from a wand or other item) directly aimed at the wearer of the ring is partially reflected back at the caster. Roll a percentile die to see how much of the spell's power bounces back; the exact determination of what happens is up to the Referee.

Telekinesis (Major). The wearer can mentally lift and move 200 pounds of weight at a range of 120 feet.

Three Wishes (Major). These rings grant the wearer three wishes. Beware of outrageous wishes; they backfire.

X-ray Vision (Major). The wearer has x-ray vision at a range of 40 feet. The maximum distance through which the wearer can see through solid rock is just over 10 feet, through solid metals (other than lead) is 1 foot, and through lead is 1 inch.

Scrolls

All scrolls, besides protection scrolls, are spells for magic-users, and regardless of the level of the spell, they can be used by any magic-user capable of reading them.

All protection scrolls can be used by any character who is able to read. After reading a spell from a scroll the writing disappears, so the spell is usable one time only!

Spell Scrolls

Scrolls that have Cleric or Magic-User spells on them. Once used they disintegrate, disappear, or are otherwise rendered useless.

Protection Scroll Descriptions (Minor)
Protection vs. ...

Demons. All within a NEAR radius around the reader are protected from the attacks of 1 demon per round.
Duration: 40 minutes.

Drowning. All within a CLOSE radius of the reader gain the ability to breathe underwater.
Duration: 1 full day.

Elementals. This scroll protects against a single elemental.
Duration: 40 minutes.

Magic. An anti-magic shell with a radius of CLOSE surrounds and moves with the reader; spells cannot pass in or out of the shell.
Duration: 1 hour

Metal. Metal cannot harm the reader.
Duration: 1 hour.

Poison. Poisons have no effect upon one who reads such a scroll aloud; moreover, any poisons, active or quiescent, in the scroll reader's body are instantly removed.
Duration: 6 hours.

Undead. All within a NEAR radius of the reader are protected against undead, but only to a limited degree. In any given round, 2d12 undead with fewer than 4 HD, 2d6 undead with 4-5 HD, and 1d6 undead with 6+ HD are foiled by the protection of the scroll. Thus, the scroll is effective against all but a vast horde of undead.
Duration: 1 hour.

Were-creatures. All within a NEAR radius around the reader are protected from lycanthropes.
Duration. 1 hour.

Cursed Scrolls

Cursed scrolls can inflict curses ranging from the amusing to the annoying, and all the way to the unbelievably catastrophic. The Referee is encouraged to invent interesting curses that might be written on scrolls, in addition to the possibilities shown on the table. A successful saving throw will allow the reader to avoid the curse. Most curses can be removed with a remove curse spell.

Staffs

Like wands, most staffs operate by using up charges. However, staffs are not as easily

Absorption (Major). Absorbs up to 100 levels of spells directed at the holder before its absorption properties cease forever. The holder can cast spells from the staff in response to hostile spells, using the staff's stored levels, of the exact level of the hostile spell directed at the caster, but the spell must be chosen from the list of spells the caster has prepared.

Beguiling (Medium). Foes within NEAR range must make a NORMAL CHA saving throw or consider the holder to be a loyal friend for 4d4 rounds (uses one charge).

Command (Medium). A charge can be used to control humans (as per a charm person spell), plants, or animals.

Healing (Medium). Cures 1d6+1 hit points of damage per charge.

Power (Major). Casts light (no charge used), casts fireball (4d6 damage), cold as a Wand of Cold, Lightning Bolts (4d6 damage), acts as a Ring of Telekinesis (costs one charge) and hits for 2d6 damage (no charge used, & gain proficiency in staffs).

Snake (Medium). In combat, a Staff of the Snake is +1 to hit and +1 damage and you are considered proficient. When commanded (by using a charge) the staff coils around the target (with a successful hit) and pinions the victim for 1d4 x10 minutes. This attack is only useful on a victim about the size of a human or smaller. The staff will slither back to its owner afterward at a speed of Normal. Only Clerics can employ a Staff of the Snake.

Striking (Medium). This staff inflicts 2d6 points of damage with a successful hit (does not use charges) and you are considered proficient when using.

Withering (Medium). The dreaded Staff of Withering adds ten years of physical aging with a successful hit and you are considered proficient when using it.

Wizardry (Major). The most powerful of staffs is a Staff of Power with additional abilities. At the cost of one charge, it allows invisibility, summoning elementals (calling 1d4 at a time), hold person, a wall of fire, passwall, a web spell, or fly.

Wands

Wands may only be used by Magic-users.

The Wands that cast spells become useless when they reach zero charges, but can be recharged by casting the spell into the wand. Each such recharge, where a spell is cast into the wand, has a 5% chance of destroying the wand irrevocably. In some cases, a non-rechargeable wand might be found with a large number of charges (e.g., 100). Wands may be used while in melee combat.

Wand of Cold (Medium). The wand casts a Cone of Cold out to NEAR. Creatures caught in the cone take 6d6 damage (NORMAL CON saving throw applies for half damage). The wand holds 25 charges and cannot be recharged.

Wand of Detection, enemies (Major). These wands detect enemies within a radius of NEAR, if the enemies are thinking hostile thoughts. The wand is always active when held, and does not use charges.

Wand of Detection, magic (Medium). Wands of magic detection function as a Detect Magic spell with a range of CLOSE. The user gets a vague sense of what sort of magic is being detected. The wand is always active when held, and does not use charges.

Wand of Detection, metal (Medium). Such wands detect large caches of metal, within a range of NEAR. The wand's user also gets a vague sense of the metal's type. The wand is always active when held, and does not use charges.

Wand of Fear (Medium). A wand of fear causes creatures in a cone-shaped path to flee (NORMAL CHA saving throw negates). There is a 60% chance that they will drop whatever they are holding. The cone extends out to NEAR. The wand holds 25 charges, and cannot be recharged.

Wand of Paralyzing (Medium). This sort of wand casts a cone of paralysis out to NEAR. Creatures in the cone are paralyzed for 3d6 turns (NORMAL STR saving throw negates). The wand holds 25 charges, and cannot be recharged.

Wand of Polymorph (Medium). Such wands are of two types. One type casts polymorph self, and the other casts polymorph other. The wand carries 10 charges, and cannot be recharged.

Weapons

+1 weapons (Minor). Gives a +1 bonus to hit and damage rolls.

+2 weapons (Medium). Give a +2 bonus to hit and damage rolls.

+3 weapons (Major). Gives a +3 bonus to hit and damage rolls.

+1 Blunt weapon that destroys undead (Medium). Can be a mace, hammer, sling, or club (determine type randomly). Lesser types of undead don't get a saving throw, though more powerful types do.

Intelligent Weapon There is a % chance that such a weapon may have the ability to cast a particular spell once per day at the wielder's command. The spell will be either Cleric (50%) or Magic-User (50%), and the Level will be determined by the sword. Such weapons generally can communicate with their bearers, and sometimes (25% chance) can speak audibly. Even if the weapon cannot speak audibly, it will communicate with its wielder by telepathy when held.
+1 Intelligent Weapon (Minor). 10% chance that it may cast and the spell will be of Level 1d3.
+2 Intelligent Weapon (Medium). 20% chance that it may cast and the spell will be of 1d4.
+3 Intelligent Weapon (Major). 30% chance that it may cast and the spell will be of Level 1d4+1.

+1 thrown weapon that returns to hand (Minor). This axe or spear will eventually return to the thrower's hand.

+1 weapon, extra attack (Minor). This weapon grants 1 additional attack for the user once per day.

+1 weapons (Minor). Gives a +1 bonus to hit and damage rolls.

+1, +2 vs particular type of foe (Minor). This weapon provides a +1 bonus to hit and damage rolls, +2 vs. a particular type of foe (were-creatures, undead, giants, goblinoids, dragons, etc.).

+1, +3 vs particular type of foe (Medium). This weapon provides a +1 bonus to hit and damage rolls, +3 vs. a particular type of foe (were-creatures, undead, giants, goblinoids, dragons, etc.).

+2, +4 vs particular type of foe (Medium). This weapon provides a +2 bonus to hit and damage rolls, +4 vs. a particular type of foe (were-creatures, undead, giants, orcs, dragons, etc.) to be determined randomly.

Dancing Weapon (Major). A dancing weapon levitates to fight beside its owner without the need to be held. In the first round, it is a +1 weapon, in the second round, it is a +2 weapon, and in the third round, it is a +3 weapon. After 3 rounds, the weapon dances no further until it is directed at a new opponent, but is +1 regardless. It takes one action to direct the weapon to a target after which the sword attacks independently on the same initiative as the owner.

Flaming Weapon (Medium). The weapon burns with enchanted fire when held, inflicting an additional 1d6 points of damage with successful hits in combat. It can also be used as a light source with a NEAR radius.

Freezing Weapon (Minor). This weapon is freezing cold, inflicting an additional 1d6 points of damage with successful hits.

Misc. Magic Items

Amulet Against Scrying (Medium). The amulet protects the wearer from all scrying, such as esp or being viewed through a crystal ball. Usable by: All Classes.

Amulet of Demon Control (Medium). This amulet functions as a Protection from Evil spell and allows the wearer to attempt to "Charm Monster" upon a demon. Success means that the demon is enslaved for 1d6 weeks, whereupon it becomes free. Usable by: Magic-Users and Clerics.

Arrow of Direction (Medium). Such a magic arrow points the direction of whatever the owner requests. It may be used only seven times in a single week. Usable by: All Classes.

Bag of Holding (Medium). The inside of this bag is larger than the outside. The inside dimensions are roughly 10x5x3 feet, but the bag cannot carry more than 1,000 pounds of weight (roughly 100 items). If it is not empty, the bag weighs 50 pounds, no matter how much weight it actually contains. Usable by: All Classes.

Beaker of Potions (Medium). This small jug fills itself with the requested potion, out of the 1d4+1 potions it is able to produce. The jug can be used as many times per week as the number of different potions it can produce. Usable by: All Classes.

Boots of Elvenkind (Medium). The wearer of the boots moves with complete silence. Usable by: All Classes.

Boots of Leaping (Medium). Boots of Leaping allow the wearer to make prodigious leaps 10 feet high and up to 30 feet horizontally. These boots also double movement rates, but outdoors only. They do not require the wearer to rest after using them. Usable by: All Classes.

Boots of Levitation (Medium).

These boots allow the wearer to Levitate (as per the spell), with unlimited duration. Usable by: All Classes.

Boots of Speed (Medium). Boots of Speed double the wearer's movement rate but require complete rest for a period of time equivalent to the amount of time they were used. Usable by: All Classes.

Bracers of Defense, AC 13, AC 15, or AC 17 (Medium). These bracers improve the wearer's armor class to the stated level; there is no effect if the wearer is already armored to the same or higher degree. The armor class granted by the bracers can be increased by magical rings or other protective magics. Usable by: All Classes.

Carpet of Flying (Medium). Flying carpets can carry as many as three people, and travel at a Movement Rate of Normal if they carry more than one passenger. With only one rider, the carpet moves at a Movement Rate of Fast. Usable by: All Classes.

Censer, Bowl, Brazier, or Stone of Controlling Elementals (Major). Censers control air elementals, bowls (when filled) control water elementals, braziers control fire elementals, and stones control earth elementals. These items can be used to summon a 12 HD elemental of the appropriate type. Generally, it takes 10 minutes to prepare the object for use. Usable by: Magic-Users.

Chime of Opening (Medium). Sounding this small chime opens any door, even if the door is barred or Wizard Locked. Usable by: All Classes.

Cloak of Displacement (Medium). The wearer appears to be in a slightly different location, off from reality by a foot or so. The wearer's armor class improves by 2, and the cloak also grants a +2 saving throw against any targeted attack upon the one wearing it. Usable by: All Classes.

Cloak of Elvenkind (Major). The wearer becomes almost, but not quite, invisible. Usable by: All Classes.

Cloak of Protection, +1 (Minor). This cloak improves the wearer's armor class by 1, and grants a bonus of +1 on saving throws. Usable by: All but Fighter class.

Cloak of Protection, +2 (Medium). This cloak improves the wearer's armor class by 2 and grants a bonus of +2 on saving throws. Usable by: All but Fighter class.

Cloak of Protection, +3 (Major). This cloak improves the wearer's armor class by 3 and grants a bonus of +3 on saving throws. Usable by: All but Fighter class.

Crystal Ball (Medium). A crystal ball allows the user to see what is transpiring in whatever location they desire to see, over a considerable distance. Such a magic item may not be used more than thrice per day, or the user will be driven mad. Certain spells and other precautions may be used to prevent being seen through a crystal ball. Some of these items may communicate sound, or even thoughts, from the area being scryed, although these are rare. Usable by: Magic-Users.

Decanter of Endless Water (Medium). This jug pours out one gallon of water per minute when unstoppered. Usable by: All Classes.

Dust of Appearance (Medium). Dust of Appearance is tossed in a NEAR radius around the user, and makes any invisible, astral, displaced, out-of-phase, or dimensional thing completely visible. The dust generally comes in a pouch, with enough for 20–30 uses. Usable by: All Classes.

Dust of Disappearance (Medium). When sprinkled in a NEAR radius, everything therein becomes invisible for 5d6 x 10 minutes. Normal means of detecting invisibility (such as a Detect Invisibility spell) are not strong enough to work against the dust's powerful enchantment. Usable by: All Classes.

Dust of Sneezing and Choking (Minor). Pouches containing this dust ordinarily contain only enough for one "dose." When scattered in a radius of NEAR, the dust forces all in the area to make a HARD CON saving throw or drop to 0 hit points (effectively killing monsters). If the nature of the dust is identified before it is experimented with, it can be used as a devastating thrown weapon. Usable by: All Classes.

Efreeti Bottle (Major). The efreeti that inhabits such a bottle will serve the bottle's owner for a year and a day unless it is accidentally released from servitude. Usable by: All Classes.

Figurine of the Golden Lion (Medium). This is a small stone figurine that transforms into a lion when the command word is spoken, fighting at its owner's orders. If it is slain, it turns back into a figurine but may be used again. The figurine may be used once per week, and no more. Usable by: All Classes.

Figurine of the Onyx Dog (Medium). This stone figure transforms into a living hound of stone when its command word is spoken. It will seek whatever the owner tells it to find, without stopping until it succeeds or is killed. It has a 75% chance to detect objects that are invisible or hidden, and of course, its sense of smell detects invisible and hidden creatures with almost perfect success. For purposes of defense and attack, the stone dog is treated as a wolf. It may be used twelve times before the statuette becomes non-magical. Usable by: All Classes.

Gauntlets of Dexterity (Medium). When worn, these gloves grant a bonus of +2 to the wearer's Dexterity (to a maximum of 22). Usable by: All Classes.

Gauntlets of Ogre Power (Medium). These gauntlets raise the wearer's Strength to that of an ogre (STR 19). Usable by: all but Magic-Users.

Gauntlets of Swimming and Climbing (Medium). These gloves permit the wearer to swim at a rate of Fast and climb sheer walls with a 95% chance of success per ten feet of climbing. Usable by: all but Magic- Users.

Gem of Seeing (Medium). A Gem of Seeing is used as a lens. It shows the truth of what it sees, cutting through illusions of all kinds, even very powerful ones.Usable by: All Classes.

Girdle of Giant Strength (Major). Increases a characters Strength to 22. Usable by: All Classes.

Helm of Fiery Brilliance (Medium). This prodigiously powerful helm grants many benefits to the wearer. Anyone donning the helm gains a +10 on saving throws against fire damage and can create a Wall of Fire. Fighters wearing the helm may command a weapon in hand to flame (+1d6 damage). Magic- Users wearing the helm can add +1 to each die of damage inflicted by a fireball or delayed blast fireball spell. Clerics wearing the helm can ignite objects within NEAR at will and may cast two light or continual light spells for each one the Cleric has actually prepared. The wearer of the helmet is likely to be attacked by any air elemental creatures, but fire elemental types (such as efreet or salamanders) will be favorably disposed. Usable by: All Classes.

Helm of Reading Magic and Languages (Medium). The wearer of the helm can read all languages, including magic script. Usable by: All Classes.

Helm of Teleportation (Medium). When the wearer casts a Teleportation spell on themselves, while wearing the helm, the teleportation is made without risk of error, anywhere the wearer desires. This may be done repeatedly (without further casting of the spell) for a period of one hour before the concatenation of spell and helm ends, and it may be done only once per day. The helm does not assist with Teleportation spells cast on anyone other than the wearer. Usable by: Magic-Users.

Hole, Portable (Major). A portable hole is physically a piece of dark cloth, about 5 feet in diameter. However, it is also the mouth of an interdimensional hole 10 feet deep—items and people can fall or climb down into it once it is placed on the ground. The piece of cloth can actually be pulled in from the inside to close the hole off entirely, although there is no source of fresh air within, and staying inside will asphyxiate the inhabitant in a short time. The piece of cloth can be picked up and carried off whenever desired—hence the name "portable." Usable by: All Classes.

Horn of Blasting (Major). This horn, when blown, has the same effect on structures as a catapult, and causes 2d6 points of damage to creatures, deafening them for 10 minutes as well. The cone of sound goes out to FAR The "point" of the cone, at the horn's mouth, is 10 feet wide. Usable by: All Classes.

Horn of Valhalla, Bronze (Medium). The horn summons 2d4 berserk warriors (3 HD) to assist the one who blew the horn. Usable by: Fighters and Clerics.

Horn of Valhalla, Iron (Major). The horn summons 2d4 berserk warriors (4 HD) to assist the one who blew the horn. Usable by: Fighters.

Horn of Valhalla, Silver (Minor). The horn summons 2d4 berserk warriors (2 HD) to assist the one who blew the horn. Usable by: All Classes.

Horseshoes of Speed (Medium). These horseshoes double a horse's movement rate. Usable by: Horses.

Jug of Alchemy (Medium). This jug produces whatever liquid is desired, in a commonly used large quantity (e.g., 10 gallons of water, but only 5 gallons of wine). It may be used no more than seven times per day, and will produce only one type of liquid per day. It does not produce magical liquids. Usable by: All Classes.

Lenses of Charming (Major). These lenses, when placed over the eyes, give the wearer the ability to charm those who meet their gaze (acting as per a Charm Person spell). The saving throw against the power of the lenses is made disadvantage. Usable by: All Classes.

Libram, Magical (level gain) (Medium). Magical librams grant a level of experience to the reader if the reader is of the appropriate character class. Randomly determine the class for which the libram is written, from all character classes.

Luckstone (Medium). This stone grants +1 to saving throws and attack rolls. Usable by: All Classes.

Manual of Beneficial Exercise (medium). Reading this tome increases the reader's Strength by 1 point (to a maximum of 20). Usable by: All Classes.

Manual of Golems (Medium). This book contains the basic instructions and formulae for creating a single type of golem. The process is expensive, and the creator must have achieved a certain level of magical expertise in order to use the book, but these are priceless repositories of forgotten lore. Such books are often warded by the original owner, against the touch of anyone not of the Magic-User class, being enchanted to inflict damage or even the loss of a level. Usable by: Magic-Users only.

Manual of Intelligence (Medium). Reading this tome increases the reader's Intelligence by 1 point (to a maximum of 20). Usable by: All Classes.

Manual of Quickness (Medium). Reading this tome increases the reader's Dexterity by 1 point (to a maximum of 20). Usable by: All Classes.

Manual of Wisdom (Medium). Reading this tome increases the reader's Wisdom by 1 point (to a maximum of 20). Usable by: All Classes.

Medallion of ESP (Major). Functions as an ESP spell within NEAR (75%) or FAR(25%). Usable by: All Classes.

Mirror of Mental Scrying (Medium). This hand-mirror (it might also be found as a smaller mirror on a necklace) allows the user to cast clairaudience, clairvoyance, and esp, with the normal range, but for an unlimited time. The mirror will also answer a question about what it portrays (the answer is likely to be quite cryptic), but only one question per week is possible. Usable by: All Classes.

Necklace of Firebaubles (Medium). This necklace is hung with 3d4 little baubles. When thrown, the baubles explode into 6d6 damage fireballs (per the spell). Usable by: All Classes.

Pipes of the Sewers (Medium). These pipes summon 10d6 giant rats. The piper does not need to concentrate once the rats arrive (which takes 1d4 x10 minutes), but it is wise to do so. When the rats arrive, there is an immediate 5% chance that they will not obey commands, and if the piper ceases to concentrate on the tune there is a 10% chance that the rats will begin to act of their own free will. Every subsequent round in which the piper fails to concentrate there is another chance to lose control, and the chance increases by 10% each time it is made (first round, 10%, second round 20%, etc.). Usable by: All Classes.

Robe of Blending (Medium). These robes make the wearer appear to be a part of the surroundings, including the ability to appear as another one of a group of nearby creatures. The robe will make the wearer appears as a small tree when in the forest surroundings, a sand formation in the desert, etc. Creatures with 10+ hit dice (or levels of experience) have a 10% chance per level (or HD) above 9th to perceive the wearer as a robed figure rather than a part of the surroundings. Usable by: All Classes.

Robe of Eyes (Major). Hundreds of eyes are woven and embroidered into the fabric of these magical robes, granting the wearer tremendous powers of supernatural perception. In a radius of FAR, anything the wearer looks upon is seen for what it is: invisible creatures become apparent, illusions are seen as such, and this sight even extends into the astral plane. The wearer cannot be ambushed or otherwise taken by surprise, and can follow the trail of anything that has passed by within the last day. Usable by: Magic-Users only.

Robe of Wizardry (Major). This robe grants the wearer the ability to cast charm, polymorph, and hold spells with a 95% chance of success. The robes may be tied to specific alignments. Usable by: Magic- Users only.

Rope of Climbing (Medium). This item is a 50-foot length of rope that leaps magically upward when commanded and can tie and untie itself upon command. Usable by: All Classes.

Rope of Entanglement (Medium). This rope, on command, twines itself around as many as 2d4+1 human-sized foes. The rope cannot be hit except with a natural roll of 20 (it is magical), and can sustain 20 hit points of damage before fraying and becoming useless. Usable by: All Classes.

Spade of Excavation (Minor). This ordinary-looking spade digs by itself when commanded, shoveling out one cubic yard (27 cubic feet) per ten minutes.

Cursed Items

Cursed items come in many shapes and forms; most likely they are ancient magical items whose magic has deteriorated or changed with age, although some of them were clearly fashioned to serve as traps for the unwary (or for the maker's enemies, perhaps). Note that cursed items cannot usually be dropped or removed without the assistance of a Remove Curse spell. Although the Referee is encouraged to dream up individualized cursed items, the samples below should prove useful as guidance:

Bag of Devouring. A Bag of Devouring functions as a bag of holding, but then devours any item placed into it within 1d4+1 hours.

Censer of Hostile Elementals. This is a censer (or brazier, bowl, or stone) that summons elementals— but the elementals are hostile instead of under the summoner's control.

Cloak of Poison. Upon donning this cloak, the wearer's body is suffused with magical poisons of many kinds, and drops to 0 hit points (see Death Saving Throws p.133) instantly, without the chance of a saving throw.

Crystal Ball of Suggestion: This cursed item does not function as a crystal ball, but rather implants a Suggestion (per the spell) in the viewer's mind.

Dancing Boots. These boots function as boots of elvenkind or speed until the wearer is in combat or fleeing. Suddenly, at that point, the unfortunate victim will begin to dance a jig, or perhaps a stately pavane.

Flask of Stoppered Curses. This flask releases a curse of some kind when its seal is broken.

Horn of Collapse. When sounded, this horn causes a blast of destruction straight upwards, destroying any ceiling overhead and causing it to collapse.

Medallion of Projecting Thoughts. While this medallion is around a character's neck, the wearer's thoughts can be "heard" by all nearby.

Mirror of Opposition. All persons looking into this mirror are attacked by evil versions of themselves, exact duplicates including spells and magic items. When the mirror opposites are slain, their bodies and equipment disappear into mist and return to the mirror.

Robe of Feeblemindedness. Anyone donning this cloak has their intelligence reduced to that of a garden snail (INT 1).

Appendix A: Conditions

Conditions alter a creature's capabilities in a variety of ways and can arise as a result of a spell, a class feature, a monster's attack, or other effect. Most conditions, such as blinded, are impairments, but a few, such as invisible, can be advantageous.

A condition lasts either until it is countered (the prone condition is countered by standing up, for example) or for a duration specified by the effect that imposed the condition.

If multiple effects impose the same condition on a creature, each instance of the condition has its own duration, but the condition's effects don't get worse. A creature either has a condition or doesn't.

The following definitions specify what happens to a creature while it is subjected to a condition.

Blinded

- » A blinded creature can't see and automatically fails any ability check that requires sight.
- » Attack rolls against the creature have advantage, and the creature's attack rolls have disadvantage.

Charmed

- » A charmed creature can't attack the charmer or target the charmer with harmful abilities or magical effects.
- » The charmer has advantage on any ability check to interact socially with the creature.

Deafened

- » A deafened creature can't hear and automatically fails any ability check that requires hearing.

Frightened

- » A frightened creature has disadvantage on ability checks and attack rolls while the source of its fear is within line of sight.
- » The creature can't willingly move closer to the source of its fear.

Grappled

» A grappled creature's speed becomes 0, and it can't benefit from any bonus to its speed.

» The condition ends if the grappler is incapacitated (see Incapacitated Condition p.233).

» The condition also ends if an effect removes the grappled creature from the reach of the grappler or grappling effect, such as when a creature is hurled away.

Incapacitated

» An incapacitated creature can't take actions.

Invisible

» An invisible creature is impossible to see without the aid of magic or a special sense. For the purpose of hiding, the creature is heavily obscured. The creature's location can be detected by any noise it makes or any tracks it leaves.

» Attack rolls against the creature have disadvantage, and the creature's attack rolls have advantage.

Paralyzed

» A paralyzed creature is incapacitated (see condition above) and can't move or speak.

» The creature automatically fails Strength and Dexterity saving throws.

» Attack rolls against the creature have advantage.

» Any attack that hits the creature is a critical hit if the attacker is within 5 feet of the creature.

Petrified

» A petrified creature is transformed, along with any nonmagical object it is wearing or carrying, into a solid inanimate substance (usually stone).

» Its weight increases by a factor of ten, and it ceases aging.

» The creature is incapacitated (see condition above), can't move or speak, and is unaware of its surroundings.

» Attack rolls against the creature have advantage.

» The creature automatically fails Strength and Dexterity saving throws.

» The creature has resistance to all damage.

» The creature is immune to poison and disease, although a poison or disease already in its system is suspended, not neutralized.

Poisoned

» A poisoned creature has disadvantage on attack rolls and ability checks.

Prone

» A prone creature's only movement option is to crawl unless it stands up and thereby ends the condition.
» The creature has disadvantage on attack rolls.
» An attack roll against the creature has advantage if the attacker is within 5 feet of the creature. Otherwise, the attack roll has disadvantage.

Restrained

» A restrained creature's speed becomes 0, and it can't benefit from any bonus to its speed.
» Attack rolls against the creature have advantage, and the creature's attack rolls have disadvantage.
» The creature has disadvantage on Dexterity saving throws.

Stunned

» A stunned creature is incapacitated (see p.234), can't move, and can speak only falteringly.
» The creature automatically fails Strength and Dexterity saving throws.
» Attack rolls against the creature have advantage.

Unconscious

» An unconscious creature is incapacitated (see p.234), can't move or speak, and is unaware of its surroundings
» The creature drops whatever it's holding and falls prone.
» The creature automatically fails Strength and Dexterity saving throws.
» Attack rolls against the creature have advantage.
» Any attack that hits the creature is a critical hit if the attacker is within 5 feet of the creature.

Appendix B: Example of Exploration

This is a simple run-through of a 24 hour (6 watch) period of travel.
For difficulties, please consult the DC table. Remember, the difficulties are not set in stone, if the conditions are particularly good, or bad, feel free to adjust them. It's just a case of bumping them up, or down, a level.

A party of 4 adventurers is traveling back to their hometown of Cabback, and decide that the fastest way is through Tayton Wood. It should take 3 days if all goes well.

Name	Class	Background
Ziri	Expert	Farmer
Thal'ol	Fighter	Barbarian
Felmeron	Cleric	Sailor
Gasdron	Magic-user	Nobel

They had camped the night before on the edge of the woods. They break camp at 8am and head straight in. The referee has determined that this is not a particularly dangerous forest so will roll once during the day and once during the night to see if a random encounter happens.

The GM rolls a d6 in secret before leaving. It's a 3, so there will be no random encounter during the day (see Random Encounters p.254).

Watch 1: 8AM -12pm

The party spends the first watch traveling with Thal'ol at the front and Felmeron at the back. Before the start, Thal'ol makes a navigation check (WIS) and rolls a 17.

Navigating in a Forest is Hard (DC16) and Thal'ol is not the wisest of chaps, with -2 Wisdom Modifier. This should have resulted in a fail but, his barbarian background gives him wilderness skills and natural instincts, so he asks if he can add his proficiency to the roll. The referee agrees it makes sense and the check succeeds. They proceed until mid-day when they stop, take a sip of water, and start the next watch.

As the travel speed in a forest is Slow they have 4.5miles of progress, which the referee notes.

Watch 2: 12PM - 4PM

They continue trekking into the forest, but Thal'ol rolls a 7 for navigation and they veer off course. The referee rolls a d10, which indicates that they are now moving in a south-easterly direction. By 4 pm they have made an additional 4.5 miles of progress in this new direction. The party decides to stop here for the day, as they don't think it's worth pushing on and risking exhaustion.

Watch 3: 4pm-8pm

Thal'ol - decides he's going to spend the next 2 watches hunting. He first needs to locate the prey with an EASY Wisdom check, which he fails (did we mention he's not the wisest!). So he will spend 2 watches searching the woods for prey and finding nothing.

Ziri - Decides she is going to spend a watch foraging. It's an EASY (DC8) check and she rolls a 14 + 2 for her Wisdom modifier. She finds a fruit tree, result! She rolls 1d2 + 1d2 for every 3 points she exceeded the target by a total of 3d2. To make it easier she rolls 3d4 and halves the result. A total of 4 provisions which she adds to her inventory.

Felmeron - Decides he's going to look for water but, before he rolls, asks if he can add his proficiency bonus, due to his sailor background. The referee congratulates him for creatively trying to use his background but says no, it doesn't make any sense. Everybody loves a trier! He fails the Easy roll and spends a watch searching, with no luck.

Gasdron - Being absolutely useless in the woods, he decides he's going to investigate the local area for anything interesting and Rolls a Natural 20. The referee decides that, after a few hours, he finds an old broken alter covered in strange runes. He makes a note of it so he can tie it into the story later.

Watch 4: 8pm-12am

Thal'ol - Spends this watch continuing to hunt, and comes to the conclusion that this wood is entirely devoid of life.

Ziri - Decides to find a campsite and makes an investigation check, which she succeeds. She finds the perfect spot that ensures any lookout checks will be made with advantage that evening.

As she goes about setting up the camp she quietly contemplates whether this group would survive a day without her looking after them.

Felmeron - Keeps looking for water and succeeds on his next check. Tonight everyone will not need to consume a provision for water.

Gasdron- Tries, and fails, to decipher the runes since he did not prepare the spell Read Languages. So, instead, he starts to copy the runes into one of his books and will research them further when he gets home.

Watch 5-6: 12am -8am

The group eats, consuming a provision each, and spends the next 2 watches resting and sleeping. They will spend 2 hours each on lookout, so the referee asks them what order they intend to take lookout in, and gets them all to make a Normal Wisdom check. He's quickly reminded that it should be made with advantage due to Ziri's success at finding a good campsite.

The referee checks to see if there is a random encounter and rolls a 1, which indicates there is. He rolls on their random encounter table and determines that the party will be visited by 5 opportunistic bandits. To fairly determine which player is on lookout when they attack, the referee rolls a d4, which indicates Felmeron. Felmeron had passed his Wisdom lookout check, so the party was not surprised by the Bandits, and see them off without any problems.

At 8am, after the 2 casters prepare their spells for the day, they head off again. Hopefully, Th,al'ol will do a better job navigating!

Appendix C: Converting Monsters

Converting Monsters from 5E

Converting monsters from old school games is fairly easy and can almost be done on the fly. 5e is more of an art form but once you've figured out the hit dice the rest is fairly easy.

Mimic (5E)

Medium monstrosity (shapechanger), neutral

Armor Class 12 (natural armor)
Hit Points 58 (9d8 + 18)
Speed 15 ft.

Str 17(+3) **Dex** 12(+1) **Con** 15(+2)
Int 5(-3) **Wis** 13(+1) **Cha** 8(-1)
Skills Stealth +5
Damage Immunities acid
Condition Immunities prone
Senses darkvision 60 ft., passive Perception 11
Languages —
Challenge 2 (450 XP)

Mimic (OSR)

Medium Monstrosity

HD 7 **AC** 13
HP 45(7d8+14)
Str 17(+3) **Dex** 12(+1) **Con** 15(+2)
Int 5(-3) **Wis** 13(+1) **Cha** 8(-1)

Prof. +3 **Speed** Slow
Saving Throws Phy
Senses Passive 11, darkvision
Languages -
Challenge 7 (290XP)

Step by Step

Basically I convert from the top of the stat block down. Trust yourself as getting things slightly wrong will not break things. So first up I am going to change the monster type to just monstrosity without the shapechanger just to simplify it.I'll also remove the alignment. So we now have Medium monstrosity.

AC. Can most of the time stay the same, occasionally I will look up an old school version of a monster to double check (in this case I looked up a mimic in the S&W SRD online) that has the mimic with an AC of 13. I am going to go with the 13. So we have Armor Class 13.

Hit Points. Always have to be simplified and we need to figure out a Hit Dice. Again using the S&W online SRD, the mimic in that has 7 HD. Olde Swords Reign uses a d8 HD, and checking the 5e ability scores, mimic's have a CON of 15 for a +2. So Hit Points 45 (7d8+14) with Hit Dice 7.

Speed. The 5e stat block lists the mimic having a speed of 15 ft, so that is Slow. Speed Slow.

Ability Scores. Are identical to the 5e version.

No skills, damage immunity listings, condition immunities in OSR so we skip those.

Most monsters in Olde Swords Reign have saving throw proficiencies (barring very weak monsters). Mimics don't look too intelligent so I am going to give them Physical saves, they add their proficiency bonus to their stat when rolling a STR, DEX or CON save. Saving Throws Physical (+3).

Senses are identical to 5e besides taking the measurement off of darkvision, truesight etc. So the mimic has Senses darkvision, passive Perception 11.

Languages. The mimic has none so Languages -.

Challenge. Is generally the same HD but there is a rough formula on p. 151

XP. Can be taken from the XP Table p. 151.

For those that haven't noticed the XP value of monsters in OSR is just knocking the tens digit from the 5e XP for the same Challenge.

We are going to use the S&W SRD description for the mimic and just cut and paste that into the stat block.

Next, I am going to cut and paste the actions from the 5e version and simplify them. OSR monsters get no melee or ranged bonuses for their STR or DEX so I have to change the to hit bonus to their HD +7. And I need to knock off the damage bonuses to leave one simple die roll. And that is that.... done.

Mimic (5E)

Special Traits

Shapechanger: The mimic can use its action to polymorph into an object or back into its true, amorphous form. Its statistics are the same in each form. Any equipment it is wearing or carrying isn't transformed. It reverts to its true form if it dies.

Adhesive (Object Form Only): The mimic adheres to anything that touches it. A Huge or smaller creature adhered to the mimic is also grappled by it (escape DC 13). Ability checks made to escape this grapple have disadvantage.

False Appearance (Object Form Only): While the mimic remains motionless, it is indistinguishable from an ordinary object.

Grappler: The mimic has advantage on attack rolls against any creature grappled by it.

Actions

Pseudopod: Melee Weapon **Attack:** +5 to hit, reach 5 ft., one target. Hit: 7 (1d8 + 3) bludgeoning damage. If the mimic is in object form, the target is subjected to its Adhesive trait.

Bite: Melee Weapon Attack: +5 to hit, reach 5 ft., one target. Hit: 7 (1d8 + 3) piercing damage plus 4 (1d8) acid damage.

Mimic (OSR)

Mimics are formless creatures that imitate surrounding features they have seen. In subterranean settings, they might be disguised as an archway, treasure chest, door, etc. When touched, they glue themselves to the victim with a strong adhesive, while striking with a suddenly-formed tentacle.

Actions

Attack. +7 to hit

Pseudopod. 4 (1d8) bludgeoning. If the mimic is in object form, the target is subjected to its Adhesive trait.

Bite. 4 (1d8) piercing damage plus 4 (1d8) acid damage.

Converting Monsters from Other Old School Games

Converting monsters from most old school games, like S&W, C&C, LL, BFRPG etc, is pretty straightforward.

AC. If the monsters have Descending Armor Class you will need to switch them to Ascending. Converting Armor Classes is often done by subtracting the descending AC from 20, so a descending AC of 4 becomes an ascending AC of 16. For negative ACs add the negative to 20 (AC -2 is AC 22).

Abilities. Special abilities, spells, breath weapons, etc, that have a Saving Throw you will need to convert the save to an Ability saving throw with the difficulty based on the monsters Hit Dice (See Monster DC's table P152)

Movement. Can be easily eyeballed and changed to Slow, Normal, Fast. For ability scores use the 5e versions of the monster and give them proficiency in Physical, Mental or both in saving throws.

APPENDIX D: CONVERTING OLD-SCHOOL SAVES

When converting older modules you will run across various "old-school saving throws" such as Save vs. Breath Weapon or Save vs. Wands. The table below will give you a quick and easy list of the saves and their corresponding Ability Scores for converting the saving throws to Olde Swords Reign. Some Referees may disagree with this list, and if that is the case change them as you see fit. Old School Save Conversions

Ability Score	Save
Strength	Paralysis & Constriction
Dexterity	Breath Weapon & Traps
Constitution	Disease, Energy Drain & Poison
Intelligence	Arcane Magic & Illusion
Wisdom	Confusion, Divine Magic, Gaze Attack, Petrification & Polymorph
Charisma	Death Attack, Charm & Fear

APPENDIX E: MONSTERS BY ENVIRONMENT

When figuring out where to locate monsters or putting together random encounter tables this should save a little time.

Artic

Name	CR
Bandit	1
Berserker	1
Dragon, White	6-8
Giant, Frost	10
Lycanthrope, Werebear	7
Mastadon	8
Phase Spider	3
Sabre-Tooth Tiger	8
Troll	7
Wolf	2

Desert

Name	CR
Bandit	1
Berserker	1
Efreet	10
Elemenal, Air	8-16
Hobgoblin	1
Lion	13
Lizard, Giant	3
Lycanthrope, Weretiger	7
Medusa	5
Mummy	5
Ogre	4
Ogre Mage	6
Purpleworm	17
Roc	13
Scorpion, Giant	7
Sergant-At-Arms	3
Snake, Giant Constrictor	6
Snake, Giant Viper	4
Stirge	1
Toad, Giant	3
Wight	3

Forest

Name	CR
Bandit	1
Berserker	1
Bugbear	3
Centaur	5
Dire Wolf	4
Dragon, Gold	11-13
Dragon, Green	8-10
Dryad	2
Gnoll	2
Goblin	0.5
Gorgon	9
Griffon	8
Harpy	4
Hobgoblin	1
Lizard, Giant	3
Lizardman	3
Lycanthrope, Werebear	7
Lycanthrope, Wereboar	4
Lycanthrope, Wererat	4
Lycanthrope, Weretiger	7
Lycanthrope, Werewolf	4
Mastadon	8
Ogre	4
Ogre Mage	6
Orc	1
Owlbear	6
Pegasus	4

Name	CR
Phase Spider	3
Pixie	0.5
Rat, Giant	0.5
Snake, Giant Constrictor	6
Snake, Giant Viper	4
Spider, Giant	4
Stirge	1
Toad, Giant	3
Treant	7-12
Troll	7
Unicorn	4
Weasel, Giant	3
Will'O Wisp	9
Wolf	2

Grassland

Name	CR
Bugbear	3
Centaur	5
Cockatrice	6
Dragon, Gold	11-13
Gnoll	2
Goblin	0.5
Gorgon	9
Griffon	8
Hippogriff	4
Hobgoblin	1
Lion	13
Lycanthrope, Wereboar	4
Lycanthrope, Weretiger	7
Mastadon	8
Ogre	4
Ogre Mage	6
Orc	1
Pegasus	4
Phase Spider	3
Snake, Giant Constrictor	6
Snake, Giant Viper	4
Tyrannosaurus Rex	18
Wolf	2

Hill

Name	CR
Bandit	1
Berserker	1
Dire Wolf	4
Giant, Hill	8
Giant, Stone	9
Gnoll	2
Goblin	0.5
Gorgon	9
Griffon	8
Harpy	4
Hippogriff	4
Hobgoblin	1
Lion	13
Lycanthrope, Werebear	7
Lycanthrope, Wereboar	4
Lycanthrope, Werewolf	4
Ogre	4
Ogre Mage	6
Orc	1
Pegasus	4
Phase Spider	3
Snake, Giant Viper	4
Troll	7
Weasel, Giant	3
Wolf	2
Wyvern	8

Shadow Below

Name	CR
Black Pudding	10
Bugbear	3
Elemental, Earth	8-16
Gargoyle	5
Gelatinous Cube	5
Ghoul	3
Giant, Fire	11
Giant, Stone	9
Goblin	0.5
Gray Ooze	3
Hellhound	5-8
Hobgoblin	1
Lizardman	3
Minotaur	6
Mummy	5
Ochre Jelly	5
Ogre	4
Ogre Mage	6
Orc	1
Phase Spider	3
Purpleworm	17
Rat, Giant	0.5
Rust Monster	12
Salamander	8
Skeleton	0.5
Snake, Giant Viper	4
Specter	7

Name	CR
Spider, Giant	4
Toad, Giant	3
Troll	7
Vampire	8-10
Wight	3
Wraith	4
Zombie	1

Mountain

Name	CR
Dragon, Red	10-12
Elemenal, Air	8-16
Giant, Cloud	12
Giant, Fire	11
Giant, Frost	10
Giant, Stone	9
Griffon	8
Harpy	4
Hellhound	5-8
Hippogriff	4
Lion	6
Ogre	4
Ogre Mage	6
Orc	1
Roc	13
Sabre-Tooth Tiger	8
Troll	7
Wyvern	8

Swamp

Name	CR
Crab, Giant	4
Crocodile	3
Dragon, Black	7-9
Elemental, Water	8-16
Ghoul	10
Hydra	6-13
Lizard, Giant	3
Lizardman	3
Ogre	4
Ogre Mage	6
Rat, Giant	0.5
Snake, Giant Constrictor	6
Snake, Giant Viper	4
Spider, Giant	4
Stirge	1
Toad, Giant	3
Troll	7
Wight	3
Will'O Wisp	9

Urban

Name	CR
Bandit	1
Berserker	1
Gargoyle	5
Ghoul	3
Invisable Stalker	8
Lycanthrope, Wererat	4
Ogre	1
Ogre Mage	6
Orc	1
Phase Spider	3
Rat, Giant	0.5
Skeleton	0.5
Snake, Giant Viper	4
Specter	7
Spider, Giant	4
Stirge	3
Vampire	8-10
Wight	3
Will'O Wisp	9
Zombie	1

Underwater

Name	CR
Crab, Giant	4
Crocodile	3
Sea Monster	30
Snake, Giant Constrictor	8-10

OGL

Designation of Open Game Content: The following is designated Open Game Content pursuant to the OGL v1.0a: all text and tables, pages 9-173.

Designation of Product Identity: Product identity is not Open Game Content. The following is designated as product identity pursuant to OGL v1.0a(1)(e) and (7): (none), The Olde Swords Reign name and logo. All artwork is copyright of their respective owners.

OPEN GAME LICENSE Version 1.0a: The following text is the property of Wizards of the Coast, Inc. and is Copyright 2000 Wizards of the Coast, Inc ("Wizards"). All Rights Reserved.

1. Definitions: (a)"Contributors" means the copyright and/or trademark owners who have contributed Open Game Content; (b)"Derivative Material" means copyrighted material including derivative works and translations (including into other computer languages), potation, modification, correction, addition, extension, upgrade, improvement, compilation, abridgment or other form in which an existing work may be recast, transformed or adapted; (c) "Distribute" means to reproduce, license, rent, lease, sell, broadcast, publicly display, transmit or otherwise distribute; (d)"Open Game Content" means the game mechanic and includes the methods, procedures, processes and routines to the extent such content does not embody the Product Identity and is an enhancement over the prior art and any additional content clearly identified as Open Game Content by the Contributor, and means any work covered by this License, including translations and derivative works under copyright law, but specifically excludes Product Identity. (e) "Product Identity" means product and product line names, logos and identifying marks including trade dress; artifacts; creatures characters; stories, storylines, plots, thematic elements, dialogue, incidents, language, artwork, symbols, designs, depictions, likenesses, formats, poses, concepts, themes and graphic, photographic and other visual or audio representations; names and descriptions of characters, spells, enchantments, personalities, teams, personas, likenesses and special abilities; places, locations, environments, creatures, equipment, magical or supernatural abilities or effects, logos, symbols, or graphic designs; and any other trademark or registered trademark clearly identified as Product identity by the owner of the Product Identity, and which specifically excludes the Open Game Content; (f) "Trademark" means the logos, names, mark, sign, motto, designs that are used by a Contributor to identify itself or its products or the associated products contributed to the Open Game License by the Contributor (g) "Use", "Used" or "Using" means to use, Distribute, copy, edit, format, modify, translate and otherwise create Derivative Material of Open Game Content. (h) "You" or "Your" means the licensee in terms of this agreement.

2. The License: This License applies to any Open Game Content that contains a notice indicating that the Open Game Content may only be Used under and in terms of this License. You must affix such a notice to any Open Game Content that you Use. No terms may be added to or subtracted from this License except as described by the License itself. No other terms or conditions may be applied to any Open Game Content distributed using this License.

3. Offer and Acceptance: By Using the Open Game Content You indicate Your acceptance of the terms of this License.

4. Grant and Consideration: In consideration for agreeing to use this License, the Contributors grant You a perpetual, worldwide, royalty-free, non-exclusive license with the exact terms of this License to Use, the Open Game Content.

5. Representation of Authority to Contribute: If You are contributing original material as Open Game Content, You represent that Your Contributions are Your original creation and/ or You have sufficient rights to grant the rights conveyed by this License.

6. Notice of License Copyright: You must update the COPYRIGHT NOTICE portion of this License to include the exact text of the COPYRIGHT NOTICE of any Open Game Content You are copying, modifying or distributing, and You must add the title, the copyright date, and the copyright holder's name to the COPYRIGHT NOTICE of any original Open Game Content you Distribute.

7. Use of Product Identity: You agree not to Use any Product Identity, including as an indication as to compatibility, except as expressly licensed in another, independent Agreement with the owner of each element of that Product Identity. You agree not to indicate compatibility or co-adaptability with any Trademark or Registered Trademark in conjunction with a work containing Open Game Content except as expressly licensed in another, independent Agreement with the owner of such Trademark or Registered Trademark. The use of any Product Identity in Open Game Content does not constitute a challenge to the ownership of that Product Identity. The owner of any Product Identity used in Open Game Content shall retain all rights, title and interest in and to that Product Identity.

8. Identification: If you distribute Open Game Content You must clearly indicate which portions of the work that you are distributing are Open Game Content.

9. Updating the License: Wizards or its designated Agents may publish updated versions of this License. You may use any authorized version of this

Index

Thank you

I hope you get as much enjoyment out of running as I do.

As a thank you, and to make your life a little easier, I'll be happy to email you a PDF copy of the player's guide. It's everything that your players will need to create characters and play the game. You can get your copy by heading to

https://fumbletable.com/osr-players-guide/

On the site, you should find links to our discord community, character sheets and be able to contact me directly if you need anything.

Damien

House Rules

House Rules

House Rules